Extraordinary acclaim for Ric

Dead Boy

"Short stories can be little goodies you nibble on while trying to decide which novel to read next. Or as in the case of *Dead Boys* they can be as filling as a banquet.... The writing is so fine throughout that it's almost a crime to single out 'Everything Beautiful Is Far Away' as a perfect specimen.... It's violent, it's truthful, and it's devastating."

— Marilyn Stasio, *New York Times Book Review*

"Stylistically brilliant, painfully and truly observed and rendered, *Dead Boys* is not just one of the best collections thus far this decade: it is one of the best short story collections of the past fifty years, right up there with Barry Hannah's *Airships,* Chris Offutt's *Kentucky Straight,* James Baldwin's *Going to Meet the Man,* and Flannery O'Connor's *A Good Man Is Hard to Find.*"

— Eric Williamson, *San Francisco Chronicle*

"Lange brings Raymond Carver's minimalism to the back alley with tales of California drifters, salesmen, and bank robbers. Violence and crime are never far away, though *Dead Boys* focuses not on the perfect heist but on the emotional wreckage it can leave behind."   — *Details*

"*Dead Boys* marks the emergence of a compelling new talent.... Lange's stories are richest on the level of atmosphere, and though there are haunting, dead-on details throughout the collection, it's the stories that go beyond mood that are most successful."

— Joshua Henkin, *Los Angeles Times*

"Any writer who draws a gritty portrait of L.A. will inevitably be compared to the great Nathanael West. Richard Lange is that rare author who actually earns such an accolade. This is a fantastic collection of stories: both heartfelt and unflinching. If you're an admirer of Raymond Carver's writing — or Tobias Wolff's, or Denis Johnson's, or Joy Williams's — I suspect you'll love Richard Lange's, too."   — Scott Smith, author of *The Ruins*

"This stark collection of stories is essential reading for any fan of gritty, macho, West Coast noir. It's the stuff of wayward deliverymen and hard-up strippers, something you'd see in a Tarantino film or a bad dream."   — *Men's Health*

"Lange's stories are knockouts. Gritty, humane, and utterly urban."   — Alice Sebold, author of *The Almost Moon*

"*Dead Boys* features outcasts and forgotten souls, men on the fringe, nearing oblivion but hanging on by dirt-encrusted fingernails. Lange's realism and ability to find empathy for these characters are stunning achievements."
            — *Pittsburgh Tribune-Review*

"Richard Lange breathes new life into the mythology of Los Angeles. The stories are achingly accurate and always telling of the hardscrabble lives caught on the grid work of the big city sprawl. This is the work of a writer who has come to know well the territory he is exploring."
            — Michael Connelly, author of *The Brass Verdict*

"A gritty, affecting debut. . . . Intensely human and compelling, these narratives crackle with the noir-like atmosphere of Raymond Chandler, the minimalism of Raymond Carver, and the stark poeticism of Denis Johnson."
            — John Vigna, *Vancouver Sun*

"A dozen of the best damned short stories you'll read this or any other year."   — Clayton Moore, *Bookslut*

"Heartbreaking stories. . . . Lange's slice-of-life scenarios, emotionally wrecked characters, and piercingly funny dialogue make for a powerful combination that recalls the work of Thomas McGuane and Denis Johnson." —Joanne Wilkinson, *Booklist*

"Richard Lange has got it right about Los Angeles. . . . What's most impressive about Lange's tales is how his L.A. bypasses the usual accounts of nihilism and dystopia to signify instead the hard-luck optimism of the losers who are drawn to it. . . . Like Raymond Carver and Amy Hempel, Lange is able to phrase a highly specific emotion or state of mind compactly, but his sentences are rangier, spackled with oddly beautiful imagery pieced together from unlikely materials. . . . There is no doubt that on the shop-worn territory of literary Los Angeles, Lange has mapped entirely new topography." —Benjamin Strong, *Bookforum*

"Twelve jaw-dropping stories, written in crisp, minimalist fashion. Lange focuses on men on the fringes of civilized society: the barflies, bank robbers, and just plain lowlifes. But there isn't a 'bad guy' among them, as Lange gives depth to their plights, painting in glorious shades of gray. Anyone who appreciates the work of Raymond Carver, William Burroughs, and Charles Bukowski will find pleasure in these deeply disquieting, heartfelt—and ultimately unforgettable—noir-tinged stories."
—*Rocky Mountain News*

"At a time when literary fiction is more inclined to plumb the travails of thirtyish Manhattan media types and Chicago ad-agency loafers than the nation's barely-scraping-by, this debut story collection from tenderhearted L.A. gritster Richard Lange is a balm." —Mark Holcomb, *Time Out New York*

"Superbly crafted. . . . Lange provides his vividly real characters with a space in which they can finally release all the emotions—the rage, the longing, the bewilderment—that they work so hard to suppress, and he compels his creations to a level of honesty. . . . The men who people this collection may engage in macho posturing, but their author never does. Superlative short fiction, and an arresting debut." —*Kirkus Reviews*

"A first short story collection filled with gripping Hollywood noir that's every bit as good as Dennis Lehane." —*Velocity*

"Lange's short pieces have a direct lineage to Raymond Chandler, and he salts them with a nice dose of literary flair." —Martin Zimmerman, *San Diego Union-Tribune*

"Lange's fine debut collection takes the so-called normal guy — husband, father, working stiff — and throws a heap of trouble at him. . . . A considered, colloquial understatement marks nearly all of the first-person protagonists over the course of these twelve stories, in a manner that's marvelously effective. Lange's characters are well-intentioned screwups, deeply flawed and utterly convincing." —*Publishers Weekly*

"A dark and delicious collection. . . . Lange's addled, low-life tales of Southern California suggest a Charles Bukowski for the painkiller generation. But there's a difference. . . . Call the difference 'hope.' . . . You can't help liking Lange's boys even when their worst traits are showing." —Bill Kohlhaase, *Inland Empire Weekly*

"Funny, tough, and tragic, with earned humanity, street style, and a shooter's eye for detail . . . Mr. Lange has talent to burn." —George Pelecanos, author of *The Turnaround*

"A killer debut. . . . These are traditional stories written in a classic style — you could shelve Lange between Denis Johnson, Richard Ford, and Richard Yates and no fights would break out. . . . Lange writes with tremendous heart, his characters' inner turmoil as rich and varied as any of the above masters. . . . *Dead Boys* will live, we think, for a very long time." —Tod Goldberg, *E! Online*

Dead Boys

Stories

RICHARD LANGE

BACK BAY BOOKS
Little, Brown and Company
New York   Boston   London

Back Bay Books / Little, Brown and Company
Hachette Book Group
237 Park Avenue, New York, NY 10017
Visit our Web site at www.HachetteBookGroup.com

Originally published in hardcover by Little, Brown and Company, August 2007
First Back Bay paperback edition, October 2008

Back Bay Books is an imprint of Little, Brown and Company. The Back Bay
Books name and logo are trademarks of Hachette Book Group, Inc.

The characters and events in this book are fictitious. Any similarity to real
persons, living or dead, is coincidental and not intended by the author.

Grateful acknowledgment is made to the publishers of earlier versions of these
stories: *New Delta Review,* "Loss Prevention"; *The Cream City Review,* "Telephone
Bird"; *CutBank,* "Love Lifted Me"; *Story,* "Culver City"; *The Southern Review,*
"The Bogo-Indian Defense"; *The Sun,* "Everything Beautiful Is Far Away";
Mid-American Review, "Long Lost"; *The Georgia Review,* "Fuzzyland";
StoryQuarterly, The Best American Mystery Stories 2004, "Bank of America";
The Iowa Review, "Blind-Made Products." Excerpt from "Out on the Weekend,"
words and music by Neil Young, © 1971 Silver Fiddle. All rights reserved. Used by
permission. John Kenyon's conversation with Richard Lange, which appears in the
reading group guide at the back of this book, was originally posted at the Things
I'd Rather Be Doing blog at www.tirbd.com. Copyright © 2007 by John Kenyon.
Reprinted with permission. Richard Lange's playlist for *Dead Boys,* which also
appears in the reading group guide, was originally published on the Largehearted
Boy music and literature blog at www.blog.largeheartedboy.com. Copyright
© 2007 by David Gutowski. Reprinted with permission.

Library of Congress Cataloging-in-Publication Data
Lange, Richard.
   Dead boys : stories / Richard Lange.— 1st ed.
     p. cm.
   ISBN 978-0-316-01736-7 (hc) / 978-0-316-01880-7 (pb)
   I. Title.
   PS3612.A565D43   2007
   813'.6—dc22   2006026482

10 9 8 7 6 5 4 3 2 1

RRD-IN

Book design by Bernard Klein

Printed in the United States of America

For Kim Turner
"Remember when we were flowers?"

See the lonely boy,
Out on the weekend
Trying to make it pay.
Can't relate to joy,
He tries to speak and
Can't begin to say.

—Neil Young
"Out on the Weekend"

Contents

———

Dead Boys

Fuzzyland

———

B<small>IG MIKE INSISTS I TRY ON HIS RING. I TELL HIM THAT'S</small>
okay, but he's a pushy bastard. He bought it in Reno or won it,
which makes it lucky or something. I wasn't listening; the
guy's stories go nowhere. He wears the ring on his pinky, but it
slips easily over my thumb. He laughs to see that and piles lox
onto a bagel.

"You're going to miss me," he says to the waitress.

Upon his retirement next month, I'll inherit some of his accounts. It's supposed to be an honor. This deli, for example. I'll
be stopping in once a month for the rest of my life, pushing flat-
ware and dishes and, say, did I mention our special on toothpicks? Unless I screw up, that is. Which happens. Ask any

salesman. Buy him a drink. Greek tragedies, man. One word too many, one wayward glance, and we are up shit creek.

The owner slides into our booth. My read is he's a little skittish coming out of the box. His hand is soaking wet when Mike makes the introduction. I'm cool, though. I don't grab a napkin or go for my pant leg. He and Mike pick up where they left off last time, and I put it on automatic. Not that I'm missing anything: golf, golf, golf. It's a gift knowing when to smile or nod or raise my eyebrows without really having to listen, but I worry sometimes that it makes me lazy.

There's a movie star at the next table, some second stringer whose name I'll never recall. My wife's the one who's great with that stuff. The waitress gets the giggles pouring him coffee, and he smiles. She must be new in town. The flickering of the overhead light is killing me, the silverware clatters. I don't like where my mind's at. A bomb goes off in my stomach, and everything in it climbs back into my throat. I'm thinking about the movie star's money. With money like that you could hire people — a whole squad of detectives, bounty hunters, hit men.

"What do you say?" Mike asks me, darting his eyes at the owner, then giving me a look like it's time I jumped in.

"They raped my little sister," I reply.

"Whoa. Jesus."

That's not what I meant to say, but now that it's out — "Some motherfucker. Last night. Down in San Diego."

Rule number one is you do not bring real life into the sales environment; it's not about you. I know that, and I'm sorry, but I am going crazy here.

THE BEE MAN interrupts me while I'm shining shoes. Every pair I own, and all of Liz's, too, are laid out on the dining room table. I woke up with a wild hair this morning, and I've been at it since dawn. My fingers are black with polish. I'm so far gone, the doorbell gives me a heart attack.

The bee man's name is Zeus. His head is shaved, and he has a lightning bolt tattooed on his scalp, above his right ear.

"They let city employees do that?" I ask as I lead him down the side of the house to the backyard.

"We're contract workers. We don't have to wear uniforms either," he says. That explains the Lakers jersey.

The hive is in the avocado tree. I discovered it last week when I heard buzzing while watering the lawn. The gardener quit, so I've been doing all kinds of extra stuff around here. Bees were so thick on the trunk, they looked like one big thing rather than a lot of little ones. They shivered in unison, and their wings caught the sun. I didn't get too close. We have the killer variety now, up from Mexico. They stung an old guy to death in Riverside last year, and, I think, a dog.

"Whoa," Zeus says.

"Are they Africanized?"

"Can't tell. The killers look pretty much like the others, except for they're more aggressive. I'll send a few to the lab when I'm done."

I thought I read in the paper that they relocated the hives to somewhere they'd be useful, but Zeus tells me that's too much trouble anymore. He has a foam that'll smother the whole colony, queen and all, in nothing flat. No sooner are these words out of his mouth than a bee lands on his arm and stings him.

"*Hijo de puta,*" he says as he and I hurry away. "Those bitches are gonna pay for that."

LIZ IS DRINKING coffee in the breakfast nook. She uses both hands to lift the cup, wincing as it touches her lips. Her eyes are red and puffy. Neither of us slept much last night. It's been that way since we heard about my sister a few days ago. Guys laugh when I say Liz is my best friend. They think I'm pulling something high and mighty. Only Jesus freaks love their wives.

"Maybe it's time for a new mattress," I say.

She yawns and shrugs. "Maybe."

"The guy's here to kill the bees."

"What's that, lightning on his head?"

I have to eat something, so I scramble a couple of eggs and toast some bread. I smear mayonnaise on the toast and make a sandwich with the eggs. Liz has an apple and a slice of cheese. I get about three bites down before the phone rings.

It's my sister, Tracy, and she's crying. In our first conversations following the assault she was all facts and figures. Yes, it was horrible; yes, she was pretty banged up; no, the cops hadn't caught her attacker; no, there was no need to drive down, she already had a friend staying with her. This morning, though, she's a wreck. She can't get two words out without battling a sob.

Her ex-husband is up to no good, she says, using the attack as an excuse to press for temporary custody of their daughters. Her attorney has assured her it'll never fly, but she's worried all the same. She keeps apologizing for bothering me, which begins to piss me off. I throw the rest of my sandwich into the trash and pour myself another cup of coffee.

"We're on our way," I say.

"It's hard, all of this. I can handle it, but it's hard."

"Shouldn't take us a couple of hours, depending on traffic."

After I hang up, I grab the sponge and start washing dishes. It's one of those days when normal things feel strange. The soap smells bubblegummy, but when I get some in my eye, it hurts like hell. The window over the sink faces the avocado tree, where Zeus, wearing a beekeeper getup now, is spraying with what looks like a fire extinguisher. The hive is soon covered with thick white foam. Liz comes up behind me and yanks on the waistband of my sweats.

"I'll drive," she says.

"I saw an actor at Canter's the other day. Big guy, dark hair. He was in *Private Ryan* and that Denzel Washington movie. Went out with Heidi Fleiss."

"Oh, I know. Tom . . . Tom . . ."

She screws up her face and stares at the ceiling, folding and unfolding the dish towel. The grass is dying out back, even though I have watered and fertilized. A few bees trail after Zeus as he carries the foam dispenser to his truck. One of them veers off and begins bashing its brains out against the kitchen window with a fury that is truly humbling.

THE FREEWAY IS clear until we get into Santa Ana, a few miles past Disneyland, then it locks up. I punch over to the traffic report. Whichever lane Liz chooses stops moving as soon as she weasels her way into it. She keeps humming three notes of a song she has stuck in her head. My mouth goes dry when I spot flashing lights.

"There's an exit right here," Liz says.

"I'm okay," I reply.

Car wrecks twist me all around. My parents died in one ten years ago now, out there in the desert, on their way back from Laughlin. Big rig, head-on, whatnot. It was an awful mess. My sister lost it. She'd just graduated from high school. She was arrested twice for shoplifting in one week. The second conviction got her a month in jail. I intended to visit, but I was working twelve-hour days selling time on an AM oldies station where the general manager told everyone I was gay when he caught me crying at my desk shortly after my parents' funeral.

When Tracy was released, she moved to a marijuana plantation in Hawaii. I still have the one letter she sent. In it she asks for money to buy cough syrup and says she's learning to thread flowers into leis. She spends half a page describing a sunset. There's dirt on the envelope. The stamp has a picture of a fish. It made me angry back then, but envy can be like that.

I try to keep my eyes closed until we're past the accident, but the part of me that thinks that's silly makes me look. A truck hauling oranges has overturned, the fruit spilling out across the freeway. Two lanes are still open, and traffic crawls past, crushing the load into bright, fragrant pulp. The truck's driver, uninjured, stands with a highway patrolman. The driver keeps slapping his forehead with the palm of his hand and stomping his feet. The patrolman lights a flare.

Things clear up after that. We zip through Irvine and Capistrano and right past the nuclear plant at San Onofre, which looks like two big tits pointing at the sky. The ocean lolls flat and glassy all the way to the horizon, sparking where the sun touches it. At Camp Pendleton, the marines are on maneuvers. Tanks race back and forth on both sides of the freeway, and the dust they kick up rolls across the road like a thick fog. The radio fades out, and when the signal returns, it's in Spanish.

We stop in Oceanside for a hamburger. The place is crawling with jarheads who look pretty badass with their muscles and regulation haircuts, but then I see the acne and peach fuzz and realize they're boys, mostly, having what will likely turn out to be the time of their lives. I convince Liz that we deserve a beer, so we step into a bar next to the diner. The walls are covered with USMC this and USMC that, pennants and flags, and Metallica blasts out of the jukebox. It's not yet noon, but a few grunts are already at it. I have the bartender send them another pitcher on me. They raise their mugs and shout, "To the corps." I can't figure out what it is that I hate about them.

A FIRE ENGINE forces us to the side of the road as soon as we get off the freeway at Tracy's exit. I see smoke in the distance. The condo development she lives in rambles across a dry hillside north of San Diego, block after block of identical town houses with Cape Cod accents. The wiry grass and twisted, oily shrubs that pick up where the roads dead-end and the sprinkler systems peter out are just waiting for an excuse to burst into flame. There have been a number of close calls since Tracy moved in. Only last year a blaze was stopped at the edge of the development by a miraculous change in wind direction.

We get lost on our way up to her place. There's a system to the streets, but I haven't been here enough times to figure it out. The neighborhood watch signs are no help, and the jogger who gives us a dirty look, well, better that than gangbangers. They keep a tight rein here. The association once sent Tracy a letter ordering her to remove an umbrella that shaded the table on her patio because it violated some sort of bylaw. I'd go nuts, but Tracy says it's a good place to raise kids. A lucky turn brings us to her unit, and we pull into a parking space labeled VISITOR.

Her youngest, Cassie, opens the door at my knock. She's four, a shy, careful girl.

"Hello, baby," I say.

Her eyes widen, and she runs to hide behind her mother in the kitchen.

"Cassie," Tracy scolds. "It's Uncle Jack and Auntie Liz. You remember."

Cassie buries her face in her mother's thigh. Her older sister, Kendra, who's eight, doesn't look up from the coloring book she's working on.

It's been almost a week since Tracy was attacked, and she still has an ugly greenish bruise on her cheek and broken blood vessels in one eye. She herds us into the living room, asking what we want to drink. The place smells like food, something familiar. "Cabbage rolls," Tracy says. "You loved Mom's."

"So how are you?" I ask. That's broad enough in front of the kids.

"Better every day, which is how it goes, they say. There are experts and things, counselors. It's amazing."

"You see it on TV, on those shows. I bet it helps. I mean, does it?"

"Oh, yeah. Sure. Time's the main thing, though."

"Come sit with me," Liz says to Cassie. She's trying to draw her out of Tracy's lap, give Mommy a break.

"No," Cassie whines as she wraps her arms tighter around Tracy's neck.

My beer tastes funny. I hold the can to my ear and shake it. This big brother business is new to me. Tracy and I have never been close. We were in different worlds as kids, and since our parents died we've seen each other maybe twice a year. She came back from Hawaii, settled in San Diego, and met Tony. They married in Vegas without telling anyone. *Whew!* I thought. *I'm finally off the hook.*

But Tony's been gone six months now. Tracy used star 69 to catch him cheating. He was that stupid, or maybe he wanted to be caught. I notice that some of the furniture is different, new but cheaper. The couch used to be leather. Tony took his share when he left. Everything had to be negotiated. Tracy got to keep the kids' beds, and he got the TV, a guy who makes a hundred grand a year. It's been downhill since then. Battle after battle.

"You owe me a hug," I say to Kendra. "I sent you that post-card from Florida."

Exasperated, she slaps down her crayon and marches over. We scared the hell out of her when she was younger, showing up one Halloween dressed in a cow costume, Liz in the front half, me in back. She'll never trust me again.

She grimaces when I pull her up onto the couch. "What's the deal?" I ask.

"What?"

"What's shaking? What's new? How's school?"

"It's okay, but my teacher's too old. She screamed at us the other day, like, 'Shut up! Shut up!'" She has to scream, too, to show me how it went.

"Kendra!" Tracy says.

Cassie sees her sister getting attention and decides that she wants some. She leaves her mother to pick up a stuffed pig, which she brings to Liz, who soon has both girls laughing by giving the pig a lisp and making it beg for marshmallows and ketchup. There's a creepy picture of an angel on the wall. I ask Tracy what that's about. We weren't raised religious. We weren't raised anything at all.

"It was Kendra's idea. We saw it at the mall, and she was like, 'Mommy, Mommy, we need that.'" Tracy shrugs and shakes her head. Her fingers go to the bruise on her cheek. She taps it rhythmically.

"Angels, huh," I say to Kendra.

"They watch us all the time and keep us safe."

"Who taught you that?"

"Leave me alone," she snaps.

I walk into the kitchen with my empty beer can. Everything shines like it's brand-new. Our mother would wake up at four in the morning sometimes and pull every pot and pan we owned out of the cupboards and wash them. Dad called it her therapy, but that's bullshit. She'd be cursing under her breath as she scrubbed, and her eyes were full of rage.

Something is burning. I smell it. The fire must be closer than it seemed. I press my face to the window, trying to see the sky, while the girls laugh at another of Auntie Liz's jokes.

ASH DRIFTS DOWN like the lightest of snowfalls, disappearing as soon as it touches the ground. It sticks to the hood of a black Explorer, and more floats on the surface of the development's swimming pool, where the girls are splashing with Liz. The sun forces woozy red light through the smoke, and it feels later than it is.

I tug at the crotch of my borrowed bathing suit, one thing Tony left behind. My sister sits beside me in a chaise, fully clothed, to hide more bruises, I bet. The rapist got her as she was leaving a restaurant. That's all she told me. In a parking garage. That's all I know. "I'm lucky he didn't kill me," she said afterward. Her hand shakes when she adjusts her sunglasses; the pages of her magazine rattle.

"Come swim with us, Uncle Jack," Kendra calls. She can paddle across the deep end by herself, while Cassie, wearing inflatable water wings, sits on the stairs, in up to her waist. I make a big production of gearing up for my cannonball, stopping short a number of times until they are screaming for me to jump, jump, jump.

We play Marco Polo and shark attack. I teach Kendra to dive off my shoulders, and she begs to do it again and again. Cassie, on the other hand, won't let me touch her. Liz bounces her up and down and drags her around making motorboat noises, but every time I approach, she has a fit and scrambles to get away. "You're so big," Liz says, but I don't know. I'm not sure that's it.

A man unlocks the gate in the fence that surrounds the pool, and a little blond girl about Kendra's age squeezes past him and runs to the water, where she drops to all fours and dips in her hand.

"It's warm enough," she shouts to the man, who smiles and waves at Tracy.

"Hey, whassup," Tracy says.

She bends her legs so that he can sit on the end of her chaise. His hair is spiked with something greasy, and his T-shirt advertises a bar. I dive down to walk on my hands. When I come up, they are laughing together. He reaches into the pocket of his baggy shorts, and I swear I see him give Tracy money.

"Where are you going?" Liz asks as I paddle to the ladder.

"I want to swim, Daddy," the blond girl yells.

"Not right now," the man answers without looking at her. He stands at my approach, smiles. A salesman. Maybe not for a living, but I've got him pegged. We shake hands professionally.

"The big brother," he crows, jokey jokey. My sister should be more careful.

"Philip's going to paint my place," Tracy says. "All I have to pay for is the materials."

"Unless we get burned out," he says.

She frowns and puts a finger to her lips, nodding toward the kids.

I scrub my hair with a towel and find that I'm sucking in my gut. It's sick. A flock of birds scatters across the smoky sky like a handful of gravel.

"You live in L.A.?" Philip says to me. "I'm sorry."

A real tough guy, going for the dig right off the bat.

"I like the action," I reply.

"I was down there for a while. Too crazy."

"You have to know your way around."

I adjust my chair, sit. Philip fingers the soul patch under his lower lip. I'm staring at him, he's staring at me. It could go either way.

"I. Want. To. Swim. Now," Philip's daughter wails.

"Your mother'll be here any minute."

The girl begins to cry. She stretches out facedown on the pool deck and cuts loose.

"Go to it, Daddy," Tracy says, giving Philip a playful kick.

He stands and rubs his eyes. "This fucking smoke."

"Nice meeting you," I say with a slight lift of my chin.

He walks over to his daughter and peels her off the concrete. She screams even louder. He has to carry her through the gate.

"He know what happened?" I ask Tracy.

"What do you mean?"

I stare at her over the top of my sunglasses. After a few seconds she says, "I told him I was in a car wreck."

"So he's not like a friend friend?"

"Hey, really, okay?" she warns.

I throw up my hands to say forget it. She's right. I don't know what I'm doing, all of a sudden muscling into her life. The girls are calling for me again. I run to the edge of the pool and dive in, determined to get Cassie to play sea horse with me.

THE KIDS TURN up their noses at the cabbage rolls, so Tracy boils a couple of hot dogs for them. She's more accommodating than our parents were. Seems like a terrible waste of time now, the battles fought over liver and broccoli and pickled beets. And what about when Dad tried to force a lamb chop past my teeth, his other hand gripping my throat? Somehow that became a funny story, one retold at every family gathering to much laughter. Nobody ever noticed that I would leave the room so cramped with anger that it hurt to breathe.

Tracy pushes food from one side of her plate to the other as she talks about her job. She manages a Supercuts in a nasty part of town. The owner is buying a new franchise in Poway, and she once promised Tracy that when she did, Tracy could go into partnership with her. Now, though, the woman is hemming and hawing. The deal is off.

"I turned that shop around. She used me," Tracy says.

"Tough it out," I advise. "Regroup, then sell yourself to her. You have to be undeniable."

"Jack, I quit two weeks ago. I'm not going to take that kind of crap."

"Well, well," I say. "Man."

"Sounds like it was time to move on," Liz interjects.

"What I'd like to do is open my own shop."

It's not that I don't understand her disappointment. I made it to sales manager once at a Toyota dealership, but they put me back out on the lot after less than a month, saying I wasn't cutthroat enough. The owner's son took my place, and it just about killed me to keep going in every day. We had debts, though. We were in way over our heads. It was a shameful time, but I didn't crack. Two months later Sonny Boy went off to rehab, and I was back on top. A good couple of years rolled by after that.

While Liz and the girls clear the table, I follow Tracy onto the patio. She closes the sliding glass door and retrieves a pack of More menthols from its hiding place inside a birdhouse. Placing the elbow of her smoking arm into the palm of her other hand, she stands with her back to the door so the girls can't see her take a drag. It's a pose I remember from when we were kids, a skating rink pose. That's where she and her dirtbag crew hung out before they were old enough to drive. Barely thirteen, and rumor had it she was already screwing some high school coke-head. Guys called her a whore to my face.

The backyard is tiny, maybe fifteen by fifteen, no grass at all. A shoulder-high fence separates it from the neighbors' yards on all three sides. I can see right into the next unit: a Chinese guy on his couch, watching TV. The sound of a Padres game curls through his screen door. I tried to talk Tony out of buying this place, but he wouldn't listen. His deal was always that I was too negative. Now Tracy is stuck with thin walls and noisy plumbing.

"You guys are still the happy couple," Tracy says. "Obviously."

"Most of the time, sure."

"The good part is you don't seem a thing like Mom and Dad."

"We got lucky, I guess."

Tracy's shoulders jerk. She turns her head and spits vomit into a potted plant. I'm not sure what to do. It would frighten her if I took her into my arms. We're not that kind of people. I'm sorry, but we're not. She wipes her mouth with the back of her hand and hits her cigarette again, then walks past me to stand against the fence, looking into the neighbor's yard so that I can't see her face. A gritty layer of ash covers everything now, and more is sifting down. The smell of smoke is stronger than ever.

"I still have some of the insurance money from the accident," I say. "What if you take it? You should get that shop going as soon as possible."

"Everything's up in the air," Tracy replies. "Maybe I'll go back to school."

"Use it for that, then."

"You've got it all figured out, huh?"

"Hey . . ."

"It's funny, that's all."

She kneels to drink from a hose attached to a faucet at the edge of the patio. After the rape, she drove herself to the hospital. Nobody else in the family had that kind of fortitude. Our dad was a notorious hypochondriac.

Cassie slides the door open with great effort and says, "Mommy, what are you doing?"

"Watering the flowers," Tracy replies.

WE PLAY UNO and Candyland with the girls, and then it's bedtime. Sundays are their father's, and he's picking them up early in the morning. Liz manages to get them upstairs without too much whining on the promise of a story. Tracy gathers the toys scattered about and tosses them into a wooden chest in the corner of the room while I go to the refrigerator for another beer.

"They love their Auntie Liz," Tracy says.

I hope she means that in a nice way. I think she does.

There's a knock at the door. Tracy looks worried, so I stand behind her as she answers. The police officer on the porch gives us an official smile.

"Mr. and Mrs. Milano?"

"Ms. Milano. He's my brother."

The cop scribbles on his clipboard. "Okay, well, we're out warning residents that they may be asked to evacuate if this fire swings around," he says.

"Oh God," Tracy sighs.

"Right now things are looking good, but you should be prepared just in case."

"God fucking dammit."

When the cop leaves, Tracy turns on the TV, but there are no special reports or live coverage. Liz comes downstairs, and I fill her in. She asks Tracy what she wants to pack, and Tracy says, "Nothing. None of it means anything to me." It's embarrassing to hear her talk like that. Liz treats the comment as a joke, though, and soon the two of them are placing photo albums in a plastic trash bag.

I decide to venture toward the fire line to see if I can get more information. Liz insists on coming along. We drive down out of the condos to pick up a frontage road paralleling the freeway. There's an orange glow on the horizon, and we make for that. A new squeak in the car gets on my nerves. I feel around the dash, desperate to locate it, and things get a little out of control. I almost hit a guardrail because I'm not watching where I'm going.

"Dammit, Jack, pay attention," Liz snaps. "Are you drunk?"

The road we're on descends into a dark, narrow canyon dotted with houses, the lights of which wink frantic messages through the trees. We hit bottom, then climb up the other side. As we crest the hill, the source of the glow is revealed to be a monstrous driving range lit by mercury vapor lamps. The golfers lined up at the tees swing mechanically. There is ash falling here, too, and the stink of smoke, but nobody's worried.

We pull over at a spot above the range and get out of the car to watch. It feels like something teenagers might do. Balls soar through the air and bounce in the dead grass. Liz drapes my arm across her shoulders. She really is great with those kids.

"Are you sure you don't want a baby?" I ask.

I watch her face. Nothing is going to get past me. When she wants to be blank, though, she's so blank. "I've got you," she says.

"No, really."

"Let's keep it simple. That's what I like about us."

We made a decision a few years ago. Her childhood wasn't the greatest either. A gust of wind rattles the leaves of the eucalyptus trees behind us, and the shadows of the branches look like people fighting in the street. When I close my eyes for a second, my blood does something scary on its way through my heart.

TOMMY BORCHARDT HANGED himself in his garage after they gave half his accounts to a new hire. No note, no nothing. Three kids. That's what I wake up thinking about after tossing and turning all night, waiting for another knock at the door.

We're in the girls' room, in their little beds. They're sleeping with Tracy. On a shelf near the ceiling, beyond the kids' reach, sits a collection of porcelain dolls. The sun shining through the window lights up their eyes and peeks up their frilly dresses. Their hair looks so real, I finally have to stand and touch it. Liz coughs and rolls over. Her clothes are folded neatly on the floor. She was in a rock band in high school. I wish I could have seen that.

Downstairs, I find some news on TV and learn that the fire has changed course and is headed away from any structures. They believe it was started by lightning. Tracy's coffeemaker is different from ours, but I figure it out. It's fun to poke around in her cupboard and see what kind of canned goods she buys.

The kids sneak up on me. I turn, and there they are. I ask if they want me to fix them breakfast, but Kendra says that's her job. She stands on a stool to reach the counter and pours two bowls of cereal. I still remember learning to cook bacon. As far as I was concerned, I was ready to live on my own after that. Kendra slices a banana with a butter knife. She won't even let me get the milk out of the refrigerator for her. Tracy shouts at them to hurry and eat, their dad will be waiting.

"Is it fun at your dad's?" I ask as they sit at the table, shoveling Cheerios.

"It's okay," Kendra says, like that's what she's been told to say.

"We have bikes over there," Cassie adds.

HUNDREDS OF PIGEONS have occupied the shopping center parking lot where Tracy meets Tony to hand off the kids. They

perch on the streetlamps and telephone poles and march about
pecking at garbage. Everything is streaked with their shit. When
a car approaches, the birds wait until the last possible second to
scoot out of its way. Tracy and Tony meet here because it's equi-
distant from both their places. He won't drive any farther than
he's required to by the court.

I had to beg Tracy to let me come with her. She's worried that
I'll start something. I like that, that she's worried, but I assure
her that I'll hold my tongue. My hope is that when Tony sees
me, he'll figure that she's pulled together some support and back
off his custody demands. He's a hardhead, though. We almost
came to blows once over who was going to pick up a check at
dinner.

The girls wait like little diplomats, wise in their silence. Cassie,
strapped into her car seat, reaches out to touch the window of the
minivan. Five minutes pass with just the radio playing. I watch
the pigeons, the people pushing their carts out of the supermarket and filling their trunks with groceries. A cloud wanders
across the sky, and I track the progress of its shadow.

After ten minutes I ask, "Is this normal?"

"He's very busy," Tracy replies, sarcastic.

There's a candy store next to the market. It's just opening up.
"Take the kids in there," I say. "You guys want candy? Take
them in there and buy them something. Here's some money. I'll
keep an eye out for him."

The girls are imbued with new energy. They screech and bicker
and fight for the handle that slides open the side of the van.

"Look what you started," Tracy says.

I shrug as she flips down the sun visor and checks herself in
the mirror there. The girls, already outside, practice tightrope
walking on the yellow lines painted on the asphalt.

"Calm down," Tracy yells. "You want to get hit by a car just
for some candy?"

Tony pulls up next to the van shortly after they enter the store.

He's driving a new Volvo. He squints when he sees me, then gives a lazy wave. I'm all smiles as I hop out and walk around to his open window. He grew up on the East Coast somewhere and moved to California after college. Tracy cut his hair, that's how they met. He works in computers. I rest my palms on the roof of his car and bend over to talk to him.

"Yo, Adrian," I say. I used to kid him that he sounded like Rocky.

"Jack."

"They should just be a minute. The girls were getting cranky, waiting so long."

Tony lights a cigarette. The ashtray is overflowing with butts. *Don't you sometimes see a chick and just want to tie her up and slap her around?* He asked me that once while he was still married to Tracy. We were camping in Yosemite, all of us. The women and kids had gone to bed. I remember looking up at the stars and down at the fire and thinking, *Whoops!* He pushes his sunglasses up on his nose and flicks ash out the window, between me and the car door.

"How's Liz?" he asks. "Good, I hope."

"You know us. Slow and steady."

"Are you still selling, what, restaurant stuff?"

"Why do you have to be that way, showing up late and everything?"

"Did she tell you to say that?"

I check to make sure Tracy and the kids are still in the store before continuing.

"She was raped, man, and you're coming at her with lawyers? Have a little compassion. Act like a human being."

"I said, did she tell you to talk to me?"

"I'm her brother. I took it upon myself."

I meant to approach this a bit more obliquely. Three years ago, two, I'd have had him eating from my hand, but these days

I feel like all the juice has been drained out of me. We stare at each other for a second, then look away at the same time.

"She was wasted," he says. "Ask her. She was coming out of a bar. She barely remembers. Read the police report. There are doubts."

My vision flickers and blurs. I feel like I've been poisoned. Kendra runs out of the store toward us, followed by Cassie. I push myself away from the car and search the ground for something—a stick, a rock. The pigeons make horrible fluttering noises in their throats.

"Hi, Daddy," the girls sing. They climb into Tony's car. Tracy watches from the store, half in and half out. I wish I was a gun. I wish I was a bullet. The girls wave bye-bye as Tony drives off.

"Can you believe that a-hole has a Volvo, and I'm driving this piece of shit?" Tracy says.

"He shouldn't smoke in front of the kids," I reply.

We pass an accident on the way back to her place, just a fender bender, but still my thoughts go to our parents. When they died I was almost to the point where I could see them as people. With a little more time I might even have started loving them again. What did they stand for? What secrets did they take with them? It was the first great loss of my life.

TRACY WANTS TO treat us to lunch in Tijuana. We'll ride the trolley down and walk over the border to a steak house that was written up in the newspaper. That's fine with me. Let's keep moving. What Tony said about her is trying to take root, and I won't have it. She's my sister, see, and what she says goes. I don't want to be one of those people who need to get to the bottom of things.

We drive to the station. The crowd that boards the trolley with us is made up primarily of tourists, but there are also a few Mexicans headed for Sunday visits. They carry shopping bags, and their children sit quietly beside them. Tracy and Liz find two seats together. I'm at the far end of the car, in the middle of a French family.

We skirt the harbor, rocking past gray destroyers big as buildings. Then the tracks turn inland, and it's the back side of trailer parks and self-storage places. The faded pennants corralling a used car lot flap maniacally, and there's always a McDonald's lurking on the horizon. Liz and Tracy are talking to each other — something light, if their smiles are any indication. I wave, trying to get their attention, but it's no use.

The young son in the French family decides to sing. He's wearing a Disneyland T-shirt. The song is in French, but there are little fart sounds in it that make his sister laugh. His mom says something snippy to him, but he ignores her. Dad steps in, giving the kid a shot with his elbow that jolts him into silence. There's a faded tattoo on Dad's forearm. Whatever it is has teeth, that's about all I can make out.

To cross into Mexico, we walk over the freeway on a bridge and pass through a turnstile. I did this once before, in high school, me and a couple of buddies. If you were tall enough to see over the bar, you could get a drink. That was the joke. I remember a stripper in a gorilla suit. Tacos were a quarter. The only problem was that the cops were always shaking someone down. The system is rotten here. You have to watch where you're going.

Tracy's got things wired, though. Apparently she's down here all the time. It's fun, she says. She leads us to a taxi, and we head into town, passing ramshackle body shops and upholstery shops and something dead squished flat. Dirt roads scurry off into the hills, where entire neighborhoods are built out of old garage doors and corrugated tin. The smell of burning rubber sneaks in now and then and tickles the back of my throat.

Calle Revolución is still the main drag, a disco on every corner. It looks tired during the day, like Bourbon Street or downtown Vegas. Hungover, sad, and a little embarrassed. It's a town that needs neon. We step out of the cab, and Tracy laughs with the driver as she pays him off. I didn't know she spoke Spanish.

I want a drink. The place we go into is painted bright green. Coco Loco. They sell bumper stickers and T-shirts. We get a table on the second-floor terrace, overlooking the street. Music is blasting inside, and lights flash, but the dance floor is empty except for a hippie chick deep into her own thing. The waiter is all over us as soon as we sit down.

I order tequila and a beer; Tracy and Liz get margaritas. Some poor guy in a ridiculous sombrero cha-chas around with a bottle of mescal in one hand and a bottle of Sprite in the other. For a couple of bucks he pours a little of each into your mouth and shakes your head, all the while blowing on a whistle. The sound of it makes my stomach jump. I'm startled every time. When my tequila arrives, I drink it down and guzzle half the beer.

"You guys wait here," Tracy says. "I have to run an errand."

"In Tijuana?"

"Tylenol with codeine, for a friend who hurt her leg. They sell it in the pharmacies."

"Wait a minute, Trace —"

"It's cool. I'll be right back."

She's gone before I can figure out how to stop her.

Everybody around us is a little shady. It hits me all of a sudden. Not quite criminal, but open to suggestion. A man wearing mirrored sunglasses and smoking a cigar gets up from his chair and leans over the railing to signal someone in the street. His partner is having his shoes shined by a kid with the crookedest teeth I've ever seen. The sombrero guy blows his whistle again, and a big black raven lights on the roof and cocks his head to stare down at us.

LIZ INSISTS THAT Tony is full of shit when I tell her what he said in the parking lot. I lean in close and speak quietly so no one else can hear. She says that men always cast aspersions on rape victims, even the cops. "You should know better," she says.

"I didn't mean anything like that."

"I hope not."

"She can do whatever the fuck she wants. Get her head chopped off, whatever."

"That's nice. That's just lovely."

It's the alcohol. It makes me pissy sometimes. Liz doesn't know the worst of it. Like the time I went out for a few with one of my bosses and ended up on top of him with my hands around his throat. He didn't press charges, but he also wasn't going to be signing any more checks for me. To Liz it was just another lay-off. Quite a few of my messes have been of my own making. I'm man enough to admit it.

The bathroom is nasty, and there is nothing to dry my hands with. My anger at Tracy rises. She's been gone almost an hour. "Hey," I yell to a busboy from the bathroom door. "You need towels in here." He brings me some napkins. I have to walk across the dance floor to get back to the terrace. A kid bumps me and gives me his whole life like a disease. I see it all from beginning to end. "Fly, fly, flyyyyy," the music yowls. "Fly, fly, flyyyyyy."

THEY STILL HAVE those donkeys painted like zebras down on the street, hitched to little wagons. I remember them from last time. You climb up on the seat, and they put a sombrero on your head that says KISS ME or CISCO and take a picture with some kind of ancient camera. Liz and I hug. We look like honeymooners in the photo, or cheaters.

There are those kids, too, the ones selling Chiclets and silver rings that turn your fingers green. Or sometimes they aren't selling anything. They just hold out their hands. Barefoot and dirty — babies, really. So many that after a while you don't see them anymore, but they're still there, like the saddest thing that ever happened to you.

Liz and I stand on the sidewalk in front of the bar, waiting. The power lines overhead, tangled and frayed, slice the sky into wild shapes. Boys cruise past in fancy cars, the songs on their stereos speaking for them. The barker for the strip club next door invites us in for a happy hour special, two for one. It's all a little too loud, a little too sharp. I'm about to suggest we have another drink when Tracy floats up to us like a ghost.

"You know, Trace, fuck," I say.

"What a hassle. Sorry."

A hot wind scours the street, flinging dust into our eyes.

THE RESTAURANT IS on a side street, a couple blocks away. We don't say anything during the short walk. Men in cowboy hats cook steaks on an iron grill out front, and we pass through a cloud of greasy smoke to join the other gringos inside. It's that kind of place. I order the special, a sirloin stuffed with guacamole.

Tracy pretends to be interested in what Liz is saying, something about Cassie and Kendra, but her restless fingers and darting eyes give her away. When she turns to call for another bottle of water, Liz shoots me a quizzical look. I shake my head and drink my beer. The booze has deadened my taste buds so that I can't enjoy my steak. Tracy cuts into hers but doesn't eat a bite. The waiter asks if anything is wrong.

We go back to Revolución to get a cab. The sidewalks are crazy, tilting this way and that and sometimes disappearing completely. You step off the curb, and suddenly it's three feet down to the pavement. Tracy begins to cry. She doesn't hide it. She walks in and out of the purple afternoon shadows of the buildings, dragging on a cigarette, tears shining.

"Must be one of those days," she says when I ask what's wrong.

We leave it at that.

She cleans herself up in the cab, staring into a little round mirror, before we join the long line of people waiting to pass through customs. We stand shoulder to shoulder with strangers, and the fluorescent lights make everyone look guilty of something. There are no secrets in this room. Every word echoes, and I can smell the sweat of the guy in front of me. Four or five officers are checking IDs. They ask people how long they've been down and what they've brought back with them. When it's my turn, a fat blond woman glances down at my license, matches my face to the picture, and waves me through. We're all waved right through.

Tracy's mood brightens immediately. In fact, she laughs and laughs as we leave the building and board the trolley. Everything's funny to her, everything's great. The train is less crowded this time. We each get our own row of seats. Just some marines at the other end of the car, talking about whores. "Oh, this little bitch, she went to *town*," one of them groans.

Tracy reaches into her purse and takes out a bottle of pills, opens it and pops one into her mouth. She smiles when she catches me watching her.

The trolley clicks and clacks like it's made of bones. I stretch out, put my feet up. The reflection of my face is wrapped around a stainless steel pole dulled by a day's worth of fingerprints. Tracy dozes off, head lolling. Liz, too. I watch the sun set through rattling windows, and all the red that comes with it.

The trolley lurches, and Tracy's purse tips over. It's one of those big bags you carry over your shoulder. A half-dozen bottles of pills spill out and roll noisily across the floor. I chase them down, mortified. Tracy opens one eye. I spread the bag wide. It's full of pills, maybe twenty bottles, all with Spanish labels.

"You've got kids," I whisper. "Beautiful kids."

"That's right." She grabs the bag away from me and hugs it to her chest.

"Tracy."

"Look, I didn't ask you to show up; I just didn't say no."

"I wanted to help."

"I fully realize that."

I try to talk to her some more, but she pretends to be asleep. Nothing I say means anything anyway, because she thinks I've had it easy. Liz is suddenly beside me. She takes my hand in both of hers. The jarheads are rapping. *Bitch. Skeez. Muthafucka.* I could kill them. I could.

WE CAN SEE the fire from the freeway. The entire hillside is ablaze. Tracy's condo is up there somewhere. Flames claw at the night sky, and smoke blots out the stars. I don't even know how you'd begin to fight a thing like that. Maybe that's what the helicopters are for. They circle and dip, lights flashing.

Tracy is still asleep. She could barely walk from the trolley to the car but wouldn't let us touch her. "Stop laughing," she yelled, so messed up she was imagining things. She's curled up on the backseat now, her arms protecting her head. We decide not to wake her until we're sure of something.

The police at the roadblock can't tell us much. The wind picked up, and everything went to shit. The gymnasium of a nearby high school has been pressed into service as a shelter. We are to go there and wait for more information. A fire truck arrives, and they pull aside the barricades to let it through.

"How bad are we looking?" I ask a cop.

He ignores me.

I back the car up and turn around, and Liz guides me to the school. We pass a carnival on the way, in the parking lot of a church. A Ferris wheel, a merry-go-round, a few games. People wander from ride to ride, booth to booth, swiping at the ash that tickles their noses. A beer sign sputters in the window of a pizza parlor. A kid in a white shirt and black vest sweeps the sidewalk in front of the multiplex. His friend makes him laugh. A mile away everything is burning.

My stomach is cramped by the time we get to the school. I can see into the gym from where I park. Cots are lined up beneath posters shouting GO TIGERS!!! Two women sit at a table near the door, signing people in, and farther away, in the shadows by the drinking fountains, a group of men stand and smoke. That's about it. Most people have somewhere better to go. Tony must have told Kendra about angels. What a thing to put into a kid's mind.

A news crew is interviewing a girl who just arrived. She's carrying a knapsack and a cardboard box full of china. They shine a light in her face and ask about what she lost and where she'll go. She says something about her cat. She had to leave it behind.

I close my eyes and bring my fists to my temples. I have to be at work early for a meeting. I can see Big Mike sliding out of his Caddy, squeezing his gut past the steering wheel. He's my mentor, he likes to say. He's been married four times. He gets winded walking to the john. There's nothing lucky about him.

"I want a baby," I say. The words just get away from me.

"Jack," Liz says. I'm afraid to open my eyes to look at her. Tracy giggles in the backseat, and we both turn. She reaches up to scratch her face and grins in her sleep.

Bank of America

———

AFTER WE TAKE CONTROL OF A BANK AND SUBDUE THE security guard, it's my job to watch the customers while Moriarty slides over the counter and empties the tills. I'm not sure why this task fell to me. Even after all this time, I'm not the most convincing bad guy. I've worked on my posture and stuff in the mirror, practiced evil glares and unnerving twitches, but I still worry that someone is going to see through me.

The gun I carry helps. A big, ugly, silver thing, it's fairly undeniable. I'm careful not to abuse the upper hand it gives me, though. You see psychos playing those games in movies, and you're always glad when they get theirs. And I've been on the other end of it, too, shortly after I moved to L.A. I know what it feels like. As I left a liquor store one night, a couple of peewees rushed me and flashed a piece. My wallet practically flew out of my pocket and into their hands. It took me weeks to stop shaking. I vomited right there on the sidewalk. I keep that in mind when we're doing our thing. No need to push it.

IT'S A SPECIAL day. We're gathered in the cramped little office that Moriarty peddles cut-rate car insurance out of to review his plans for our final job. Moriarty, because he's the mastermind of our crew. Under his direction, we've pulled off twenty-seven successful bank robberies in three years—more than Jesse James—and in all that time we've never been caught, never had the cops on our trail, never even fired our weapons.

It must be a thousand degrees outside. Even with two fans whirring and all the windows open, the air just lies there, hot and thick as bacon grease. One story below, down on Hollywood, an old Armenian woman is crying. She sits on a bus bench, rocking back and forth, a black scarf wrapped around her head. Her sobs distract me from Moriarty's presentation. He asks a question, and I don't even hear him.

"Hey, man," he scolds. "Come on. Really."

"I'm with you, I'm with you." I get up off the windowsill and go to the Coke machine he keeps stocked with beer. The can I extract is nice and cold, and I press it to the back of my neck and motion for him to continue.

It's the same scenario as the last job and the one before. There's not much finesse at our level. We're not blowing vaults or breaching high-tech security systems. Basically it's hit-and-run stuff. We grab as much cash as we can before someone activates an alarm, then run like hell to our stolen getaway car. Moriarty has always wanted us to look like amateurs. He has a theory that the cops will pay less attention to us that way. We've taken other precautions as well. No two jobs are ever less than twenty miles apart, and we vary our disguises: ski masks, nylons, wigs and fake beards. We wore alien heads once, and once we went in turbans and shoe polish, trying to have a little fun with it.

Moriarty has me trace our route in and out with my finger, then crumples the map and burns it in an ashtray. I admire his thoroughness. It makes me proud to be his partner. And the control he exerts over himself—my God! He has mastered the messy business of life. Every day he eats a banana for breakfast and a tuna sandwich for lunch. Every day! And his whole week is similarly cast in stone. Thursday nights: pool at the Smog Cutter from nine to eleven and two beers—no more, no less. Saturdays, a movie, target practice, an hour of meditation, and the evening spent studying history. Sundays he's up at six to read the *New York* and *L.A. Times* from cover to cover. I believe him when he says that living this way gives him time to think. It makes perfect sense: He's a speeding train, and his routine is the track; all he has to concentrate on is moving forward. That doesn't mean he's perfect—he still lives with his mother, gets a little too spitty when he talks about guns, and seriously believes Waco was just a taste of things to come. But that will of his!

"So everybody's clear?" he asks. "No muss, no fuss?"

"Clear, *mon commandant.*" This from Belushi, the third member of our crew, who's lying on the couch, smoking another cigarette.

Moriarty steps out from behind his desk and opens the office refrigerator. He tosses a Popsicle to Belushi and one to me, and we sit sucking them in silence. The Armenian woman is still crying downstairs, and it starts to get to all of us. Belushi snaps first, growling, "For fuck's sake, put on some music or something." Moriarty slips a CD into the boom box, and "Whole Lotta Rosie" blasts out of the speakers.

"Maybe we should go down and see what's wrong," I suggest.

"I'll tell you what's wrong," Belushi says, a chuckle rattling the phlegm coating his throat. "It's too hot, the air's for shit, and the world is run by evil old men. You could rip your eyeballs out, and the tears would keep right on coming."

He's one of those hard-core doomsayers, Belushi, and a junkie, too—hence the nickname—but he also understands money like nobody I've ever met before. Rumor has it he comes from a rich family, so maybe it's in his blood. He's been the driver on all our jobs, and our accountant. Our goal when we started this thing was a quarter million each—serious fuck-you money—and today the balance of my Swiss bank account stands at $248,320. You'd never guess it, seeing him sprawled out like he is now, grinning that yellow, broken-toothed grin, but Belushi has taken all of our booty and, through some serious offshore hanky-panky, more than tripled it. That's why this is our last gig. It'll be little more than a formality, but we have to stick to the plan, because sticking to the plan is what brought us this far.

Moriarty plugs in his vintage Ms. Pac-Man machine, and it comes to life with a barrage of beeps and whines. A sticky drop from his rapidly melting Popsicle falls onto the screen, and he wipes it away with his thumb.

"So how's your love life?" he asks Belushi. Here they go again.

"None of your business."

"There's nothing wrong with paying for it, you know. It's a victimless crime."

"Not according to the women who end up with you."

"Is your mom bad-mouthing me again?"

Belushi fakes a belly laugh and draws his long, thin arms and legs in to push himself up off the couch. The hottest day of the year, and he's dressed all in black. "I'll see you bastards Thursday," he says.

When the door closes behind him, Moriarty shakes his head.

"My man's a trip, ain't he?" he says.

"He's something," I reply.

A sheet of paper with the current scores for our never-ending tournament is taped to the side of the Ms. Pac-Man machine.

Moriarty checks it, then starts his game. I move back to the windowsill to drink my beer and try to catch a breeze. From there, I watch Belushi exit the building and approach the Armenian woman, who's still crying, even though I can't hear her over the music. I can't hear what Belushi says to her either, but whatever it is stops her frenzied rocking. He reaches into his pocket for some money and gives it to her. She takes his hand in both of hers and kisses it, and he pats her on the back before scuttling down the street.

Yes, my man is definitely a trip.

Belushi and Moriarty call me John Q because I'm the normal one, which means I've got the wife and kid, and I hit the floor running every morning, looking for some way to scrape together the cash it takes to keep my family afloat. When we reach our goal after this last job and finally, by mutual consent, get access to our money, Belushi is splitting for Amsterdam, where he's going to register as an addict so he can receive free government-issue heroin, and Moriarty's finally moving out on his own, to Idaho, the last free place in America, or something like that. Me, I just want a Subway franchise somewhere quiet with good schools. A three-bedroom Kaufman and Broad and a decent car. Bank robbery is a hell of a way to get a little boost up the ladder, I know, but aren't they always saying to go where the money is? You can make anything mean anything if you try.

WHEN I GET home Maria's peeling potatoes in the kitchen for her famous french fries, to go with the burgers I'll throw on the barbecue. I told her I was going out to bid on a painting job. She asks me how it went.

"Looks good," I say. "It's a big place. Might keep me busy for a month or so."

"Hooray for our team, huh?"

"We'll see, we'll see."

She picks up a knife and slices the potatoes into long, thin strips, which she places in a bowl of water.

"Someone broke in next door and stole their television," she says.

"You're kidding."

"They were asleep when it happened. Didn't hear a thing."

"Man oh man."

"I know. Scary."

She's not trying to make me feel bad, but I do. I should have pulled her and Sam out of this neighborhood years ago, when the graffiti first sprouted, the first time the car was broken into. I kept thinking things would turn around. I was like that back then, all silver linings and never say die. Now, though, I acknowledge the impossible. And after Thursday—the Hole in the Wall Gang's last ride—we're saying good-bye to bad luck.

"Let's start looking for another place," I say, moving up behind Maria to wrap my arms around her and bury my face in her hair. I love her hair. I have always loved her hair.

"Maybe over in Glendale," she says.

"How about farther? How about the mountains? Completely the hell away from here."

"Don't be a joker."

"Baby, I'm serious. It's time."

She turns to kiss me. Her wet hands on my face smell of potatoes and dirt. She's Cuban, brown and smooth-skinned. Her parents begged her not to marry me. They had a friend of the family lined up, a medical student, but she was as stubborn then as she is now.

"Okay, the mountains," she says.

"The mountains."

We rest against each other for a second, then she laughs and pushes me away. "Ahh, you're crazy. I brought some quizzes home to correct. Go check on Sam and let me work."

I pause in the doorway and watch as she sits at the table and takes up her pen. The curtains billow in the window behind her and dance in the evening breeze, and the shadows of the refrigerator and the toaster grow longer and cooler by the minute. She rests her forehead in her hand and smiles, and I finally understand why people are so afraid of dying. I want to be with her forever.

"Papi," Sam says. "Hey, Papi, look."

I jerk back out of a deep and dreamless catnap, and the sudden return of sight stings my eyes. One minute I was contemplating the brittle droop of the fronds of the palm tree outside our living room window, and the next I was gone. Even when I'm not working I'm tired all the time.

"Papi!"

Sam is almost five. He told me last week that he wants to be a doctor when he grows up so he can fix broken hearts. This evening he's busy pulling apart his collection of action figures and recombining the pieces to create new forms of life. He slides one across the coffee table for me to look at.

"This is the man who found out he was a robot," he explains. "He watched in the mirror and took off his face, and there was a robot head underneath. Now he drinks oil and is very, very sad. He gets mad sometimes and breaks things."

"Does he have any friends?" I ask.

Sam purses his lips, thinking. "He's too scary and too sad. He cries too much. If he had some money, he would buy a new head, but he doesn't."

"How much would a new head cost?"

"Around ten dollars, I think."

"Here," I say, pretending to hand the little man something. "Here's ten dollars. Go buy yourself a new head."

"He can't hear you," Sam says. "He's got robot ears, too."

Sam splashes in his inflatable wading pool while I set up the grill and start the briquettes. Some of the people who live in the other bungalows in our complex are cooking outside, too, and we wave at each other across the courtyard all of our doors open onto. There's plenty of shade now. The sun is low on the horizon, coating every leaf of every tree with honey, and the birds are deep into their happy hour. The air is filled with raucous screeches as they swarm a freshly seeded patch of lawn.

"Look, Papi."

Sam lies on his stomach and drops his face beneath the water. Bubbles fizz around his head. He rises and waits for my smile and nod, then goes under again. One of the neighbors turns on a radio, and Mexican music competes with the chatter of the birds. When we move to the mountains, I'll build our house myself. One of those wooden dome jobbies you can order plans for, kind of a futuristic log cabin kind of a thing. I picture myself sawing boards and pounding nails. It seems entirely possible.

We eat on the porch, citronella candles pushing back the bugs and the darkening night. Burgers, Maria's fries, and a salad of avocados and sliced ripe tomatoes dressed with oil and vinegar and lots of pepper. Sam's damp hair clings to his forehead, and the towel Maria dried him with is still draped around his shoulders. Maria scolds him when he burps, but then I burp, too. She wrinkles her nose in disgust and pours more iced tea. The birds have quieted, and in the distance there is the faint *pop pop pop* of gunfire. I glance at Maria and Sam, but neither reacts, and I tell myself that it's because they haven't heard the shots, not that they've grown used to the sound.

Later we watch an old monster movie together, that one about the giant tarantula running amok in the desert. I switch from iced tea to beer. Sam is curled around a pillow on the floor in front of the television, and Maria lies with me on the couch. The weight of the day presses down upon me, and my eyelids grow unbearably heavy. I fall asleep to the sound of a woman screaming. When I awaken after midnight, Maria has moved to the floor, next to Sam, and they've both sacked out. I pick Sam up and carry him to bed, then gently rouse Maria, who wobbles into the bathroom.

Someone famous is selling something cheap on TV. I shut it off. A rustling outside the front door tightens everything in me like a knot. I turn out the light and edge over to the window. Pulling the curtains aside just a bit, I peek out at the porch, but there's nothing there, just a napkin we missed when we cleaned up. Maria returns in her bathrobe and wants to know what's wrong. I tell her not to worry, that I'm just paranoid after what happened next door. We share a glass of ice water and go to bed.

In the morning, Sam's wading pool is gone.

MORIARTY HAS ME meet him up at Lake Hollywood. They call it a lake, but it's actually a reservoir tucked into the hills where the movie stars live, a concrete-lined hole surrounded by a chain-link fence. Pretty enough, if you squint. Moriarty does six miles a day on the road that circles it, round and round, rain or shine. He makes me feel like a slob.

I park where he instructed me to and walk over to the fence. The still, black water is covered with a layer of dust that sparkles in the sunlight, and the smog is so thick the trees on the far shore are barely visible. Above me a big house juts out from a hill, propped up by a few spindly wooden supports. The view from the deck must be terrific in October or November, when the air clears; you can probably see all the way to the ocean, and I bet the people who live there step out every evening to lean on the railing and watch the sun set.

Moriarty pounds past me in a flat-out sprint and continues on for another hundred yards or so before turning around. He returns at a jog, throwing punches.

"Hey," he huffs. "How you doing?"

"I'm good," I reply.

He lifts his T-shirt and wipes away the sweat on his face with it. Another runner passes by, and they exchange nods.

"Wait at your truck," he says to me.

I walk across the road and lean against my Nissan. Fingers intertwined behind my head, I stare out at the reservoir and contemplate the golden film of dust that floats upon it. It doesn't seem very sanitary, this system of storage. Maria's been after me to spring for bottled water, and I'm beginning to see her point. If the stuff that comes out of our tap originates here, who knows what kind of deadly crap it's laced with.

Moriarty is parked a short distance up the road. He pulls a duffel bag out of his trunk. I know the song he's whistling as he approaches. It's a Sousa march my dad had a set of dirty lyrics for:

> *Oh, the monkey wrapped his tail around the flagpole*
> *To watch the grass grow*
> *Right up his asshole.*

Something like that. Used to crack me up when I was a kid.

Moriarty sets the bag in the bed of my truck and unzips it to show me the sawed-off shotgun inside.

"There's a box of shells, too," he says.

"Thanks."

"Lock it away where the kid can't get at it. Don't be stupid."

"Come on, man."

"Do you know how to use it? You probably won't have to, because the sound of the shells sliding into the chamber will send your average burglar packing with a pantload, but just in case?"

"I can't imagine it's too difficult."

Moriarty grins and closes the bag. "Just point and shoot."

An old lady steps out of his car and shouts, "Stuart, I don't want to be late."

"Yeah, Ma, okay," Moriarty shouts back. "Church," he says to me with rolling eyes. "See you Thursday."

"You betcha."

We shake hands and he jogs to his car. I take another look at the big house above me, and I can't help it—call it jealousy, whatever you want, but I can't help picturing the Big One hitting and the surprise and terror on the owners' faces when those supports snap like toothpicks and they end up riding that fancy sonofabitch down the hill and through the fence and straight to the bottom of poisonous goddamn Lake Hollywood.

I WAS A wreck when Moriarty happened upon me, so twisted inside that at times I couldn't even breathe deeply enough to fill my lungs. Driving along the freeway or standing in line at the supermarket I'd find myself gasping for air like an astronaut unmasked on Mars. A year earlier, after my third paycheck in a row had bounced, I'd told the contractor I'd been working for to get fucked and drawn out all of our savings to set myself up as an independent. I didn't love painting houses, but I figured that in a short while I'd have enough capital to move into buying and renovating neglected properties and reselling them at a profit. Twelve months later, though, I'd only had four jobs, and to get those I had to bid so low that I barely broke even. One beer in the evening turned into three, then six. "What kind of idiot did you marry?" I'd ask Maria, and she'd say something nice, but that's not what I wanted to hear, so I'd ask again, "What kind of idiot did you marry?" I'd keep asking until I brought her to tears.

Moriarty found me at the unemployment office in Hollywood. I ignored him on his first approach, because everybody there seemed so strung out and crazy, and who knew what this blond bastard with the crooked smile was up to. *Just let me fill out my forms and be on my way* was my philosophy that morning, but he kept at me, asking to borrow some of my newspaper and following me outside to the catering truck parked at the curb, where we stood eyeing each other through the steam rising from our coffee.

He says he could tell right then that I was the one, but I don't know how. That first conversation, as I recall it, was nothing more than your standard two strangers shooting the shit kind of thing: a little sports, a little music, and each of us maybe trying a little too hard to convince the other that we were worth more than the three hundred bucks a week we were waiting in line for. In my version it wasn't until later — when we retreated to a bar to wash the shame of the morning from our craws — that the truth began to come out. When Moriarty wrapped his hands around his beer like he was praying and sighed, "I'll tell you what, getting by is killing me," that's when I first thought we might have something in common.

Turned out we lived in the same part of Hollywood, so we started getting together for drinks once a week or so. Bank robbery was a running joke from the beginning, or at least I took it as a joke. Moriarty would say, "I'm serious," and I'd laugh and say, "I know you are." To me it was like, "Hey, let's make a movie," or, "Let's open a pizza place," one of those shared pipe dreams guys sometimes use as an excuse to keep meeting when they're too up-tight to admit they enjoy each other's company. You know, "This isn't just drinking; we've got business to discuss." You get to fanta-size together, share your plans for all the money you're going to make, act a little foolish.

Even when Belushi came into the picture — an old college buddy of Moriarty's — and Moriarty got into the insurance racket, and we started meeting at his office instead of the bar because he decided we shouldn't be seen together in public any-more, I still didn't take it seriously. And how could I? I mean, the three of us — us! — sitting around hefting pistols and dis-cussing timing while studying maps Moriarty had drawn of the various banks he'd cased — it was hilarious. I remember laugh-ing to myself the first time we actually drove out to scout an es-cape route, because I knew an hour later I was going to be home playing patty-cake with Sam and helping Maria clean the bath-room. That was real life. My life.

So how, then, do I explain what happened next? I don't. I can't. Boom! There I am, standing in one of those same banks on legs that are shaking like a pair of Slinkys. I've got a gun in my hand and pantyhose pulled over my head, and when I yell, "Get down on the floor!" you'd think it was the voice of God rumbling out of a thundercloud, the way the customers throw themselves at my feet. I'd always imagined that when you crossed the line you saw it coming, but it turned out to be more like gliding over the equator on the open sea. Don't let them kid you, it's nothing momentous, going from that to this.

El Jefe phones early Monday morning with an offer of a few days' work on a house in Los Feliz. He was a bigwig in the Nicaraguan army until they ran his ass out on a rail after the revolution. Now he's got a rinky-dink painting business here, with most of his jobs coming through flyers he leaves in mailboxes and under windshield wipers. When white people hire him, he calls me in, because he jacks up his prices for Caucasians and figures they won't complain as much if some of it is going to a fellow gringo. Besides that, white women feel more comfortable with one of their own around, he says, "to keep an eye on us thieves and rapists." It's a hundred tax-free bucks a day, and it'll keep my mind off the heist.

The house is a big, two-story Spanish-style that we're taking from dull tan to something slightly darker. It's me and a couple of short, silent Guatemalan Indians doing the labor, with El Jefe supervising between cigars and chats on his cell phone.

The best thing about painting is that it has a rhythm that allows you to drift away. On this morning I run through our first Christmas in the mountains, tweaking the vision bit by bit until it snaps into perfect focus, right down to the broken-glass sparkle of the new snow, the pop and hiss of the logs burning in the fireplace, and the smell of the tree that Sam and I will cut down and drag home through the wintry woods.

It's such a pretty picture that the sun chewing on the back of my neck doesn't bother me at all, and I'm almost reluctant to put down my brush and descend the ladder when lunch rolls around.

I get the sandwiches and thermos of lemonade that Maria made for me out of the cooler in the bed of my truck and settle against the shady side of one of the palm trees planted in the strip of grass between the street and the sidewalk. The Guatemalans sit on the curb some distance away, talking quietly as they peel back the foil from their burritos. We haven't exchanged two words all morning, but that's the way it goes on these jobs. I think they know why El Jefe brings me around, and I'm not about to stroll over and plop myself down beside them and give them a "we're all in the same boat" speech, because we're not, and they know that, too.

El Jefe pulls himself out of his dented BMW, where he's been sitting with the air conditioner blasting for the last half hour. He mutters something to the Guatemalans, who bow their heads and nod, reluctant to meet his gaze, then marches across the yard to check our progress. Out of habit, I guess, he still carries himself like a military man — back straight, shoulders squared, one hand always resting on his hip, where his sidearm would be if he were in uniform. It's funny seeing him strut around like this now that he's gone soft and sprouted a belly, but I don't dare laugh, not with those crazy eyes of his and his history.

He walks into the backyard and then returns a few minutes later and motions with a quick snap of his wrist for me to join him. We step softly along a stone path that leads to a covered patio where we can look down onto the swimming pool, which sits at a lower elevation than the house. Two nude men are sunning themselves, side by side on chaise lounges. As we watch, one of them stands and kisses the other before diving into the water.

"Fucking *maricones*," El Jefe whispers. He raises an imaginary rifle to his shoulder and aims it at the men.

"What's the big deal?" I ask.

"It makes me sick, those *putos*." He removes his mirrored sunglasses and wipes the sweat from his eyes with the palm of his hand. "We flushed our shit in Managua."

I shrug and say, "Free country and all that."

"And this is freedom, to fuck another man?"

"To fuck whoever you want, I guess. Who cares?"

"What?" he says, staring at me with disgust.

I don't want to get into it, so I return to the front yard and prepare to go back to work. El Jefe's all fired up, though, and won't leave it alone. He hovers behind me and says, "This country has lost its way."

"Yeah yeah," I snap. "And you used to be hell with a cattle prod and a pair of pliers. I'm busy here, okay?"

I've never popped off to him like this before, and I'm afraid to look up to see what effect it's had on him. Sweat is running down my forehead, my nose, my cheeks, and a few drops fall into the can of paint I'm stirring. After a while his shadow slides away, and I hear him walking across the lawn. When he reaches his BMW, he calls to me.

"Hey, gringo."

I try to strike a defiant pose as I stand to face him.

"You think I am a bad man?"

He looks almost sad now, almost ashamed, but I'm not about to back down. "I think you've done bad things," I reply.

An unripe date drops from a palm tree above his car and bounces off the hood with a loud bang. He stiffens at the sound, a slight flinch, then relaxes again and says, "So it's lucky that only God will be the judge of both of us."

Before I can fish up a response, he gives me a quick salute and slides into his car and drives away. At quitting time he returns with liquor on his breath and hands each of us our pay sealed inside an envelope, as is his usual custom. I open mine at a stop sign on the way home and find an extra fifty-dollar bill tucked among the twenties.

THE BEDROOM IS dark; darker still the figure filling the doorway. I strain my arms and legs, try to sit, roll to the floor, yell, but nothing works. He walks slowly to the side of the bed and jams the barrel of a pistol into my mouth, twists it past my lips and teeth, pulls the trigger. An awful goddamn dream. I awaken with ringing ears, my heart heaving against my ribs like an animal struggling to escape a trap. I taste gunpowder and oiled metal, and even before the world has fully congealed, I'm on my feet. The shotgun and shells Moriarty loaned me are hidden on the top shelf of the closet, inside an old gym bag. I carry them out to the living room and sit on the couch.

The porch light stains the curtains orange. A moth's shadow flashes huge across them. It's bright enough in the room for me to make out the TV, the DVD player, the stereo, everything where it should be. I've never been out here naked before. My balls feel funny, resting on the cool vinyl of the couch. I raise the gun to my nose, and the smell brings back my nightmare. A shudder runs through me.

There's something sharp beneath my bare foot. I reach down to pick up whatever it is, one of Sam's toys, the man who found out he was a robot. It seems important that I help the little guy by giving him the new head he wants. I'll fix him and leave him for Sam to find in the morning, a kind of miracle. Thinking there must be more of the figures scattered about, I slide to the floor and lie on my stomach. I sweep my hand through the dark and dusty cavern beneath the couch, but find nothing except an old soda straw and a penny.

"Honey?"

Maria startles me. I roll over and grab the shotgun and point it at her, and then lower it just as quickly when I realize what I've done. My God. My fucking God.

"What's going on?" she asks.

"Nothing."

"Is that a gun?"

The refrigerator grumbles under its breath in the kitchen.

"I got it from a friend," I say. "With all the burglaries, I thought it might be good to have around."

"So you're going to shoot someone?"

"Scare them maybe."

I pull myself back onto the sofa, upsetting the box of shells. They fall to the floor one by one, clank and roll, clank and roll. I'm an idiot. Maria slips into the orange glow, arms crossed over the front of her robe, her worried look tempered by a quizzical smile. My shame only burns more intensely when she sits beside me and reaches out, probably afraid, to lay a hand on my shoulder. Her lips touch my cheek, and I feel as soft and black as a piece of wormy fruit. I squeeze the man who found out he was a robot so hard he cuts into my palm. How do normal people live with all the mistakes they've made?

AFTER WORK ON Wednesday I stop off at the supermarket to pick up milk and eggs, and who do I spot but Belushi. He's slouched in the condiment aisle, brow furrowed, rubbing his temples with his index fingers. His black-clad frame sways like a tree rocked by the wind.

I know he lives in the neighborhood, but our paths have never crossed before, and I marvel at how strange he looks compared to the other shoppers. Big bubble sunglasses hide his eyes, and tattooed leopard spots tumble out of the sleeve of his T-shirt, which advertises five-cent mustache rides.

I don't have it in me, the guts it takes to set yourself apart like that. I had my ear pierced once, but it only lasted a week, until a carpenter on the job I was working at the time made a smart remark.

"Boo," I say to Belushi when I finally sidle up next to him.

He glances over at me and smiles like we do this every day. "Twenty-five kinds of barbecue sauce," he says. "And all that mustard, man." His speech is slurred, and thick strings of saliva stretch between his lips.

"You shopping?" I ask.

"Nah, nah. I came in for cigarettes and got distracted."

He loses his balance and almost topples over. A security guard at the end of the aisle pays close attention.

"Truthfully, I'm pretty fucked up. Could you give me a ride home?"

His apartment is only a couple of blocks away, in a nice building, much nicer than mine. It must be true what Moriarty says about him coming from money. He invites me in for a beer, and I say sure, because it looks like he might need help getting to his door.

The walls and ceiling of the elevator are covered with a mosaic of tiny mirrors. I crouch and make a monkey face, and it's like watching myself on thousands of little TVs. Belushi staggers into the kitchen when we reach his apartment. He's got a computer and a plasma screen, and there are two or three electric guitars lying about. Instead of a couch, fat pillows surround a low table covered with those religious candles they sell in Mexican stores.

Belushi returns with a bottle of Heineken and hands it to me, then drops onto one of the pillows. It feels a little hippy-dippy, but I join him. I wish he'd open a window or at least twist the blinds to let some sun through. It's like an animal's den in here, or the end of some dark road. I imagine bones in the shadows, jagged rocks, old burned wood. He takes a noisy hit from a purple bong and asks in a high, choking voice whether I'm nervous about tomorrow's job.

"Sure," I reply. "I've barely been sleeping. You?"

"I'm a fucking mess," he says with a smile. "This is the last one. The big one. Your old lady doesn't know what's up, does she?"

"No way. No. She'd flip."

"How are you going to explain coming into money?"

I shrug to avoid answering. I've given the matter a lot of thought, but he doesn't need to know that. He's got plenty of other things to make fun of me about.

"You and Moriarty have been friends for a long time, huh?" I say.

Belushi lights a cigarette. The ashtray is a coiled rattlesnake with red rhinestone eyes.

"Yep. Me and the buttfucker go way back. He's my favorite Martian. The same spaceship stranded both of us on this prison planet, and we've been looking for a way off ever since."

"Is that right?" I reply.

"It is," he snaps.

"Can you do this?" I ask, flashing the Vulcan salute from *Star Trek*.

He laughs and says, "Make it so." Picking up the remote, he turns on the stereo. Strange music fills the apartment, layer upon layer of squealing guitars over a flat *chunk chunk* drumbeat. It sounds like a factory coming apart in a hurricane. Belushi's fist keeps time, pounding against his knee. There's a poster on the wall of the pope marching with Nazis.

"I know what you're thinking," Belushi says, gesturing at the TV and guitars and everything, "but I need this money as much as you."

"I understand," I reply, and I guess I do. There's more than one kind of miserable.

"I'm going to miss you when this is over," he says.

This blindsides me, but I nod and say, "And I'll miss you."

I carry Maria's coffee in to her, set the cup on the dresser while she's getting ready for work. She smiles at me in the mirror when I crouch beside her and rest my chin on her shoulder. I run my hands up under her nightgown and cup her breasts. Turning my face to her neck, I tongue the beauty mark there and inhale deeply. I need to memorize it all in case something goes wrong.

"You have dark circles," she says. "Still not sleeping?"

"I'm fine. Don't worry."

The big day is finally here. I could be rich by nightfall, or dead. What a wide-open feeling. I can't put my finger on it.

Sam is sitting on the living room floor in front of the TV, a bowl of cereal in his lap. His eyes are locked onto the screen, where a cartoon spaceship goes down in flames.

"Invader X neutralized," he declares, imitating the voice of some hero in a visored helmet.

I remember the joy of losing myself like that as a child. What a gift it seems now. I resist the urge to pick him up, to intrude, and instead sit on the couch and love him from afar.

The three of us leave the bungalow together, and I walk Maria and Sam to the Sentra. She'll drop him off at kindergarten on her way to school. I kiss them both and wait to make sure the car starts, because the battery hasn't been holding a charge lately. It's hard to let them go this morning. Tears sting my eyes as the car crests the hill in front of our complex and pops out of the shadows and into the ravenous sunlight.

THE PLAN IS to meet at three o'clock in the parking lot of a minimall a few blocks from the bank. Until then it's business as usual. The Guatemalans are already up on their ladders when I arrive at the house in Los Feliz. El Jefe steps out of his BMW and watches me unload my truck. He's smoking a cigar and drinking from a quart carton of orange juice.

I'm painting up under the eaves this morning, which is nice because it keeps me out of reach of the sun, but hell because of the spiders. If this was my job, I'd have sprayed the webs down with a garden hose yesterday and let the wall dry overnight, but El Jefe's not much for prep, so I use a brush to sweep the webs away. They're as thick as cotton in places, and studded with dried-out flies that jump and crackle. The webs wrap around me when they fall, cling to my face with ghostly tautness, and slither into my lungs on the current of my breath. And the monsters that spun them! Fat black spiders drop like poison rain. I swat them away when they scrabble over my arms, my neck, but it's too much. I have to take a break, sit on the lawn with my head between my knees.

After lunch I begin to work myself up to sticking my finger down my throat. That's how I'll get away, by vomiting and telling El Jefe I'm too sick to keep going, maybe blame it on a spider bite. I'm prying open a new can of paint when my phone rings. It's Maria. There's worry in her voice. Sam has fallen at kindergarten and may have broken his leg. She can't leave school right now and wonders if I can pick him up and drive him to the hospital. No problem, I say. Relax. Everything'll be okay.

"Jefe!" I yell, approaching his car at a run. "I've got to go. It's an emergency."

He rolls down the window. Chilled air breaks over me like a wave. "I'm not paying you for today, then," he says. "You have to work the whole day to get paid."

"Do whatever you want. I'll pick my shit up later."

It's not until I'm driving away that I think to look at my watch. Quarter after one. I'm supposed to have a gun in my hand and a bulletproof soul in less than two hours.

SAM IS LYING on his back on a cot in the school nurse's office. He stares at the ceiling, afraid to move, his face pale and sweaty.

"I'm hurt," he says, "but not bleeding."

He whimpers when I scoop him up, cries for his shoes, which the nurse has removed. She gives them to him, and he twines his fingers through the laces, clutching them tightly. I shield his eyes from the sun as I carry him across the parking lot. A bell rings behind us, doors open with a *whoosh,* and hordes of screaming children run for the playground.

He lies across the seat of the truck. The top of his head rests against my thigh. He looks up at me as I drive, his bottom lip held between his teeth. I know he's in pain, but he doesn't complain once, though every block seems to have a pothole that makes the truck shake like an unwatered drunk.

"Want to play music?" I ask. He's not usually allowed, but I need to see him smile. I turn on the radio and say, "Go ahead."

He reaches out tentatively, as if this might be a trick, and pushes one of the buttons, changing stations. When no scolding follows, he sets to work in earnest. We listen to snatches of some rapper, the Eagles, news, a Mexican station, and back again, and he laughs at the cacophony he's creating. I feel awful for ever depriving him of this pleasure, for ever slapping his hand and shouting, *Knock it off.*

Meanwhile my partners are waiting, and the ticking of my watch grows louder with each passing second. If I don't show up, they'll call the job off, but I know Moriarty and his completion principle. He'll just plan another, and that's unacceptable. I want this to be over now. I want to be a citizen again. I want to spend my fucking money.

I lay my hand on Sam's chest. His heart is beating as fast as mine.

"I'll teach you a song," I say. *"Oh, the monkey wrapped his tail around the flagpole . . ."*

WHEN THEY WHEEL Sam off for his X-rays, I call Maria at school. Her phone is off, so I try the office. The secretary puts me on hold, then comes back on to ask if I'd like to leave a message, because Mrs. Blackburn is unavailable at the moment.

"This is her husband. Tell her I've got our son here at Kaiser in Hollywood."

"Let me write it down," she says. "You're her husband?"

I don't have time for this, so I hang up on her and call Moriarty. No answer, but I decide not to leave a message. You never know who's listening. Then I try the school again. The same woman answers, and I slam the receiver down.

I'm clenching my jaw so tight, my teeth hurt. Any minute something inside me is going to burst. I lean against the wall, close my eyes, and breathe deeply, which only makes me feel worse, because the air in the corridor reeks of shit and medicine. There's a TV on somewhere. A woman on it asks, "Do you love me?" and a man answers, "I don't know right now." "Do you love me?" the woman screams. I begin to pace, ten steps up the hall and ten steps back. The world narrows into a strip of snot-green linoleum over which I have complete control. It should always be this easy.

Suddenly Maria arrives, flushed and sweaty-palmed. Another teacher took over her class, allowing her to leave school early. She'd left her phone in her desk. The doctor informs us that Sam has a hairline fracture of the tibia. Nothing serious, but he'll need a cast. It's two-thirty. I can still make my rendezvous with Moriarty and Belushi if I go now.

"Hey, I left my stuff at the site," I tell Maria. "I should probably pick it up before they quit for the day."

"Okay. Go ahead."

"You'll be fine here by yourself?"

"See you at home."

I kiss her on the cheek and force myself to walk until I'm out of her sight.

Boom! Here we go, rolling in out of the heat and noise and destroying the silky air-conditioned calm of the bank. Today it's Mexican wrestling masks and happy-face T-shirts, party clothes to commemorate our final heist. "Get down," I yell, "down on the floor," showing my gun. There are one, two, three customers, and they drop like trapdoors have opened beneath them. Moriarty beelines for the security guard, who meekly holds out his

hands to be cuffed. One, two, three customers, all secure. I wonder if the plants standing in the corners are real or made of plastic. Something tickles my neck. I reach up and snag it, a long
black hair, Maria's. I raise it to my lips as Moriarty hurdles the
counter and makes his way down the line of tellers. No trouble
there. They've been trained not to resist. Just push the silent
alarm and back off. Well, supposedly silent. The signal zips up
my spine like a thimble on a washboard, and all of my pores are
screaming. One, two, three, old lady, fat man, vato. Each second
is disconnected from the one that came before it, so that they
bounce around like pearls cut loose from a necklace. Moriarty's
finished. He heads for the door, the bag slung over his shoulder. I
follow him out to the car, dive inside, and Belushi slams his hand
against the steering wheel and screams, *"Yes!"* He swings out
into traffic and we're gobbled up into the steaming maw of the
city, where we disappear for good.

IF IT'S TRUE that the same God will judge both El Jefe and
me, I want this added to the record: In the end, I didn't lie to my
wife. When she wondered about the money, I came clean. I
hadn't planned to, but I did.

"Where did you get it?" she asked.

"I robbed a bank. Lots of banks."

She stiffened in my arms — we were in bed at the time — then
rolled over to watch my face.

"Will they catch you?"

"No."

It took the rest of the night to work through it. Maria felt I'd
put the family's future in jeopardy and wanted answers to a lot
of questions I hadn't dared ask myself before for fear that the
answers would have pulled me up short, destroying the ruthless
momentum that had enabled me to do what had to be done. I
explained as best I could while she waffled between tears and
outrage. Dawn found us silent and drained at the kitchen table,

sharing a pot of coffee. The walls of the bungalow ticked and popped in the gathering heat, and the fresh light of the new day stumbled over the cracks in the plaster left by the last earthquake. Her decision was conveyed by a simple gesture. She reached across the table and took my hands into hers: We would go on.

I'M SITTING ON the couch, using a Magic Marker to draw a spaceman on Sam's cast. He keeps leaning forward to monitor my efforts, and isn't pleased with how it's turning out.

"No, Papi, his body's not right."

The phone rings, and Maria picks it up in the kitchen. Another real estate agent. We're driving up to Big Bear on Saturday to look at houses. Only a week has passed since the robbery, and already things are changing. So many options, so many decisions. To tell you the truth, it leaves me a little dizzy. I'm like a dog that's finally managed to jump the fence and, rather than running like hell, sits in front of the gate, waiting for his master to let him back in.

Sam asks me to give him the pen so that he can finish the spaceman himself. I leave him to his work and walk into the kitchen, where Maria is making notes on a legal pad, the phone's receiver pressed to her ear with her shoulder. I'm too big for the bungalow tonight. If I move too quickly, I'll break something.

"I'm going out," I whisper, motioning to the door.

Maria frowns and holds up her hand to indicate that I should wait for her to finish. When I come out of the bedroom after putting on a clean shirt, she's still on the phone, so I just wave and go. Sam is busy with his drawing. He doesn't hear me when I say good-bye.

I stop in at the Smog Cutter. There's a country song playing on the karaoke machine, and old Fred is singing. I grab a stool and settle in to see if Moriarty will show up for his regular Thursday-night session at the pool table. We haven't seen each other since the robbery, since Belushi presented us with our account numbers and the partnership was dissolved. For security reasons we agreed to go our separate ways from that moment on, but I just want to say hey and find out how he's doing.

Because I can, I buy a round for the house, and I'm everybody's best friend for five minutes. It makes me laugh to see how easy it is, and how quickly it fades.

Nine comes and goes, then ten, and still no Moriarty. He must have changed his routine. Hell, he may already be in Idaho. And Belushi's not home either, or at least he doesn't answer when I push the button for his apartment on the intercom downstairs. Well, fuck it, then. "Here's to us, fellas," I say, raising a pint of bourbon in the parking lot of a liquor store. The only good thing about the moment is that I'm pretty sure that as long as I live I'll never feel this lonely again.

The shotgun Moriarty loaned me is locked in the toolbox in the bed of my truck, where I put it when Maria told me to get it out of the house that night. I've been meaning to dispose of it, and this seems as good a time as any.

I drive up to Lake Hollywood. The lights from the mansions in the hills circling the reservoir are reflected in its inky blackness. I press my face against the chain-link fence, then turn to gaze up at the stilt house that caught my attention on my earlier visit. Someone inside is playing a piano. Another belt of bourbon, and I swing the shotgun up and fire twice into the air. The blasts roll across the reservoir and back.

I toss the shotgun over the fence, where it plops into the water and sinks from sight. The piano is silent, and a shadowy figure crouches on the deck of the house, watching me. I stare up at him and tip the bottle again, hoping to spook him even more, but when I slink away, it's with darkened headlights, so that he can't make out my license plates.

THREE POLICE CARS are parked on the street in front of the bungalows when I get back. Their lights, red and blue, wash over the trees. My hands begin to shake as I drive slowly past, trying to see what's happening. The cops are gathered in the courtyard, and the doors to all the units are open.

I should keep going, return later just in case, but I can't. My family is there, frightened probably, worried. I park down the block and head up the hill on foot. I'll go easy if it comes to that. They won't have to club me or twist my arms to get the cuffs on. If Sam saw that, it could scar him for life.

The cops tense up as I step into the courtyard. A few hands move toward guns.

"Papi," Sam yells. He hobbles to me, dragging his cast, Maria right behind him. "A burglar was here," he says. I reach down and pick him up.

"The Floreses surprised somebody breaking into their place," Maria says. "He ran out the back when they came in the front."

"Jesus," I say.

The cops go back to their discussion, ignoring us.

Maria hugs me close and whispers in my ear, "I was so scared." I apologize to her, tell her everything will be okay.

We'll be like this for a while, tightening at the sight of police cars, losing hope every time there's a knock at the door. But the years will pass, the fear will fade, Maria will stop wondering what other secrets I'm keeping, and someday I won't even be the same man who took down those banks. It will be more like a crazy story I heard than something I lived.

Sam won't let me put him down. He wants to be carried. I put my other arm around Maria, and we walk to the bungalow, step inside, and lock the door behind us. Safe — oh, please let us be safe — for at least another day.

The Bogo-Indian Defense

SOMETHING HAD CHANGED. I SENSED IT AS SOON AS I walked into the doughnut shop. Nobody was playing chess, where always before there had been at least one game going on. All the guys just sat glumly at the little plastic tables, staring into their coffee or fiddling with empty sugar packets. And the radio was off. No Dodgers. In the middle of the season. Impossible.

I thought it might be me. I have this tendency. I'll pick a bar, for example, and stop in for a drink every evening for six months, a year, know all the bartenders' names, all the regulars, get slipped a free one now and then, feel right at home, but then one day, out of nowhere, it turns to shit. Same bar, same stool, same gin and tonic, but suddenly the mole on the face of my favorite waitress makes me sick, the Christmas lights framing the bottles

56

are a terrible joke, and the ice cubes feel like broken glass in my mouth. I hurry out in what always seems like the nick of time, never to return. I've fled bowling alleys in the same cold sweat, restaurants, apartments I loved, too many jobs to count, an entire city. Denver—just the thought of that place makes me shudder.

So that's what I assumed was going on when I saw those men I'd never known to be anything but cheerful fighting back tears and not even Cocaine Bill could muster a greeting. I stepped to the counter for a coffee, waiting for that inexplicable dread to grab me by the throat and once again force me out onto the street. It was no use even sitting. I stood in the corner, holding my cup in one hand, jingling the change in my pocket with the other.

But then Whitey roused himself with a heavy sigh, running his fingers and thumb over his big silver mustache. He glanced at me with bloodshot eyes before turning back to the window, on the other side of which cars raced up and down Sunset on missions of great importance.

"Bud passed away," he said, letting me in on the reason for the pall. "Heart attack, apparently, yesterday afternoon."

José crossed his tattooed arms on the table in front of him, bowed his head, and began to sob, while Bill, that miswired fuck, ran out the front door and attacked a parking meter, kicking and punching it until Ray Ray screamed at him to stop.

I got a refill on my coffee and settled in for a long night in my usual spot next to the video game. Yes, things had changed. But this time it was the world, not me. Was it selfish to feel relieved? I couldn't decide.

BUD LEARNED TO dream in Vietnam. Before that, back on the ranch—Montana, Idaho, wherever it was he grew up—he'd turn to stone as soon as he hit the sack. His mind shut down till morning, when his father's voice resurrected him, calling him to breakfast and days heavy with heat and dust and endless chores.

At first it scared him. He'd be sleeping in a bunker deep in the jungle, and his head would fill with yellow or red or green. He thought he was going crazy, like the private from Tulsa who came off a long night at a listening post on the perimeter and started in with "Pete and Repeat were sitting on a log. Pete fell off. Who was left?" and was still at it two days later when they choppered him out. But then Bud discovered that if he focused—*squinted* was how he put it—the colors coalesced and he'd find himself starring in the wildest movies.

It was a revelation. In the midst of all that desperation and fear, where even the birds made sounds like people dying, he could turn in and visit his mom or bang Raquel Welch or eat a steak that doubled in size every time he took a bite. At first he dreamed exclusively of home, but after a while crazier scenarios played themselves out. One night it was pirates, all pirates; the next he rode a bike through Rome, Italy, wearing nothing but skivvies and flip-flops.

When his tour was up, he returned to the ranch, but he could no longer stomach the early mornings. He wanted to sleep, to dream, till noon, then maybe nap again after lunch, which didn't sit well with his father, who expected him to pull his weight as he had before. A friend from the army invited him to Buffalo, and the two of them boozed away a couple of good years, screwing hippie chicks and shoveling snow, until the friend started talking to God and decided to shack up with a waitress. Bud split for Florida then, but the humidity down there brought on his first nightmare. He was back in the jungle, carrying a severed hand that had little mouths that wouldn't stop screaming on the tips of each finger. *Fuck this shit,* he decided, and set out for California.

It took him ten years to get here. On the way he married and divorced a couple of times, went to barber college, did time for burglary and aggravated assault, learned to weld, and lost the sight in one eye. L.A. was everything he'd hoped it would be, though. As soon as he hit town, he said, he put it in neutral.

When I met him at the doughnut shop, he was living off VA money in a garage apartment owned by a Filipino slumlord. He slept twelve hours a day and once a month took a five-dollar turnaround bus to Vegas to work on a keno system that was going to make him rich, something that had come to him in one of his dreams. He was full of shit and worse, but who among us wasn't? I was rooting for him. We all were.

WHITEY MADE THE arrangements. Apparently he and Bud had discussed the inevitable a number of times and shared with each other their last wishes. That kind of foresight was astonishing to me.

I'd never been to a funeral before, but I'd seen them on TV, so I knew to wear a tie. Bill asked me to pick him up because his license had been suspended again. "I will be high," he said, "but ignore it." I did my best. The whole way there he played bongos on the dashboard and rocked back and forth in his seat. Every so often he'd unpin the fist-size rose he'd stuck to the lapel of his jacket and shove it under my nose and say, "Smell that. Pretty, huh?"

It was a big church, and new. The ceiling arched over us like an umbrella, and every little sound had an echo. I'd never known Bud to be religious. In fact, the only comment I'd ever heard him make on the subject, while gloating over a particularly profitable chess victory, was "The devil is in the details." But I guess there were certain times when certain words had to be said, and where else outside of a courtroom were you going to get people to shut up long enough to listen?

We only took up the first two pews; the rest stretched out behind us like some kind of tricky maze. The mourners were all men except for Nita, the Cambodian lady from the doughnut shop. It was nice that she showed up. A thing like that needed a woman's tears. I felt the pew vibrating beneath me and noticed that Bill was shaking like a car with its idle out of whack. Ray Ray was on one side of him, Dennis on the other. They each reached over and held one of his hands to calm him.

Bud's ashes were in an urn on the altar. The cross suspended behind it was smooth and clean, without a nail hole or a drop of blood. The preacher did the best he could with his send-off, being a stranger. He told a few stories Whitey had fed him, like the time Bud took up a collection to buy José's kids presents when José got laid off right before Christmas, and how he once gave a whore his only pair of shoes, then walked around barefoot for a week because he said he needed a lesson in humility.

Toward the end of the service a man slipped through the door and stood in the shadows at the rear of the church. He stayed only a few minutes, was gone before we'd raised our heads following the final prayer. Whitey insisted it was Bud's brother, the only member of his family to make an appearance, but I don't know about that. With a life like Bud's, the possibilities were endlessly exotic.

WE ALL MET up at the doughnut shop later. Everyone was on the program except Bill and me, so the two of us kept stepping outside to guzzle bourbon between cups of coffee. Nita had made chicken and rice, and someone brought a couple of supermarket pies. The radio was on, and the urn containing Bud's ashes had a table to itself. Pretty soon Ray Ray and Dennis set up their pieces for a game.

Whitey seemed old that night. His hand trembled when he lifted his coffee. Various people sat down across from him and tried to get him talking, but he just nodded or said, "Oh, really?" never picking up his end of it. Even when Bill and I played the video game, the noise of which Whitey always claimed gave him a migraine, he couldn't muster the energy to cuss us out. My guy had iron fists, and Bill's shot fire from an amulet on his chest. We fought in a ring in the middle of a desert.

Whitey followed me when I stepped outside for a smoke. A line of people waited to get into the nightclub across the street. We watched a couple of pretty girls jaywalk to join it. The door opened, and the music and laughter that spilled out were louder than the traffic. I wondered what the fuck was wrong with me.

"Youngblood," Whitey said, pointing at my cigarette. "Those things will kill you."

"Don't worry about it."

"Give me one," he demanded, and I handed him the pack.

"I've got a job for you," he said.

"I have a job," I replied, and it was true. I'd been working at U-Haul for six months.

"Someone's got to deliver Bud's ashes to his daughter. It's what he wanted done."

"His daughter?"

"She moved out here from Florida a while back. Her and Bud only met once, and it didn't go so well, but it's what he wanted done. She lives in Downey with her husband and kid. Won't take you an hour."

Family shit. I hadn't spoken to my own mother in ages.

"You were his best friend," I said. "I'll drive you."

"I'm not up to it."

"One of the other guys, then."

We turned to look in the window of the doughnut shop, at everyone hanging out. "Who?" Whitey said. "José? The man has a goddamned tear tattooed on his cheek. Ray Ray? You think I'm going to trust this to a dude who forgets to put his teeth in half the time? Or Bill?" At that moment Bill was standing in the corner, doing math problems in midair and laughing to himself. "Get up in the morning, shower, shave. I'll spring for a haircut and gas," Whitey said.

I turned back to the nightclub, thinking again that I should have been there instead of at the doughnut shop. I didn't dance, but that wasn't a problem. You could sit at the bar, buy a girl a drink. It worked that way, too. Whitey put his hand on my shoulder and gave it a squeeze. The booze felt like it was chewing a hole in my stomach. When the traffic signal switched to green, everything started moving at once.

I LEFT BUD's ashes in the trunk of my car that night. It wasn't the smartest thing I've ever done, but after splitting another pint with Bill, I got a little squeamish. My grandma used to tell me ghost stories when I was a kid. Then, after I was asleep, she'd sneak into my room with a sheet over her head and scream bloody murder. I peed my pants once, she scared me so bad, and everybody died laughing. She was trying to teach me something, I think, but the dark still gets to me.

When I went down to go to work the next morning, the trunk was wide open. Some asshole had punched out the lock. My spare was gone, my jack, and the urn containing the ashes. The sun can seem so cruel in a moment like that. And the trees, the way they just stand there, and every dog in the neighborhood snickering at you. Your own skin feels like a punishment.

ALL KINDS OF people came into the U-Haul place. Happy people, sad people. We entered their names into the computer, checked their credit cards, and led them out to their vehicles. You were entitled to a bonus if you could talk them into extra insurance. The boss was always on us about it. "Push the cheese," he'd say. "Push the cheese." He was a young black guy. Cedrick. Very ambitious. But all I could think about that morning was Bud's ashes and what an idiot I'd been for leaving them in the trunk. I wanted to hurt the person who'd taken them. I wanted to hurt myself.

The man with the funny teeth had a million questions, but his grin made it obvious that he already knew the answers and was just fucking with me. Certain types get a kick out of doing that to people who work behind counters. All my life I've had to deal with them.

"How much gas is in the truck now?"

"It's full, sir."

"And what if it's not full when I return it?"

"We'll fill it up and charge it to your card."

"How much a gallon?"

"Five dollars."

"Do you really think that's fair?"

My hands began to sweat so much I could hardly hold the pen, and the neck of my T-shirt tightened across my windpipe. The man with the funny teeth grinned even wider, so that his mouth cut his face in half. I excused myself and stepped into the back room. My tongue wouldn't lie still, and I was terrified that I'd swallow it. Someone out front said "refrigerator," and someone else said "who." The floor seemed about a million miles away. It was Denver all over again. I didn't want to cry, but that's usually how it went.

Cedrick found me with my arms wrapped around the watercooler, my head resting on top of it. There was such kindness in his voice when he told me to take a break. On my way out I dropped my nametag onto his desk, because I knew I wouldn't, couldn't, come back.

THERE WAS QUITE a selection of urns at the mortuary. They were displayed on shelves in a room full of caskets. An old woman with hair like a puff of smoke tried to steer me toward the high-end models, but I stood my ground. The basic copper container cost me sixty dollars.

I borrowed my neighbor's hibachi and dumped in half a bag of charcoal. After it had flamed and crumbled and cooled, I scooped the ashes into the urn. It was the only way I could think of to make things right. Bud would have approved, I'm sure. He always enjoyed a good fake-out. I took the urn up to my apartment and opened a can of chili. It was the first food I'd eaten all day. Sleep didn't come any easier, but I wasn't expecting miracles.

THE HOUSES IN her neighborhood all looked alike: square, flat-roofed little bungalows the color and texture of after-dinner mints. I drove around the block a few times, smoking and noticing the bars on the windows and how some people pulled their cars right up into their yards. She had a lawn, though, and there was a waist-high chain-link fence to separate it from the sidewalk. I made sure to latch the gate behind me.

I could hear the TV through the door when I rang the bell. It took a while for her to answer. Her dark hair was cut short and combed like a boy's, and she had green eyes. I thought maybe I had the wrong place. There wasn't much of Bud about her.

"Yes," she said, like she was expecting trouble.

"I'm looking for Kate, Bud Herman's daughter."

"That's me."

"He . . . he died last week."

"I heard."

She opened the screen door. A little girl with the same green eyes came up behind her and peeked at me around her legs. I wished I'd worn nicer clothes, maybe my tie.

"I was asked to deliver these. His ashes. He wanted you to have them."

Kate glanced down at the urn, then looked back up at me with a smile.

"Is that ridiculous or what?" she said.

I smiled, too, and shrugged. A car alarm went off a few houses away. "People put them on their mantels," I said.

She laughed out loud at that and brought her hand up to cover her mouth. There was a ring on every finger. "The mantel, huh. Well, all right."

I wanted to keep her laughing. The sound had a sweetness to it that cut through everything. The little girl stared up at her, puzzled, as Kate took the urn.

"Thanks," Kate said. "Really."

I turned sideways and pointed at the grass with my thumb. "Nice yard."

"It's a little shaggy."

"Do you have a mower?"

I don't know what Bud had intended by having her take charge of his ashes, but it suddenly seemed to me a very weak gesture. It took a few minutes of convincing, but she eventually led me to the garage. I fired up the lawnmower and went to work.

There were two squares of grass separated by a concrete walkway that ran from the gate to the house. I cut one square, then the other, then started over. Sweat ran down my face, and I thought about taking off my shirt but decided against it. The little girl stood on the porch the whole time with her fingers in her ears, watching.

When I finished, Kate gave me a 7 Up. We stood in a sliver of shade between the garage and the house. She uncoiled a hose and watered the flowers planted there. A hummingbird flickered above us like some strange gift, and I thought, "Summer. Wow," remembering yards and hoses and cold drinks that had been lost to me for years.

"Tell your husband the mower needs gas," I said.

"He left months ago," she replied without looking at me. "But you already guessed that."

She was right. I had.

BILL CUT HIS finger scrounging cans from recycling bins. He kept taking off the gauze he'd wrapped around it to show all of us in the doughnut shop the flash of bone that could be glimpsed when he pulled the edges of the wound apart.

"It's my pussy finger," he said over and over. "Ain't that a bitch."

"You best look after that," José advised.

I joined the circle gathered around the table where Whitey was taking on a walk-in. It was a ten-dollar blitz match, five minutes on each clock, and Whitey already had his opponent's queen and both bishops. The chess played there was a million miles away from the solemn, sedate pastime I'd always associated with Persian rugs and smoking jackets. The doughnut shop crew had picked up the game in jails and psych wards. You didn't take pieces, you killed them, the object being complete annihilation. Kamikaze assaults were the norm, and there was always money at stake, even if it was just the price of a cup of coffee.

Whitey darted in and out, eating pawns just for the hell of it and foiling every attack his opponent mounted. The walk-in was a gigantic Samoan who scowled down at the board as we urged Whitey on. "Whack that fucker," someone yelled. "Off with his fucking head." In the end, the Samoan's king stood alone, surrounded by black marauders. The Samoan reached across the table and shook Whitey's hand, then left without a word.

The guys drifted outside to smoke or to the counter for refills, and Whitey motioned me into the empty chair across from him while he arranged the pieces for another game.

"How'd it go?" he asked.

"Nice girl," I replied.

"She cry or anything? Was it a scene?"

"Not at all."

Whitey always knew the right thing to do or say, but only because he'd spent his whole life making mistakes. It seemed a high price to pay for wisdom—a ruined liver, a bullet nestled against his spine, a family broken and lost along the way. I hoped I'd somehow stumble upon a shortcut.

The Dodgers were on the radio, ahead by two in the bottom of the eighth. It was still hot outside. I could feel it when I pressed my palm to the window. The smell of freshly mown grass clung to me.

"Ready for a lesson?" Whitey asked, leaning back in the chair and rubbing his neck.

Bud had been teaching me the game before he died. Every night he'd walk me through a match, slapping my hand when I reached for the wrong piece. I had the basic moves down and a few dirty tricks under my belt, but it never meant as much to me as it did to Bud. I just liked to see the light in his eyes when I finally picked up something he'd been drilling me on.

"Sure," I said to Whitey.

"I'm a different breed of player than Bud was, a little more tactical. I actually read a few books."

"So I'll have the best of both worlds, right?"

"That's right. Good. Why don't we start with a few openings."

Outside, Bill poured whiskey on his finger and howled and jumped up and down like an angry coyote in a cartoon.

THE NIGHTCLUB ACROSS the street from the doughnut shop opened at nine o'clock. I arrived at 9:05 in order to beat the line. It was just me and the bartender for the first hour. Louise, originally from Nebraska. She didn't want to talk about it, though. She didn't want to talk about anything. The place was smaller than I'd imagined. The walls were painted black, and there was no door on the bathroom stall.

I stuck to beer as more and more people showed up and the music grew louder. The bass bounced in my chest like a second heart. It was difficult to get a good look at anyone, the way the lights flashed and wobbled. Faces bloomed and faded and dropped away before I could draw a bead. I kept telling myself something good would happen, but wasn't quite sure what I was expecting.

The thing I was most afraid of was appearing desperate. A girl danced alone in a dark corner of the club. She knew the words to every song, even the Mexican ones. I came up with fifteen ways to introduce myself to her, but all of them turned my stomach.

Last call came as a shock. I wanted one more drink, but when I reached into my pocket, I discovered I was out of money. It was useless to ask Louise to cut me some slack. She'd given away my stool when I'd gone to the men's room, and to get it back I'd had to mad-dog the squatter, who turned out to be her boyfriend. The girl in the dark corner, though, we'd exchanged a few glances, so I walked over and offered to write her a check for double the cost of a shot and a beer. She made a sort of clawing motion at my eyes and then put her hands over her ears and yawned. Sirens wailed and the house lights came up and bouncers started throwing people out. Everybody looked like they were about to cry.

LUCKILY, KATE SMILED when she came to the screen door and saw me standing on her porch. I don't know what I would have done if she hadn't. Such presumptuousness was out of character for me, and I hoped my showing up unannounced wouldn't frighten her.

I raised the tray of pansies I'd picked up at Home Depot and said, "It's freaky, I know, but I thought these might look good in your yard."

"It's freaky," she confirmed. She was wearing cutoff denim shorts and a red tank top, under which I could see a scallop of black bra strap.

"I can just leave them, or if you want you can show me where, and I'll put them in for you."

Her bottom lip slid up over her top one, and she furrowed her brow for an instant before opening the screen and calling over her shoulder, "Hey, guys, ready for some gardening?"

I could see past her then, into the living room, where her

daughter and a big balding man about my age were playing with Barbies on the couch. The man held up one of the dolls in my direction and called out in a high voice, "Just a minute. I'm not dressed yet."

His name was Heinz — that's what he went by, anyway — and he and Kate had met at the supermarket or some such place. He had all kinds of suggestions about where to plant the flowers, but Kate ignored him and let her daughter, Monica, decide instead. While the girls placed the dog-faced blossoms in holes they scooped in an empty bed at the edge of the front yard, I leaned against the fence with Heinz.

He tried to get the lowdown on me and Kate, but I sidestepped his gentle probing. He'd have to come right out into the open if he intended to cock-block me, and I didn't think he had it in him. Someone had gone after every tree on the street with a can of spray paint. The loopy blue letters circling the trunks didn't make any sense at all. The house next door still had a Christmas wreath in the window and a plastic jack-o'-lantern on the porch.

Heinz's earring sparkled as he flexed his thick biceps, showing me how he once reeled in a shark he hooked on a day boat out of San Pedro. His pale eyebrows were almost invisible against the pink expanse of his sunburned forehead.

"Hey, Kate, you fish?" he called out.

She was on all fours, but raised herself to her knees to shoot him a sarcastic look. "Oh, yeah. Love it."

Monica, bored with the flowers, walked over to stand between me and Heinz. A man in a wheelchair passed by, rolling himself along the buckling sidewalk. Monica hooked her fingers through the fence and closed her eyes. "Don't stare," she hissed at us. "It's not polite. You have to peek."

KATE INVITED ME to stay for dinner. Heinz sold steaks door to door and had brought along some samples. If my continued presence was a disappointment to him, he didn't let on. We moved to the backyard, and he started the barbecue while I helped Kate set the picnic table and mix tiny canned shrimp into the salad. Crickets began to chirp as day folded smoothly into night. I was finally able to relax a bit. The sharp edges of everything lost their gleam, and you could feel the dusk, like a feather, on your eyelids and the backs of your hands.

After we'd eaten, we dragged chairs onto the grass to watch the stars come out. The sky soaked up so much light from the city that only ten or so were visible, but that was all we needed. Monica, in her bathing suit, skipped to and fro through a sprinkler that hissed quietly in a corner of the yard while Kate told us funny stories about the lawyer she worked for, a man so reviled that someone once shit in his desk drawer while he was out to lunch.

"I love her," Heinz said when Kate took Monica into the house to get her ready for bed.

I nodded, staring at the distant lights of a plane headed for LAX.

"The first time I saw her . . . you know what I mean?" he continued.

A dog barked in the next yard, and both of us flinched. It seemed only fair that I leave before him. Kate walked me to the gate. She said I should call first next time and gave me a business card with her home number written on the back. Her lips on my cheek turned me inside out.

"Didn't think I'd find a white man for this job," Frank said. He hired me without even reading my application. There were not even any questions about why I'd left U-Haul. According to him, the Oasis was the last American-owned motel in the city. I liked it because it was within walking distance of my apartment. I worked nights at the front desk, "fighting off the zombies," as Frank put it. The lobby was locked after ten, so I dealt with the guests from behind a sheet of bulletproof Plexiglas. Money and keys were exchanged by means of a sliding drawer.

People didn't plan to stay at the Oasis; bad luck and lack of options forced them to. They arrived angry or in tears or so fucked up they had to lean against the window to pull their wallets out of their back pockets. I treated them all the same. You got a smile at the beginning of the transaction, a smile at the end. The porno channel was five dollars extra.

As far as jobs went, I'd had worse. Things usually calmed down around three or so, enough on some nights that I actually got in a nap before the maids came on at six. Either that or I listened to the radio. There was this crazy show where people called in to talk about UFOs, ghosts, and the Book of Revelation. Barricaded in the office, watching ambulances rocket past and helicopters flush suspects from the alleys, I couldn't understand why anyone would search for new things to be frightened of.

One morning, as I was hosing down the parking lot just after dawn, a man came out of a room on the first floor, got into a car, and sped away. He left the door to his room wide open, and I stood there waiting for someone to close it. When that didn't happen, I walked over and peeked inside. A naked woman lay on the carpet, her face and upper body covered by the bedspread. "Hey," I said. "Hey, you." Her toenails were painted black, and there was blood everywhere. I didn't realize what I was seeing until it was too late, until one more bad thing had sneaked in and taken up space I'd been saving for the good. The police hypnotized me afterward, but I was no help at all.

KATE KEPT THE urn on a bookshelf, high enough up that Monica couldn't reach. I learned to ignore it after a while, but in the beginning I'd catch myself staring while we played cards or ate breakfast. I was afraid Kate would notice and start asking questions, and then the truth would dribble out, that it was just charcoal in there, not really old Bud. It probably wouldn't have mattered, she probably would have laughed, but those kinds of things will come back to haunt you.

One night soon after I found the dead woman, Kate and I were watching a DVD. I sat on the couch; she lay with her head in my lap. Monica was with her dad. The T-shirt Kate wore as a nightgown had climbed above her hips, and she wasn't wearing panties. My hand was resting on her thigh when something about the way her ankles crossed reminded me of the corpse. There was the bluish glow from the TV, too, a color akin to morning.

The chemicals began to flow, mixing and matching and doing a number on me. My chest filled with gravel, and each breath was like a finger down my throat. Kate's voice worked its way through the muck. She asked why I was shaking. "It's not me," I wanted to say, "it's everything else," but all that came out was a cough.

Denver again. Instinct urged me to flee. The shadows grew thick and painful, and I could have sworn someone was hiding in the kitchen. I fought the panic as long as I was able, but there wasn't enough air in the room, and I didn't want Kate to see me that way.

She stopped me on the porch just by calling my name. I waited cramped and panting, one hand cradling my racing heart. The lawn shone silver in the moonlight, like a bed of nails. We sat back to back, the screen door between us, Kate inside the house, me out. I told her some things about myself that had been secrets before; I put some things into words for the first time. It felt good to get through it. My pulse slowed and my fists unclenched.

"Running away's a bad habit," Kate said when I was done. "Have you ever tried to stand your ground?"

"I will. I would. For you."

"I have a child. I have a life. Jesus Christ, man."

"Invite me back in. You'll see."

She opened the screen door, and I stepped inside. While she made a pot of coffee, I started the DVD over again.

H*EY,* EVERYBODY SAID when I dropped by the doughnut shop. *What's up? Where you been?* Not much had changed. Ray Ray was trying to sell an old Buick, and Whitey had shaved his mustache. I told them about living in Downey, near Kate, and my new job at an auto-parts warehouse.

José said, "Oh, shit. Bud's got to be rolling in his grave, you with his daughter."

"You're gonna thank me for that, right?" Whitey asked. "Who sent you out there in the first place?"

We took our coffee to one of the outside tables, where we could smoke. The sun reflected off the bumpers of passing cars and sliced into us like laser beams, and the exhaust hanging in the air made everything taste funny, but nobody complained. That's how it was with them.

"I taught her to play chess," I said. "She whips my ass every time."

"So it's for real, then. You guys are a thing?" Ray Ray asked.

Whitey laughed at him. "A thing? A thing?"

Bill appeared out of nowhere. He didn't recognize me right away. The guys all stared at their shoes and watches. His lips were cracked and bloody, and a black smear of something dirtied his forehead.

"Do I owe you money?" he asked.

"We're good."

"Speak for youself."

"Okay, I'm good."

Bill laughed at that, spat on the sidewalk.

He was more like me than most. I had problems staying put, and he couldn't ever seem to get away. I tried to explain it to

Kate that night, but back then I was just getting used to saying what I meant. I still felt like I was learning the logic of a brand-new dream. She listened to me fumble for words, then put her arms around me and told me she was proud of me. *I could lie here forever,* I thought.

Long Lost

═══

THREE ASTRONAUTS ARE SIGNING AUTOGRAPHS AT THE mall, side by side at a long table next to Santa's castle. A red, white, and blue banner behind them screams YOUR AMERICAN HEROES, but Santa is a bigger draw, with his fake snow and plywood candy canes. It's Christmas, after all! Mommies in sweatpants and stained T-shirts drag their children past the table and into the castle, where an elf will snap a Polaroid to send to Grandma or maybe Daddy and his new wife, while the astronauts, ignored, sip from cans of soda and dream of Thai bar girls.

One of them cups his ear whenever anybody speaks to him, an old man with a face like the end of an orange. He once walked on the moon — the moon! I watched it on TV as a kid.

Fucked me up for years. I couldn't wait to blast off. He must
have some answers, the ancient astronaut. If I could muster the
energy, I'd get up off this bench and ask him why my hands
sometimes feel like they belong to somebody else. I'd sing along
to the Christmas carols and take the See's candy lady dancing.
Or maybe I'd fill a bottle with gasoline, stopper it with a sock,
and set fire to this circus. I don't know.

I MEET ANOTHER husband at the bar. He offers to buy me a
drink, which is supposed to be a joke, because all the booze is free.
He's loosened his tie so that the knot hangs to the middle of his
chest, and he can't stop running his fingers through his hair.

"Which one's yours?" he asks, and I point to Judy. She has
a good job, management, and this is her company Christmas
party. I tried every way I could to get out of coming, but she put
her foot down. She has that right, I guess.

"Do you love her?" the other husband asks.

Of course I do.

"I love mine, too," he says with a grin.

Judy is talking to her boss over at the buffet. I watch from
across the room as she smiles one minute, nods seriously the
next, the transition so smooth and professional it seems almost
rehearsed. She's lucky that way. The seams never show. "All you
have to do is try," she'll say when I ask how she does it, and every
time she says it, my spit turns to battery acid and my head hurts
for days.

Mostly, though, we're fine. We keep it simple. She likes
strawberry daiquiris, silver jewelry, and anything with Gene
Kelly in it. I know what kind of flowers to buy on her birthday, and we need about the same amount of sleep. I have heard
her crying in the bathroom when she thinks the shower is
drowning it out, but we're still rolling along, and that's better
than most.

The other husband's wife joins us at the bar. She's wearing Frosty the Snowman earrings. "So you're Mr. Judy," she says. "You're in publishing, right?"

"Is that how Judy puts it? I'm a proofreader."

"Proofreader," her husband says. "What the hell's that?"

"A job. A bullshit job. Lots of people have them."

"I'll drink to that."

"So you'd rather be doing something else," the wife says to me.

"Not really."

She eyes me over the rim of her wineglass. I can tell she's not going to back down. It's these kinds of conversations that will kill me.

"What are you two doing for the holidays?" she asks.

"We're not real big on the whole holiday thing."

"What does that mean?"

I answer with a shrug.

"When you have kids it'll be different," she says. "They really make this time of year special."

Judy finally motions for me to join her. I excuse myself and follow her out to the patio of the restaurant.

"Float me a smoke," she says.

Two men, coworkers of hers, approach us with their arms around each other. They are singing "Silent Night" and try to get Judy to join in, but she pats them on their backs and steers them inside.

"Wash your hands," I say. "This place is a hotbed of Yuletide cheer."

"Best behavior. You promised," she says.

People are dancing in the restaurant. The windows are beginning to fog. There's a small black spot on my white shirt. I can't figure out where it came from.

Judy takes her cell phone from her purse and dials our answering machine. After listening for a minute, she looks confused, then presses the code to replay the messages and holds the phone out to me.

"Your brother called," she says.

"I don't have a brother."

"Merry Christmas."

Spencer Wright, this is your life. No, really, hey, my name is Karl Wright, and I'm your brother, half-brother, whatever. It's a hell of a story, but I tracked our old man down and he gave me your name and they had computers at the library. He said he thought you were living in L.A., so it was pretty easy. Do you know about me? He married my momma after he married yours. Anyway, I'm gonna tell you right off the bat, I've been away for a time, and where I was locked down they had a shrink who said a lot of my anger and stuff comes from not having family ties and missing out on that, so I'm doing something about it, or trying to anyway. I said back off, nigger! Sorry about that. I bet this tape's gonna run out, so let me get to it. I'm in town, I've got a room down here at the Hotel Cecil, and I'd love to hook up with you for a few minutes, lunch, whatever you can spare. Seeing your face and hearing your voice is all that's important. Leave a message at the desk for Karl Wright. If I don't hear from you, don't worry, I'll get the hint. Love you, bro. Already. Merry Christmas and Happy New Year.

The desk clerk sits behind bulletproof glass. All transactions are conducted via a sliding drawer, and one must be buzzed in through a security gate to get upstairs. The sign warning against drugs, prostitution, and firearms makes me smile. Have you never dreamed of such lodgings?

The clerk is Indian. Turban, the whole bit.

"I'm here to see Karl Wright," I say.

He checks the register and then the cubbyholes where the keys are stored.

"Wright is out," he says.

"He told me to meet him here."

The clerk grabs a key and taps it three or four times against the thick Plexiglas separating us. "He is out, out, out. This is his key."

"What's that music you're listening to?"

It's a woman wailing over some kind of half-assed bagpipes and penny whistles dipped in mud.

"Indian music. From my country."

"What's she saying?"

The clerk shrugs. "She loves him. He has robbed her heart."

I step back into the lobby. A few men are hunched on the spavined couches, rapt before a silent television chained to a shelf up near the ceiling. I take a seat and do my best to mimic their institutional quietude. *These boys know how to wait,* I think to myself while the audience on TV applauds us soundlessly. In one corner of the room, a small aluminum Christmas tree lists under its burden of twinkle lights and tinsel.

The old guy beside me is wearing a blue polyester suit coat, the cuffs of which hang past his knuckles. He smells like yeast and mothballs. For a while he stares openmouthed at the screen, his tongue worrying his dentures. Then he stands and faces me.

"Hit the road, punk," he wheezes.

"Say what?"

"Time's up."

"Sit down, you crazy fuck," one of the other men shouts.

"Yeah, asshole," another chimes in.

The old man's chin trembles; his eyes shine with tears. He returns to his spot on the couch and sits with his head in his hands. I'd trade any ten people I know for one of him. His desolation is as beautiful as a broken mirror.

My brother laughs. He's been watching everything from an easy chair by the door. He's handsomer than me, taller, more graceful as he strides across the lobby, muscular arms outstretched.

"Karl?" I ask, knowing full well.

He wraps himself around me. I feel his fists on my back, drawing me closer until my mouth and nose are pressed against his shoulder. I want to return the embrace, I should, but it's awkward. I can't figure out where to put my hands.

"My bro," he whispers. "My big bro."

We separate, and he wipes his eyes with the ball of his thumb. He's wearing a denim shirt and a pair of tan chinos, and I wonder if these are the clothes the prison provided when they released him. Everyone in the lobby is smiling at us, as if our meeting has allowed hope to slice its way through the scar tissue surrounding their hearts. I don't want to be responsible for that.

A siren screams past outside, and Karl doesn't even flinch. I reach out and tousle his hair like an older brother would a younger brother's. He grabs my hand and kisses it. It's one of those moments when you wish you weren't always watching yourself from across the room.

WE WALK TO a McDonald's a couple of blocks off Skid Row. I suggest sushi in Little Tokyo or one of the Mexican places over the river, but Karl says no, no, McDonald's is fine. The streets down here are something else. The sun never quite reaches them over the tops of the buildings, and those who have chosen to live in this constant twilight collide with those who have no choice and those who are simply, in one way or another, lost. On this cold, late December afternoon, it could be any miserable, man-eating place in the world. Cheap wine, crack, lies loudly told — these are the bonfires that keep the wolves at bay.

OH, MAN, YOU really want to get into that mess? It makes me look stupid. Like a real idiot. But okay. Me and this fucker Edgar I used to hang with, we were heavy into downers. I was staying away from smack, but anything else, bring it on. This was in OKC, before the bomb and whatnot, and Edgar knew this guy who knew this guy who . . . well, if you were a serious pill popper and you got to thinking, "Hey, where do they keep all the drugs in this town?" you might come up with this, too—the hospital, right? So Edgar tells me about this buddy of his who shot himself in the hand with a twenty-two, then went to the hospital and told them it happened while he was cleaning the gun, and they set him up with a nice, fat scrip for Percodan or Darvon or some such wonder. We're thinking right on, right. Voilà! You've got to be in pain to get painkillers! Neither of us had the balls to take a bullet, but we worked it out where we'd toss a coin and the winner would hit the loser in the head with a piece of pipe just hard enough to cut him and lump it up so it'd look like maybe he fell off a ladder, which is what we'd tell the doctor.

A few beers later, we do the toss, and I lose. Edgar gets the pipe from under his mattress and I sit at the kitchen table and he fuckin' nails me. I mean, he knocks me the fuck OUT! I wake up on the floor, blood gushing, my ears ringing, and Edgar zips me over to the emergency. Well, first off they shave half my head to stitch me up, then there's all kinds of X-rays and Y-rays and Z-rays. I must have been in there four or five hours, crying this hurts and that hurts and doc, you got to help me, and after all that, do you know what I walked out with? Tylenol. Fucking Tylenol. Long story short, we drive to this dealer's house and bust down his door and steal his stash. He ratted us out, saying we took his TV, and me being on probation already for some other rinky-dink beef, that was that. Your little brother hit the big time.

THE MCDONALD'S IS all plastic and chrome and perfect and horrible. Karl lifts the bun of his hamburger to remove the pickles. He's tattooed the letters of his name on the fingers of one hand, a sloppy, homemade job, the ink already faded to green. The one thing I see of myself in his face is its only imperfection, the bulbous tip of his nose. We can thank our father for that.

"How long's it been?" Karl asks.

"Oh, hell, what, twenty-five years maybe. He dropped by on his way to Vegas once, when he still lived out here. He was with your mother then. She was pregnant with you, as a matter of fact. We've talked on the phone a few times since."

"You never missed having a daddy?"

"My mom kept trying. There were always men around."

"But not your daddy."

I shift in my seat and fight off the exasperation his earnestness provokes in me.

"We never had pets, either. Should I feel bad about that, too?"

"You got an answer for everything," Karl says, his smile a bit too knowing.

"So what's your story?" I ask.

He shrugs, dips a fry in ketchup. "How old were you when he bailed?"

"Three."

"I was barely a year." His voice takes on a harsher tone, as if something inside him has suddenly cinched up tight and he has to force his words around it.

"Momma did her best, but it was hard in Texas. Different from here, the people and all, how they treated us. Especially her family. They were too cruel half the time, too kind the rest. By the time I was fourteen, she'd had enough, so she gave herself up to cancer. And I'm glad, you know, because look at me."

He strikes himself in the chest with his fist and would do worse, I know — tear his guts out, take an ice pick to his skull. It's the kind of self-immolating rage that drives men to decisive, if reckless, even destructive, acts, and I have often envied it in others, as the dead must surely envy the living.

I sip my coffee and watch him seethe. He closes his eyes and exhales loudly, then rotates his head from side to side, his neck cracking and popping.

"He had a house on a golf course out there in Florida, a boat in the driveway. A girl answered the door, looked like us, and there was a boy, too. Daddy wouldn't let me in, though, didn't want to upset his family, like I was somebody, I don't know, nobody. So we walked out to the garage. What did I want, he wanted to know. I said, 'Just to see you. You're my daddy.' 'Are you sure?' he asks. Are you sure? Can you believe that? I lost it. I got him by the throat and took him down to his knees."

"I've dreamed this," I say. "I've killed the fucker in my dreams."

Karl pauses, derailed momentarily by my interruption — shocked, if that's possible. He swirls his straw in his cup.

"I had a pistol," he continues, "but it's when I reached for it, when my fingers touched it, that I lost my nerve. I slapped his ass around until he gave up your name and that you were in California and all, and then I got the fuck out of Dodge. 'Son,' he called after me. 'Son.' But I didn't look back. He put another notch on his going-to-hell belt that day, that's for sure. And me, I haven't had a mean spell since."

Even if it had gone differently, if he'd confessed to murder, I don't think I would have rejected him. He is everything I could have been, everything I am, except a coward.

He wrestles his anger back into its cell, and a wry sweetness returns to his eyes. There's something of an eager child about him as he takes a bite of his burger.

"What did you do with the gun?" I ask.

"Pawned it. For traveling money."

A black girl screams at the old Mexican man behind the counter. "I told you no tartar sauce, you motherfucker, and what is this?" She throws her fish sandwich at him and stands with her hands on her hips while a stray dog that has somehow slipped inside laps at a puddle of spilled Coke.

"I can't help you," I say.

Karl purses his lips and draws his head back. "I ask for anything?"

"I mean spiritually, philosophically."

"I understand."

"Something happens, you live through it, and then another thing happens. That's all I can say."

Karl grins. "You're full of shit, bro."

"Let's go get your stuff."

"I don't want to ruin your Christmas."

"It's not a big deal. Really."

I CALL THEM the gray men, my coworkers, though there are a few women in the bunch. We sit side by side in the basement of the building, ten of us, in shoulder-high cubicles the size of barnyard stalls. The others have decorated their workspaces with comic strips clipped from the newspaper and maps and photos of their cats, but not me. Except for my company-issued lamp, desk, and chair, my cubicle is empty. I'm ready to walk away at any time.

The gray men think I'm a snob because I make fun of the detective novels and spy thrillers they pass along to one another with rave reviews. Little do they know I haven't read a book in years. I stopped because nobody was writing about me. For a while I had my screenplay to keep me occupied when I went home at night. It was about a man who killed his boss and got away with it. I let a friend read it, and he said I was crazy. "Don't you understand the good guy has to win?" he asked. Now I watch old Westerns and dream of moving to the desert, and I'm not talking about Vegas, I'm talking about some lawless spot where it's just me and rocks and the bluest blue sky. I will go months without hating my face in a mirror. I will learn to shoot a gun, set a trap, the art of ambush. My legend will deepen and spread. When I was a boy, I thought I would grow up to be some sort of poet. Now, when it's ridiculous, my heroes are bank robbers and vengeful desperados. "Don't be surprised if you wake up one morning and I'm gone," I tell Judy. "If I just disappear." God, does that make her laugh.

KARL STANDS IN front of our living room window, watching the sun set. I point out the landmarks — the Hollywood sign, the observatory, Capitol Records. It's a view I like best at night, when, with a squint, I can transform the lights of the city into stars.

"If you stretch, and it's not too smoggy, you can even see the ocean," I say.

"No shit?" Karl asks with genuine wonderment. His duffel bag is on the couch, everything he owns in a bundle small enough to be carried under one arm. I do my best to get past the envy that triggers in me.

The downstairs neighbors are throwing a party; the nose ring and platform sneaker crowd. Their music seeps right up through the floor, and every time someone slams the front door, the whole building shakes. This place will come down in the next earthquake. And I will be here. Still.

In the kitchen Judy is taking stock of the refrigerator. We eat like birds when it's just the two of us. The look she gives me when I reach around her for a beer lets me know I'd better step lightly.

"It's only for a couple of days," I say. "I'll do the cooking and everything."

"Turkey and all the fixings, huh?"

"The cleaning, whatever."

"You'd better pick up a tree, too, and some decorations."

"I'm sorry."

"Do you want a beer, Karl?" she calls out.

"Thanks, but I'm on the program."

I make a horrified face, and this gets a smile out of her. We've been together for ten years now. It's hard to believe. I never planned on knowing anyone as well as I know her. You get so comfortable after a while. You start to wonder if you could make it on your own. She grabs the beer out of my hand, snaps it open, and takes a sip, then goes back to writing the grocery list.

Karl is studying the old photos of Judy's relatives that hang on the living room wall. He touches the faces with a tattooed finger.

"These were taken in Poland, before the war," I say. I move up beside him. "This little girl, her uncle here, her great-grandmother—all of them died in the camps."

"Hitler, you mean?"

I nod.

"I never was down with the Nazis. They kept at me in the joint."

"Hey, I've got something to show you. Hold on."

I go into the extra bedroom we call the office and dig out a photo of my grandfather from my desk drawer.

"My mom gave me this. It's our dad's dad when he was about twenty or so."

Karl rests the photograph in the palm of his hand. It shows a young man in a hat and suit, smiling and squinting into the sun. Behind him, a dusty plain stretches to the horizon. I've always imagined that he's come back to West Texas for a visit, that the suit is new and worn to impress the folks. He's been to Dallas, Kansas City, Chicago, which is where he picked up the camera and the radio he's brought for his mom and pop and little sister.

"All I really know about him is that his name was Karl, like yours, and that he used to box a little and make his own wine. I never met him. I think he came from Germany or maybe Ireland."

Karl smiles and strokes his chin. "Well, you got his fucked-up nose," he says.

"So did you."

"And I guess that'll do for history."

The party downstairs is raging. The drugs must be kicking in. Someone yells, "I drink Dr. Pepper and I'm proud!" Judy comes in and asks Karl what he'd like for dinner. He ducks his head shyly and says anything's okay.

Night falls so quickly in winter. The sun has barely dropped out of the sky. We sit together watching television, the three of us, nobody speaking. Karl is perched gingerly on the edge of the couch, like he's afraid he'll be asked to leave at any moment. He finally clears his throat and says almost too loudly, "I've been to prison. He tell you?"

"Yes," Judy replies.

"So we're cool, then?"

"We're cool."

Karl leans forward and rests his forearms on his thighs and stares out the window. At what? Thinking what? I'm joyfully at a loss.

HER NAME WAS Tiffany, and I knew from the start we were gonna fuck this up. Most of the dancers you meet, you get them outside the club, and it becomes pretty clear pretty quick that it isn't really just a job, no matter what they want to believe. At least Tiffany was honest with herself. She'd been diddled by her stepdad, okay, and was born with one leg shorter than the other, which gave her a limp that made her feel ugly. There are reasons for everything, right?

I was doing a lot of speed back then but not having much fun. In fact, I was pretty desperate to crawl out of the hole I'd dug myself. Along comes Tiffany and her boy, and I don't know what I was thinking when I thought, *Hey, I can do this.* He was about six, Jack, a cute little guy, tougher than shit. I'd let him punch me in the shoulder sometimes, and it fucking hurt! I got my act together, took a job as a mechanic, and she let me move into her condo, which was in a real decent part of town. You felt like a citizen there. Our neighbor was a chiropractor. The sprinklers were all on timers. I worked in the day and watched the kid while she danced at night. We had dinners, man, Kentucky

Fried Chicken, went to the park and Little League on weekends. You want something like that to work out. You really do.

Our problem was Ed Landers, this old, rich bastard with a red Seville who started hanging around the club. Big, fat, white-haired fucker. Big tipper. Tiffany swears to me nothing's going on, but it's always Eddie, Eddie, Eddie. I'm a jealous man, I'll admit it, and the whole thing started to wind me up after a while, soured all my good intentions. She invited Ed to supper one night so I could see what it was, but the two of them, I mean, what were they thinking? That they could play me like that? We were drinking some, and he was holding the kid in his lap, telling him to call him Uncle Eddie and shit, and I just couldn't take it anymore. I went off on him right there in the living room. Broken glass, the kid crying, a real fucking mess.

Needless to say, I was out on my ass with the clothes on my back and some righteously bruised knuckles. No good-bye, nothing. You know, sometimes what we call love is something else, but it's just that there aren't enough words for all the kinds of wanting in the world, and people, bro, people are fucking lazy.

WE HAVE A good time at the supermarket, even though it's so crowded with people shopping for the holidays I can barely squeeze the cart down the aisles. I read the items off Judy's list, and Karl retrieves them from the shelves. He's wearing a red tasseled hat trimmed in fake white fur that he picked up from a display at the front of the store. "Here comes Santa Con," I sing, and, "Santa Con is coming to town."

"Ho ho ho," he bellows. We deviate from the list whenever we feel like it, grabbing potato chips, ice cream, caramel corn, and cookies.

"You sure it's okay?" Karl asks as he reaches for a box of graham crackers.

"Come on, man, it's Christmas," I reply.

He tries to give me money at the checkout counter, but I wave it off. While the clerk is ringing us up, I turn to the candy rack and casually slip five Hershey bars into my jacket pocket. It's a silly habit that took hold a few months ago. Every time I pay for something, I look for something to steal. An odd compulsion to develop at my age, I know, but I kind of enjoy it. It worries and disgusts me and gives me a thrill all at the same time.

We walk over to examine the trees for sale in the parking lot after putting the bags in the car. The night has grown colder, and neither of us is really dressed for it. Karl raises his hands to his mouth and blows on them, and they disappear in the fog his breath makes. Colored lights hang above the sad forest of misshapen pines and scrawny firs, and the bulbs are reflected in the drops of water clinging to the needles of the freshly misted branches. A Mexican kid in a stocking cap follows us as we search for the least lopsided of the bunch.

Actually, I'm not all that particular. It's Karl who seems to have some idea of what he wants. "How's this?" I ask once or twice, but he shakes his head and moves on. After two circuits of the place, I've had enough. I stroll to the flocking tent, where a fire burns inside an oil drum. Standing over it, I let the flames lick my palms, then press them to my face and cup my icy ears. A few minutes later Karl joins me, and the kid.

"What a bunch of garbage," Karl says. "Looks like they kept the best for themselves." He points with his chin into the tent, indicating a five-foot tree caked with fake snow and swaddled in lights and blue glass ornaments. A golden angel is perched on top, a trumpet raised to its lips. It's a nightmare. Really. Judy will fucking die.

"How much for that?" I ask the kid.

"It's not for sale. It's like the display."

"Lights, decorations, everything, how much?"

The kid shrugs and goes off to consult the owner.

"Forget it, bro," Karl says. "They're gonna rip you off."

I put my finger to my lips to shush him.

The kid returns and says, "Two hundred."

Karl snorts. "Yeah, right. Let's go."

"We'll take it," I tell the kid.

"What's up with you?" Karl asks, a shocked look on his face.

"Ho ho ho," I reply.

I'm for tying the thing to the roof of the car, angel and all, but Karl insists upon removing the ornaments first. The kid finds an empty cardboard box, and I watch from the oil drum as the two of them gently stack the balls inside it.

"I SAW WHAT you did in the store," Karl says on the drive home.

"So," I reply.

"What's the point?"

"I could ask you the same thing."

"Well, I was stupid and drunk and on drugs."

I feel myself blushing and hope he doesn't notice. He does, though, I can tell by his smile when I glance over at him. "It's just a game I play with myself," I say.

"You ever see a shrink?"

"Should I?"

"It helped me."

"Are you sure?"

If he answers that, I'm ready with more, but he doesn't. He turns away from me and stares out the window at a little house with bars on its windows and a plastic Nativity scene in the yard. You don't get a silence like this every day. I'd like to tear off a piece of it and keep it in my wallet for later.

I MADE A run for it once. It was before Judy and I were married, but we'd been living together for about a year, and I could see where things were headed. I was editing the employee newsletter for an aerospace firm at the time. Corporate propaganda interspersed with health tips, recipes, and announcements of promotions, anniversaries, and retirements. Every issue I'd set up the headlines so that the first letters of each of them read in sequence would spell out messages like FUCK THIS PLACE and KILL YOURSELF NOW. I waited to get caught, but never did.

It was a Monday afternoon in March, a day so bright and clear that the mountains looked close enough to walk to. I left work for lunch but kept driving right past Taco Bell to the freeway. West was the ocean and the end of everything, so I headed east, into the desert. Gradually the malls and gas stations fell away, the houses, the people. I found myself alone in a pitiless wasteland. It was lunar, perfect. The craggy hills in the distance stood firm against the sun and wind, but everything near me was well on its way to being worn down to dust. Here and there wiry plants clutched at the rocky ground for dear life.

I stopped the car and walked a few hundred feet off the road to a boulder that broke the flatness of the plain. I took off my clothes. The boulder was warm against my skin, almost silky, as I lay on top of it. A shy little lizard poked its head out of a crack, and a pair of hawks circled overhead. I held my breath, then exhaled slowly, and whatever was bent almost to breaking inside me seemed to straighten itself out.

The wind picked up toward sundown, surprisingly cold. I drove on across the border into Nevada and stopped in a little town that wasn't much more than a gas station, a motel, and a casino. "Car trouble?" the woman asked when she handed me the keys to my room, as if that was the only reason anybody would end up there. I could have kissed her.

Feeling reckless and lucky, I walked over to the casino. It was deserted except for a couple of snowbirds playing video poker. The bartender was a fat man with a handlebar mustache. When he asked me where I was from, I said, "Tonight? Right here," which got me a dirty look.

The blackjack and craps tables were dark, so I spent a few hours drinking and throwing money at the slots. What happened next has always been somewhat hazy — this was back in my hard liquor years. I hit a jackpot, fifty or sixty dollars, and tried to give it to the cocktail waitress. She wouldn't take it, and that pissed me off. I got on the bartender's bad side, too. My jokes went right over his head. "You must know where the whores are in this town," I said, and he asked me to leave.

There was blood on my pillow when I came to in the morning. My lip was busted, my left eye swollen almost shut. I vomited all the way back to L.A., pulling over to the side of the road every twenty miles or so. What can I say but that I failed? I had a spark within me, but not enough fuel to break the bonds of gravity.

I WAKE UP at five a.m. and can't get back to sleep. When it's quiet like this, before the city revs up, you hear the strangest sounds. Roosters crowing, squirrels in the trees, distant trains. Nobody believes me, but it's true. I roll over to put my arms around Judy. She shudders and pulls away, scooting to the edge of the bed.

The refrigerator is full of food. I'm not used to this. It takes me a while to notice the blood. The plastic the turkey is sealed in has a hole in it, and watery pink blood has leaked out and puddled on the bottom shelf. I take out all the beer and sodas and pickles and sour cream and clean everything off in the sink.

As the sun comes up on the morning of Christmas Eve day, I'm sitting at the kitchen table, eating the chocolate chip cookies we bought last night and drinking a glass of milk. Karl is asleep on the couch in the living room. I hear him breathing. I sense he doesn't like me much. He thinks I'm weak and bizarre, and he's right, but how do I make him understand that everyone here is weak and bizarre?

IT'S JUDY'S IDEA to drive to the beach. She suggests it after breakfast. Karl is washing the dishes, and I'm drying.

"We'll go out there and laugh at the rest of the country," she says. "Picture them shoveling snow."

"That'd be something," Karl replies.

Good. It'll be good to get out of the apartment, all of us together. My wife is a genius. I rustle up a pair of shorts for Karl. We throw the snacks he and I bought into a bag, then some towels, a blanket, and we're off.

What a day. The sky is a flawless blue, the sun a cheerful old friend. We take Judy's car. She drives, Karl sits in back, and the radio plays all my favorite songs. I start up the license plate game. We alternate calling out the letters of the alphabet as we spot them on passing cars. Karl joins right in. "What am I?" he asks, and we switch to twenty questions.

The freeway dumps us out at the beach, which is almost empty at this time of the year. It's a little colder than it was in Silver Lake, a little windier, but we tromp out and spread our blanket on the sand like it was the Fourth of July. Karl strips off his shirt, revealing a large tattoo on his chest. BROKEN-HEARTED, it reads, the letters arching over the face of a woman. "Momma," he says before Judy or I have a chance to ask. "Prison shit."

The waves are sluggish today, syrupy, breaking with only the greatest of effort. Propped on my elbows, I watch them struggle toward shore, while Judy, sitting beside me, flips through the pages of a magazine. I find that if I lie perfectly still, the sun eventually wins out over the breeze and provides a fragile warmth.

The high tide line is marked by a band of waterlogged debris, kelp mostly, driftwood, odd chunks of Styrofoam and plastic. Karl strolls along beside it, stirring up a cloud of flies every time he stops to poke around in the mess with a stick he found somewhere. In the distance, the pier stands black and skeletal against the sky, its burden of joyless fishermen and stoned teenagers placing entirely too much faith in the strength of its spindly pilings, or perhaps the possibility of collapse is all part of the fun.

"What are you thinking about?" Judy asks, her cold hand on my shoulder.

"Nothing."

"Is your brother enjoying himself? Seems like it."

"I'm doing my best."

She reaches down to scratch her ankle. "That tree you guys got is something else."

"I knew you'd like it."

"We're awful, aren't we?"

The conversation has upset my delicate relationship with the sun. I sit up and hug myself for a quick fix of warmth. "We should have brought beer," I say. "Or tequila. Tequila would have been great."

Karl approaches the blanket, carrying something on the end of his stick.

"Check it out, a jellyfish," he yells.

"That's close enough. Those things can sting even when they're dead," I caution.

"Yeah, keep it away from here," Judy chimes in.

Karl stops short, disappointed by our reaction. He examines the jellyfish up close once more, then drops it into a hole he kicks into the sand and buries it with his foot.

"I'm going swimming. Come on, bro," he says.

Judy throws down her magazine. "I'm ready."

"There's shit in that water," I scoff. "Big poisonous turds."

They laugh at me before running down to the waves together. Judy advances slowly on stiffened legs and screams as the frigid water swirls around her calves, but Karl enters at a run and dives headfirst into the breakers. By the time she's in up to her waist, he's already bobbing in the swells, not touching bottom.

I turn away from them, from the sea, and lie on my stomach. In the parking lot two young lovers wrapped in one jacket lean against the hood of a car. The girl rests her head on the boy's chest, and he strokes her hair. A thing like that isn't supposed to make you angry, I know.

A CHRISTMAS STORY? I've got one. I was sixteen, thumbing my way out of trouble somewhere down in Louisiana, I believe, and this old boy picked me up on Christmas Eve. He asked was I hungry, and I was, so he told me there was a birthday cake in the backseat I was welcome to. He worked in a bakery, see, and got to take home the leftovers and mistakes. It was chocolate with white frosting and big blue flowers, and I dug right in with my fingers and ate it all up while the dude laughed and laughed. Afterward he sparked up a bomber, and I was like, well, here we are, man, here we are.

A few miles down the road he started in. "You like cock? You sure look like you would." Ain't nothing come for free, right? I don't know what I was thinking. You gotta figure a guy must be packing if he's talking like that, so plain to a stranger, and I'm not gonna lie but I was scared. I told him I had to piss, and he asked could he watch. "Sure," I said. "Enjoy the show." As soon as the car pulled over, I was out the door and up the hill into the woods as fast as I could get. I found a good hiding place and hunkered down where I could see him through the trees. He fired a few rounds from a little pistol up my way, then got back in his car and left.

After an hour or so I started walking. Didn't even bother to stick my thumb out. It was so bitter cold and kind of sleety, and in the middle of the night with me looking such a mess, nobody was gonna stop. Up the road a ways I came upon a blanket I thought I could maybe use, but when I went to snatch it up, there was something wrapped inside it. A dog, I thought, or, I don't know why, a monkey, but it was a baby, a little blue baby. It seemed dead till it started to cry. I can't say I didn't think about just moving on down the line, but it was a baby, man. A baby. On Christmas Eve.

I shoved it up under my shirt and jacket, and it was like carrying a block of ice. I could feel its heart beating right next to mine. Cars were passing all the while, and I waved like crazy, but they went right on by. First time I ever prayed to see a cop, I can tell you that. After a few miles of walking, the little guy warmed up a bit, and you know what he did? He went right for my tit, like I was his momma. I don't think I've ever felt so hopeless, but my tears froze before they made it halfway down my face.

Finally I saw a house all lit up for the holidays. I banged on the door, and they let me in, real nice black folks, just sitting down to dinner. The lady of the family took the baby from me and set about making it comfortable till the ambulance could get there. They fixed me up with a plate, and their children sang Sunday school songs for me. The sheriff gave me an empty cell to sleep in that night and had me over to his house the next day. There was a present for me under the tree and everything, a new coat. It wasn't until he put me on the bus to New Orleans after dinner that he told me the baby had died.

OH, LOOK! JUDY and Karl are friends now. They've crossed that line. I can see it at the dinner table over the takeout Chinese. They're finally comfortable with each other, moving easily from joking to paying attention when it seems important, discovering common ground, that whole thing. This leaves me pretty much ignored. My contributions to the conversation earn a quick smile and nod, if that.

I take my beer into the living room and sit on the couch. The Christmas tree lights are on, twinkling stupidly. I think about those astronauts at the mall. What was it: Mercury, Gemini, Apollo. If I went into space, I'd want to go alone, and if I made it as far as the moon, there would be no stopping me. Judy laughs, and I turn on the TV. Loud.

"What do you think, honey," Judy shouts over it. "A tattoo."

"That's against your religion."

"What about you, then?" Karl asks.

"Not my style."

Karl stands and begins to clear the table, but Judy tells him to leave it, she'll do it later. They join me on the couch, she on one end, he on the other. Judy grabs the remote and clicks off the television.

"If we're going to do this, we might as well do it right. There have got to be some carols on the radio."

"Now you're thinking," Karl says as he jumps up and goes to the stereo. A few twists of the dial, and "We Three Kings" fills the room.

"I can play this, you got a guitar," he says.

"Nope. No guitar," I reply.

Judy says, "That baby, if you don't mind me asking, did they ever find its mother?"

Karl shakes his head and looks down at the carpet. "I've wondered about that, too, I really have."

This guy could be full of it. That's certainly something to consider. A good liar is a kind of genius. We may be playing right into his hands.

When I get up for another beer, Judy is explaining Hanukkah to him. I can see into the apartment next door through the kitchen window. A family is gathered there—old people, young people, babies. Everybody is talking at once. I don't understand Spanish, but they seem to be happy. My mother is in Hawaii with her new husband. That's where his children live. And that's fine. It's good for her to get away. Everybody should be able to enjoy themselves if they get the chance. I drink the beer, standing in the kitchen, the whole thing in three gulps, and open another.

"Come on, bro, let's have a sing-along," Karl calls.

I reclaim my spot between them on the couch. Judy has a slight sunburn from the beach. She looks healthy and happier than I've been able to make her in a long time. Karl stands and raises his arms like a choir director. He cocks an ear toward the radio.

"'Little Drummer Boy.' Let's do it," he says.

Nobody really knows how the song goes, but we give it our best shot, singing the parts we remember loudly and letting the radio carry the rest. Next up, though, is "Little Town of Bethlehem," which loses us all.

"We're pitiful," Judy says.

Karl laughs. "Well, fuck it, then," he says. "Let's just sing the easy ones."

We run through "Rudolph" and "Jingle Bells" and a few others, then give up on Christmas crap completely to serenade each other with anything that comes to mind. I do my Cub Scout cowboy repertoire — "Streets of Laredo," "Darling Clementine," "Polly Wolly Doodle" — and Judy offers something in Hebrew she memorized a thousand years ago and a few numbers from *My Fair Lady*.

When it's Karl's turn, he moves to the middle of the room and busts out with a creepy old song his grandfather taught him, something about a murdered child in a garden. He stands with his eyes closed, arms dangling at his sides, and his voice is a high graveyard whine that squeezes the breath out of me. It's as beautiful as such a thing can be.

Judy watches and listens with trembling lips, her hands clapped to her cheeks. "Karl," she exclaims when he finishes. "My God!"

He shakes himself out of his trance and smiles broadly. "Whew! That's a goody, huh?"

"You fucking jailbird," I say in a voice choked with anger and envy. "You don't have a clue, do you?"

"Take it easy, bro," he says. "Have another beer, why don't you."

I LIE QUIETLY beside Judy until I'm sure she's asleep, then roll out of bed and dress in the hallway. The only thing I think to grab is my toothbrush before creeping through the living room, past Karl sprawled on the couch, and out the front door.

I'm dizzy with excitement, tight in the belly, and I swear I can see in the dark as well as any cat. The streetlights are as bright as the sun and shadows hold no mystery. I try to work up some emotion when I turn at the bottom of the stairs for one last glance at the apartment, but all that comes is a smile. Perhaps I will change this to a tear in the retelling somewhere down the road. Perhaps not. Perhaps I will never speak of this life again.

My car is parked on the street half a block away. There is a 4-Runner in front of it, backed right onto the bumper, and a car has wedged itself in behind. I start the engine and shift into reverse, stomping on the accelerator in an attempt to gain enough space to maneuver away from the curb, but the car behind me won't budge. Neither will the 4-Runner. I get out and check the doors of both vehicles and find they're locked. And it's cold. Really cold. I should have brought a jacket.

I scoop up my steering wheel lock and look both ways on the street. The incredible clarity of a few minutes ago has faded. I draw the steel bar back over my shoulder and move up next to the 4-Runner. It should be a simple matter to slip the vehicle into neutral and push it forward a few feet to facilitate my escape. I swing the lock as hard as I can, and the window shatters into a million tinkling pieces. This is followed by the piercing whoops of an alarm, which echo off the surrounding buildings and return twice as loud as when they left.

Gutless instinct takes over, sending me sprinting down the sidewalk and up the stairs to the apartment. Karl is standing in front of the window in the living room when I burst through the door. The alarm can be heard as clearly here as it could down in the street.

"What's going on?" he asks.

"Nothing," I say, passing through without stopping. "Happens all the time. Kids and shit."

I undress in the dark. Judy doesn't stir as I climb back into bed. I bury my face in the pillow while my heart slams itself against my ribs in frustration.

I MUST HAVE been drunk, because I now have a vicious hangover, or at least it feels like a hangover. On Christmas morning. If it wasn't for Karl, that wouldn't mean anything. It would be just another day for Judy and me. No hideous tree. No turkey and cranberry sauce to deal with. Judy's up to her elbow in the bird, stuffing it. I offer to help, but she laughs and says, "No, no, go talk to your brother."

Karl is on the couch, fresh out of the shower. He sits there all big and clean and shiny.

"Hey, bro. Good morning. Merry Christmas," he says. He motions me closer with a finger, checks over my shoulder to make sure Judy's busy.

"I want to get your old lady something," he whispers. "You gotta drive me."

A kind of sureness that infuriates me has appeared in his tone. "That's not necessary. Forget it," I reply.

"No, no, really."

Judy and I should have worked out a signal beforehand. We should have been a lot smarter about this whole thing. Now it's all up to me.

"Dear," I call out. "Do we have time to go down to the Boulevard? Karl wants to see the footprints."

Judy looks up from a cookbook, pushing away a strand of hair from her face with the palm of her hand. "Do you know how long these things have to roast?" she asks. "Stop at the store and pick up some whipped cream."

Karl slaps me on the thigh and grins. My head starts throbbing again, the pain sneaking right past the aspirin.

CHRISTMAS DECORATIONS COIL like red and green snakes around the streetlights on Hollywood, and Santa and his elves fly from one side of the Boulevard to the other on banners stretched between the buildings. We join the Mexican families dressed in church clothes who are strolling past the souvenir shops and lingerie stores and the cheap restaurants with menus in five languages taped to their windows. I point out one to Karl, a burger joint where all the homeless punks gather to preen and tweak, and tell him that rumor has it you can fuck them for a corn dog, but he's more interested in the sidewalk stars, calling out the names he recognizes as we step over them.

"Lucille Ball! Bob Hope! Michael Jackson!"

A line of tour buses idles in front of the Chinese Theater. Despite the holiday, the forecourt is packed with tourists taking turns posing next to their favorite actors' and actresses' hand- and footprints. Japanese, Germans, Frenchies. Karl wades in among them, a white trash Gulliver. He stops at John Wayne's slab and stares down at it like he's all alone somewhere, in a church or a cemetery. With great solemnity, he places his tennis shoe over the impression left by Wayne's boot. "Will you look at that," he says, not to me, not to anyone, and I wish Judy were here to see him, although on second thought she'd probably find a way to twist it into something charming.

I walk out to the curb for a cigarette. I don't know how people do it, live this life. It seems incredibly difficult to me today, incredibly annoying. A few years ago, when the city spruced up this neighborhood, they mixed something sparkly into the asphalt used to repave the street. When the sun hits it, it looks like broken glass, like you'd cut yourself if you stumbled. And they wonder why there are so many lunatics around here. Even the ground beneath their feet seems to have turned against them.

THERE WASN'T MUCH open because of the holiday and all. We went into this place that had like posters and T-shirts. Junk. It wasn't what I had in mind, but my bro's like, "Fuck it, man. I got a headache and she doesn't give a fuck what you bring her, so just pick something." Whatever, right? Merry Christmas. I found this teddy bear wearing a little shirt that said LOVE, and when I showed it to him, he just smirked. I didn't care, though, because it wasn't for him, it was for his old lady, and she was good people.

This is a weird one, dude, I warned you. As we were walking back to the car, he asked me if I'd stolen anything from the store. I thought he was fucking with me, you know, 'cause that's how he was, so I said, "No, man, boosting's your trip, remember?" giving it right back to him. "Well, I don't know. Best check your pocket," he said. So I reach into my coat, and I'll be damned if there wasn't one of those little plastic things that snows when you shake them. That cocksucker must have slipped it in when I wasn't looking.

He started laughing, but I was pissed. Motherfucker was toying with my freedom. I say, "They could send me back for that, you know. I'm not even supposed to be in this state." And out of nowhere he goes off about didn't I want to go back because I missed my boyfriend so much, and by the way, how does it feel to take it up the ass? Without even thinking, I slammed him against a wall, whereupon he came at me, kicking and screaming that I was out to fuck his old lady. Dude had some serious problems. I mean, he was my bro, but for him to pull that shit. And he would not let up. He wanted to throw down right there on Hollywood Boulevard. I gave him a shot to the head to calm his ass, and he started yelling for the cops, so I gave him another that dropped him and took off running, just left him laying on the sidewalk. Broke my heart.

JUDY IS SETTING the table when I get home, with the good china, which has been buried in a closet for years. She's such a sport. I forget to acknowledge that sometimes. The radio plays Christmas carols, and the smell of food cooking almost gags me. I put my hand over my split lip so it doesn't startle her, but there's not much I can do about the blood on my shirt, so I walk quickly into the living room.

"That's that," I announce.

She turns to me with a smile. "What?"

"We don't have to do this anymore."

I pick up the tree. Ornaments and fake snow go flying. As I'm carrying it to the front door, Judy moves to block my way, and I don't understand the look on her face.

"Wait," she says.

"He attacked me. I caught him stealing something from a store, and when I confronted him, he went crazy."

I push past her and carry the tree out. More blue glass balls are dislodged, and they pop like balloons when they shatter against the stairs, collapsing into nothing. The cold yellow smear of sun in the sky is not even bright enough to give me a shadow. Down in the street, I toss the tree into the gutter. Maybe some poor family will drive by and pick it up. It might make their day.

Judy waits at the top of the stairs, arms crossed over her chest. She tenses as I climb toward her. I see all her muscles tighten at once.

"Spencer," she says.

"I'm fine. He just grazed me. Gave me a bloody nose. It was nothing."

"You're not making sense."

She follows me into the apartment, back to the kitchen. I snatch up a dish towel and open the oven. The turkey's just turning brown on top.

"Where do you want to go to dinner?" I ask. "I'm buying."

"Stop it," she says.

I slide out the rack and lift the foil pan with the bird in it. The towel isn't thick enough to stop the heat, though, and my fingers are on fire. I drop the pan onto the door of the stove, and it tips over onto the floor. The turkey hits the linoleum with a fleshy pop.

"Spencer!" Judy yells, retreating to the hallway.

"I'll clean it up. Relax."

I go to the refrigerator and grab a cold beer to stop the burning in my fingers. When I try to walk over to calm Judy down, I slip on something, turkey grease, and fall on my ass, my head smashing into the cupboards. There is a moment of glorious darkness before the pain begins. I'd like to lie here for a while, but Judy is freaking.

"Stop crying," I snap as I struggle to my feet. We've somehow gone out of alignment. Things are rattling, shuddering, threatening to come apart. I pick up the turkey with the towel and stumble out the front door and down the stairs again. Steam is rising off the bird as I drop it into the blue recycling bin. An ice-cream truck passes by, playing "Jingle Bells." I wave at the driver, and he just stares at me. What a mess I've made, trying to get everything back to normal. I almost laugh. The blisters rising on my fingertips begin to throb.

Judy is in our bedroom, stuffing clothes into a suitcase. There's nothing hurried about it. It seems like part of a longstanding plan suddenly put into dogged motion.

"Hey, come on now," I say.

"I'm going to Vince and Kylie's," she replies without looking at me. Her tears have stopped, and I want to touch her, but my arms can't reach that far. I feel like I have to yell to be heard, though she's standing right in front of me.

"Who?"

"Friends from work."

I trail her down the hall, limping and dizzy. She pauses at the front door, and here it is, my last chance.

"It's you and me again," I say.

"I can't. I can't anymore."

"Let's celebrate."

"I'm afraid of where you're headed."

"Karl, right? Am I fucking right?"

Her face flushes, and she holds her hand up, palm outward. "You are fucking crazy."

"Shhh," I say. "Not in front of the kids." I gesture at the photos of her dead relatives over the couch.

The door slams in my face. I close my eyes and listen to her footsteps grow fainter as she walks down the stairs.

I SPREAD MY booty on the coffee table. The candy bars from the other night, three pine tree car deodorizers, assorted cigarette lighters and drink cozies, a can of Vienna sausages, Karl's snow globe. Silly shit. Junk.

A football game plays on the muted television. Wherever it is, it's snowing. Drifts are forming on the sidelines and flakes stick to the camera lens, blurring the action. I stand and draw a pair of six-shooters from imaginary holsters on my hips, empty them into the set. Then I pretend I'm on my way to the moon. I tiptoe around the living room in slow motion, holding my breath and feigning weightlessness.

The phone rings. It's my father.

"I want to warn you that Karl may be on his way out there to look for you. Do you remember him? He's just been released from prison, and he showed up here unannounced a while back."

"Merry Christmas," I say.

"What?"

"Fuck you."

Karl's duffel bag is under the magazine rack at the end of the couch. I unroll it and sort through his possessions. I put on one of his T-shirts and a pair of his socks. And Judy. Oh, Judy. Who knew you, too, had dreams of escape? And who knew yours would come true?

Telephone Bird

——

In a decent world, losing the car would have been the last knot in that particular string of bad luck. The Denver boot they called it, and there it was one morning, big and orange and clamped to the left rear wheel of my Nissan. What kind of nastiness was that? A few unpaid parking tickets and they came down on you with a sledgehammer?

Bobby didn't answer. The joint he'd smoked half an hour earlier had put him into a scientific frame of mind, and he held two dead leaves he'd found on the prickly yellow lawn out at arm's length, shifting his gaze between them.

"You know what I did?" I continued, not worried if I seemed to be rambling a bit, as it was just the two of us. "I slashed the tires and cut every hose in the engine. I put dirt in the gas tank and took a screwdriver to the radiator, turned it into a sieve. What they towed away was a junker they won't even be able to auction off. They'll have to sell it as scrap. This is the new me, you see. Things used to happen to me; now I make things happen."

"You were crying, though," Bobby said, still intent on the leaves.

"Hello?"

"I heard you."

"Give me a break."

Bobby, Bobby, Bobby. He'd made it all the way to law school before his brain seized up. Now he watched too much television and labored over a trilogy of novels chronicling the Great Elven Wars of a land called Tybor. There was no sweeter kid if he took his medication and stayed away from hard liquor, but you wanted to shake him sometimes when his memory went spotty.

A bird cut loose with a trilling electronic chirp, and I nudged Bobby and pointed in the direction of the sound, somewhere near the shed at the back of the yard. It was this bird we were looking for, the one that had somehow learned to mimic the ring of my telephone. The first time it had perched outside my window just after sunrise and twittered that way, I'd sat up in bed and grabbed the receiver, certain that the temp agency was calling with a last-minute assignment. Since then, there'd been many more such false alarms, and my patience had been exhausted.

Because it was my problem, I took the lead. As stealthily as Hollywood Indians, we crept from apricot tree to lemon tree to avocado tree, finally crouching next to the rickety outbuilding. The boards of it were warm through my shirt, and I couldn't believe how much I was sweating.

I peeked around the corner, where an old orange tree twisted out of the ground. Then, lying on my back, I wormed myself to the base of the tree's trunk, my eyes fixed on the confusion of leaves and branches swaying against the sky's blue blankness.

There! Its little chest puffed, its throat swelled, and out came the ring. I watched the bird bustle from branch to branch, a feathered twitch, more motion than mass, until a sudden ripping tumult frightened it away. The fist-size rock responsible dropped from the tree and landed too close to my head.

"I get him?" Bobby asked.

"Well, he knows he's not wanted now, anyway. That might do the trick."

I was trying to be hopeful in those days, you see, hopeful but forceful.

THE BIRD WAS back the very next morning, ring, ring, ringing, at the crack of dawn. Again I snapped awake, paranoia an icicle lodged in my bowels, my lower body puckered and clenched. The bill collectors were prohibited from harassing me under the terms of the bankruptcy, but the damage had already been done. At the end, right before I filed, they were calling all the time, some even threatening me. "You never got in over your head?" I'd scream at them. "You never had a beautiful wife you couldn't say no to?"

The trap in the shower was clogged with hair, and someone had watered down my milk again, to hide their pilfering. Emma, the owner of the house, came into the kitchen while I was stewing over my cornflakes. She had her church dress on. She'd been a nun until 1988, and still went to Mass every day.

"Want some tea?" she asked. Water screamed out of the tap, thudded into the kettle.

"The milk fairies have been at it again," I said.

"I'm sorry."

"Five people in one house is just too many."

"That depends on the people."

Emma smelled funny. Everything smelled funny. A hundred years' worth of grease hung in the air, a slick of it settling on top of my coffee. What strangeness a man could get used to.

"I have to move out," I said. "This place is killing me."

"We'd sure miss you. Scrabble wouldn't be the same."

"Don't look," Sandal yodeled on his way to the refrigerator. He was wearing nothing but a pair of red bikini briefs. There was a house rule about that, about running around half-naked, but Sandal ignored it. He lived rent-free in the biggest room on the second floor in exchange for acting as handyman, and this, he felt, entitled him to certain privileges.

He leaned against the counter and tipped a container of yogurt into his mouth. With his ponytail and those panties and the dusty morning light, he could have been a woman in some screwy dream.

"Are you working today?" he asked me.

"No, Sandal," I replied. "I always dress for breakfast."

"No, really, how much are they paying you? Because this friend of mine hooked me up with an extra gig on this movie. I can probably get you on, too, and maybe Bobby. We'd make like seventy-five dollars."

"Thanks, but I already committed."

Emma brought her tea to the table and sat in the chair across from me. She was a nice lady, I liked her, but still I felt a little crowded. My knee wobbled, and the soles of my feet itched.

"What's the movie about?" she asked.

"It's a postnuclear deal, L.A. after the bomb and all that. I'm one of the zombies."

Emma smiled, then bowed her head. She lifted the rosary hanging around her neck to her lips as she whispered a prayer over her tea. I glanced at Sandal, ready to exchange smirks, but his head was ducked, too. I waited until they'd finished to light a cigarette.

I WAS WORD processing for the gas company that week. The regular employees were out on strike, and every morning and evening we scabs were bused through an angry picket line. The strikers spat and cursed at us as we passed, their faces monstrous with rage, like those you see on the news, in footage from other countries. With rumors of guns in the throng, we rode most of the way bent double, hugging our knees, and I wondered if this was what war felt like. Afterward the bus's windows would be glazed with snot and broken eggs that caught the sun and sparkled almost prettily.

SANDAL CROUCHED OVER a triple-beam scale placed on the coffee table, dividing a pound of marijuana into quarters and eighths. This was one of his jobs as handyman, because in addition to renting out rooms in her house, Emma also dealt small quantities of sinsemilla to a select and established clientele. Both Sandal and Bobby — sunk deep in a recliner, profoundly stoned — were still in makeup from their movie roles. Their faces glowed a purulent yellow and were riven with thick-lipped, oozy gashes.

"We looked even better on the set," Sandal said. "With these gnarly false teeth and contact lenses."

His elbow directed me to a stack of Polaroids he'd taken during the shoot: Skyscrapers in flames. Hordes of malformed creatures running riot. He and Bobby sharing a pint of bourbon, a severed head shrieking in the gutter between them.

"So it's a documentary," I joked, thinking of the picket line.

A baseball game fizzed on the big-screen television. It was an archaic projection model, and the lenses had been knocked out of alignment long before I'd moved in, so that three pitchers, red, green, and blue, occupied the mound at the same time, throwing to three overlapping batters. It helped to be high if you were going to watch it, and I wanted to see the game, so I reached for the joint Sandal offered.

How nicely the couch cradled me then, like the softest cloud. I lost track of the game, charting the snaky creep of darkness across the rug and up the wainscoting. The black tide slopped over onto the wallpaper, drowning the roses row by row, and

I was right there when it reached the ceiling, the only witness as night overtook us. My head tingled with exciting plans for the future, and if I'd had a pen, I might have written them down.

AFTER THE GAME Bobby and I walked to the liquor store for a six-pack. The gang members who lived in the house up the block were gathered around a car parked at the curb, trying to install a stereo by flashlight. I whispered that perhaps we should cross the street, but Bobby refused.

"It's my neighborhood, too," he said.

The gangsters grew sullen as we approached. I stiffened my arms and clenched my fists. I crammed my hands into my pockets and pulled them out again. I made my face as blank as it could be. Grim stares greeted us as we drew abreast of the gangsters. Tattooed fingers tightened around wrenches and screwdrivers.

"Hey, *ese,* you seen a puppy? A little pit bull?" This from a fat kid sitting on the hood of the car, holding a fat, naked baby.

"Not us," Bobby replied. "No puppy."

"Don't be shitting me."

"I'm not shitting you."

We were past them then, and gravity decreased with each step we took, as if we were hopping from planet to planet. Somewhere around Pluto everything went back to normal, and I was ashamed of being afraid. It was my neighborhood, too, after all.

The Korean man at the liquor store winced and averted his eyes when we brought the beer to the register. I understood why upon catching a glimpse of Bobby in the security mirror over the door. He was still wearing his makeup, and it was awful under the fluorescents.

"Take me to your leader," Bobby said to the Korean, handing him our money.

The Korean examined him more closely, then laughed. "Trick or treat," he said. "Okay, I know trick or treat."

He called to his wife, who was watching a portable TV behind the counter. She gave a little scream when she saw Bobby and almost fell off the milk box she'd been sitting on. The Korean laughed even harder, his shoulders jumping up and down.

I SMOKED ANOTHER joint, drank a couple beers, and decided to turn in. Foster was frying eggs and bacon when I stopped by the kitchen for a bowl of ice cream to take with me to my room. He worked nights unloading trucks and claimed to be a Hells Angel. Shortly after I'd moved in, he'd accused me of stealing his radio and punched me in the mouth. Emma said she'd throw him out unless he apologized, and we'd been okay with each other since then, though I suspected it was he who was sneaking my milk.

"The Donster," he said. "Donald Duck."

"Foster Freeze. The bee's knees."

I heated a spoon by running hot water over it, then dug out a few thick curls of ice cream. Foster hissed to get my attention. He drew a pistol from the waistband of his jeans and slid it under a towel on the counter.

"That's for you, for the bird," he whispered. "Don't let Emma see it, or she'll freak."

"Jesus, Foster."

"It's just a pellet gun. Like you had when you were a kid."

The pistol felt creepy in my hand, and when I stuck it in my pants the sharp edges of it scraped my stomach.

"Watch out," Foster said, dropping a slice of bread into the frying pan to soak up the bacon fat. "The Donald's packing."

I passed Bobby's room on my way upstairs. He was talking to himself, and I put my ear to the door to listen.

"No!" he said. "No! No! You won't get past me. You won't get past me."

It sounded like he was off his meds again.

THE PHOTOGRAPH I chose for target practice showed my wife and me on the beach in Mexico. Our last trip before the credit card companies cut us off. The memory of how happy I'd been then sometimes kept me awake late into the night. And her—*radiant* is the word people use to describe such a smile. It was a smile you believed, or I had, anyway.

I leaned the picture against my pillow and crouched at the foot of the bed. The pistol sighed sharply each time I squeezed the trigger. I blew both our heads off, then shot the beach up just for the hell of it. When I flipped the picture over, the scattering of raised perforations left by the pellets reminded me of braille. I closed my eyes and ran my fingertips across them. When the money ran out, Cathy did, too. There should have been signs. I should have seen them.

I turned out the light, and the darkness tightened around me, sticky as a spider's web. Lying in bed, I drew circles in the air with the cherry of my cigarette while every sound I'd ever heard in my life poured through the open window at once. I chose a single thread of the clamorous snarl to concentrate on; the plashy roar of the ocean, it might have been, or teardrops striking asphalt, amplified a thousand times. My rude lullaby.

WE WERE ON our way in one morning when the strikers broke through the police cordon and began rocking the bus. Glass shattered and a woman screamed. I lifted my face off my knees to watch somebody crawl up the aisle, an Indian named Subhash. He pressed a hand to the side of his head, blood and hair between his fingers.

"They have killed me," he wailed.

He rose to his knees as the driver gunned the engine to make a run for the gate. The sudden lurch slammed him onto his back, and he lay there silent and still. The driver ordered us not to move him, which meant that some of us had to step over his body to disembark.

Word went around later that he was fine—his cut had been fixed with a Band-Aid—but that he'd been so frightened he'd wet his pants. Curtis, whose terminal was next to mine, couldn't stop talking about it. He felt sure Subhash would sue for stress and humiliation and wind up collecting a million dollars.

"Motherfucker gets a million for pissing," he said. "I'm gonna shit myself tomorrow, see if I can get two."

Someone else heard Subhash had died, but that the company was keeping it secret. You'd be surprised how many people wanted to believe that one.

It wasn't until Saturday, when Emma shopped garage sales after church, that I could hunt in earnest. The crushed soda crackers I spread over a bare patch in the yard drew a whole flock of small brown birds, any of which might have been the one I was after. This was an unexpected complication, but I didn't let it discourage me. A picnic table and an old canvas tarp served as a blind. I had no trouble dropping a bird with my first shot. The others leaped into the air and disappeared when it fell.

The bird lay on its back, not quite dead yet, and I walked out to examine it. Its scaly little claws made me nauseous, the way they jerked and clutched as if trying to tear something apart. I rolled it over with the barrel of the pistol, and the blood welling up in its open beak was like a shiny red berry.

Suddenly it began to thrash about, its spastic wings beating the dirt into dust, and I ran to the porch and stood there shaking, my hand on the doorknob, ready to flee if the bird came at me. It quieted down quickly enough, though, and I finally worked up the nerve to approach it again and fire three more times, putting the last pellet right into its hateful black eye.

I waited for punishment then — the bird had suffered, after all — but the sun glowed just as brightly, and the ground stayed firm beneath my feet, and I knew the disappointment some criminals must feel when their most daring transgressions fail to make the papers.

I used a shovel I found leaning against the house to scoop the bird up and toss it over the fence into the neighbor's yard, and the others returned and settled onto the saltines before I'd even concealed myself again. Their greed disgusted me. There was no need to take aim, and I didn't bother to remove the bodies of those I killed after that. The flock dispersed each time one of their number went down, but reassembled out of nowhere seconds later, like something snapping suddenly into focus. They ignored the dead completely, bouncing merrily over the corpses.

I fired until the pistol was empty, which was a mistake, because some of the birds were still alive when I finally went out with the shovel to gather them up. I couldn't bring myself to wring their necks, so the wounded ended up with the dead in a hole I dug at the back of the yard.

The telephone bird rang louder than ever from a lemon tree as I smoothed topsoil over the grave, and I sat down and cried for a while, brokenhearted because I'd saddled myself with another secret, this butchery.

SANDAL SHOUTED ME out of a beautiful dream in which my wife and I were planning a ski trip, and the water-stained ceiling of my room was almost too much to bear. I'd been asleep since burying the birds, and my legs felt hollow when I got up to unlock the door.

"Bobby's on the roof again," Sandal said. "He's all whacked out."

"Can't you handle it? Or Emma?"

"The only thing I'm going to do is get the cops to haul him off to the fucking loony bin. I'm so sick of his shit. Besides, you're the one he wants."

It was usually a phone call from his mother that set Bobby off. She was kind to him, and nothing but supportive, but all he heard in her voice was pity and disappointment. He'd been royally fucked, as far as I was concerned. What good was it to be crazy if you still felt shame?

The window in Sandal's room opened onto a small balcony, and from there a ladder led up to the roof. Emma stood on the balcony, her hands cupped around her mouth, her long gray braid coiled on the back of her head. She was talking to Bobby, even though she couldn't see him.

"I said we're going bowling. Don't you want to come?"

Foster was out there, too, shirtless, his tattoos looking like some kind of disease. When I started up the ladder, he said, "If he's gonna do it, let him. Get too close, and he'll put a death grip on you."

My bare feet were sweaty and kept slipping off the thin iron rungs, and the ladder rattled against the house as I climbed. I expected Bobby to be crouched on the edge, where I'd found him before, but this time he was straddling the very peak of the dizzyingly pitched roof, holding on to the TV antenna with one hand, a bottle of Wild Turkey clutched in the other.

"Didn't you hear?" I said. "We're going bowling."

"Have fun," he replied.

"Can I get a hit of that Turkey?"

"I don't know. Can you?"

I worked my way up the steep incline backwards, like a crab. When I reached the top, I turned and swung a leg over so that I sat astride the house like him, and he passed me the bottle. I drank more than I meant to, and my throat closed off. I spit, but the wind blew it back in my face.

The sun was setting behind the scraggly palms and sagging telephone lines. In the distance, the Hollywood sign leaned rosy against its dark hillside while the sky over the Boulevard soaked up the cheap reds and greens of the tourists' neon. Bobby stared off in that direction, sliding his thick glasses up his nose with the knuckle of his thumb. What to say now was always a problem, or whether to say anything at all.

"Looks like it's going to be a nice night," I ventured.

Bobby nodded.

"Maybe we should get out, see a movie or something."

"Did you go to your high school reunion?" he asked.

"The ten-year, sure."

"But you were married then, right? You had something to show off, your wife."

"My wife? Yeah, I guess I showed her off. Somebody should have shot me."

Bobby smiled around the bottle, which he'd raised to his lips. Pulling himself up with the antenna, he stood and balanced on the peak of the roof.

"Now, hey," I said. "Bobby." If a funnier joke had ever been played on me, I couldn't remember: putting me in charge of saving someone's life.

Televisions blared from every open window in the neighborhood, and three kids chasing a soccer ball across the empty lot next door called each other dirty names in Spanish. The streetlights flared once, twice, then all snapped on at once.

"Give me another drink," I said.

Bobby edged over to hand me the bottle. A good beginning, except that now that he was away from the antenna, he held his arms out like a tightrope walker, wobbling back and forth.

"I'm not going to mine," he said. "They sent an invitation, but forget it."

"You won't be missing much."

"I was class president, you know. And valedictorian."

"Hey, meet Best Dancer *and* Best Hair."

Bobby sat down again just like that and motioned for the bottle, and my first thought was to break it over his silly head.

"I'm the biggest damn bull in the barnyard, aren't I?" he said.

"Yes," I replied. "Yes, you are."

Something tickled the back of my throat, and I coughed, catching whatever it was on my tongue and bringing it to my fingers. A feather. Bobby straddled the roof of the house again, and pretended to ride it like it was a bucking bronco, screaming,

"Yeeehaw!" his heels scraping the shingles in sync with my squirming heart.

A CHEER THAT could be heard throughout the building went up from the picket line. The strike had ended. Our supervisors thanked us for all our hard work and sent us home early, and the strikers chanted, "So long, scabs," as we were bused out for the last time. It was a solemn ride back to the underground parking lot where we'd gathered each morning for the past month. Some of the women sniffled into great wads of Kleenex.

We'd been cut loose again, and being cut loose was never pleasant, no matter how bad the job. You always took it personally, and it made for some awfully scary grudges. According to the experts, the best strategy to avoid depression was to update your résumé and stay close to the telephone. The agency would call the next day with something else, or the next week, or the next month. It helped to have a friend there, but I didn't.

Culver City

—

SHELLY'S ACTING AGAIN, ACTING LIKE SHE CARES, SAYING,
"I swear to God, honey, this will change our lives forever."
Reaching across the kitchen table, she burrows her fingers
between mine and gives me a pout and wiggle that's pure
porno, and I have to smile back even as I'm thinking, *Who is
this tramp?*

There are eight Polaroids spread on the table. Eight Polaroids
that show a famous young actor doing things with a famous
older actor. Sex things. On a bed, on a lawn, in the sparkling
water of a swimming pool like the one we've always dreamed of
owning. Shelly was at a party in the Hills last night, and she
claims the photos fell right into her purse out of a book she
pulled off a shelf. Somebody will pay for them, she's sure. First

we'll try the actors, then the *Star* or the *Enquirer* or somebody like that. She figures $100,000 easy.

It's dirty business for a Sunday morning. I'm starting my first cup of coffee, and she just got home. We spend a lot of our time like this, at opposite ends of the day. I want her to go to bed happy, but the holes in her scheme are as obvious to me as the hickey she's tried to cover with a smear of flesh-colored makeup.

I'm working on a tactful way to tell her that she's gone too far this time, when the kid, giddy at seeing us so calm for once in each other's presence, snatches a Polaroid and makes a run for it. I yell and lunge, but he's halfway to the TV, slowing to examine his prize. I go over the back of the couch like a hurdler, completely forgetting about the coffee table on the other side. It collapses with a splintery crack, and the kid's screaming even before I land on top of him. He's okay, though, just scared. I rub his head until he eases off into a whimper. His teary eyes reflect a couple of cartoon mice skidding across the TV screen, and he slips away to watch them.

Back in the kitchen I crumple the Polaroid and throw it on the table, where it blooms like a flower as soon as it hits. Shelly grabs it and shoves it into her purse with the others, out of my reach.

"People get killed behind this kind of shit," I say. "Get them the fuck out of here today."

She rolls her eyes like I'm an idiot. She was different once upon a time, or I was. Her face turns tired, her mouth hateful. "Like you'd be any help," she says and, without even a good morning for the kid, slinks off to bed. I'm left to ponder that hickey and what to do about it. I stir my coffee and watch it swirl in the cup. If it was possible for me to dive into it and drown, I can't say that I wouldn't.

CULVER CITY is south and east of everything worth anything in L.A. We're all between jobs here or between marriages, between runs of good luck. We wait out our slumps in flaking

stucco apartment buildings, count the stars on our cottage cheese
ceilings. There are three different kinds of palm trees between
me and the 7-Eleven, and, when the wind's right, the faintest
tang of ocean — just enough scraps of paradise to drive you nuts.
We've been here too long now to go back, though, no matter
how bad it gets. At least Shelly and I agree on that. The great
state of Texas can kiss our asses. It was her dream to come out
here, and I jumped at the chance to make it happen. That's how
crazy I was about her. With all the nothing I'd seen in my life
up until I met her, she seemed to be an extravagant gift from a
very stingy God.

I THROW THE kid in the truck and head out to see a man
about some work, a Mr. Caldwell, who got my number from the
sign I keep tacked to the bulletin board at the Laundromat. He
sounded drunk when he called, but that doesn't bother me.
Some of the nicest bosses I've had have been alkies. A low chain-
link fence surrounds his house, and the yard is an expanse of
white rocks that crunch like ice cubes beneath my feet. The
doorbell plays a church song.

Mr. Caldwell takes a long time to answer, an elderly black
man in a bathrobe. I smell booze right away, but like I said, so
what? I've woken him up, so we spend a few minutes getting
straight who I am, him squinting at me over the bifocals hanging on the end of his nose.

"You got something to haul something in, right?" he asks.

"Yes, sir." I point to my truck out on the curb. The kid is
pressing his face against the window, licking the glass.

"That your little partner?"

"We're letting Mom have the day off."

What Mr. Caldwell wants me to haul is his dog. It's old and
blind and arthritic and hasn't been able to get to its feet for a
week now. He wants me to take it to the vet and have it put
to sleep because he can't bear to. I say I'll do it for fifty bucks.

That's double my usual rate, but I figure I deserve it since it's Sunday and I'll have to explain to the kid what's going on and everything. Mr. Caldwell says that'll be fine and invites me in.

The dog is lying on a blanket in the middle of the living room. It's bigger than I expected, part shepherd maybe. Its cottony eyes fidget as I move closer, and a shudder ripples from its snout to its tail. Other than that, it might be dead already. A bowl of food placed near its head is busy with flies.

"He's been a good friend to me," Mr. Caldwell says.

"I'll bet," I reply.

"Sonofabitch broke in here one night a while back, and Rowdy took ahold of his ass and didn't let go until the cops showed up."

"A real watchdog, huh?"

"Smart, smart, smart, too. He could count, I swear to you, and knew all the colors. I'd say, 'Get me that red shoe,' and he'd trot over and pick it out of a whole pile of them."

Poor old dog, poor old man. I have to move things along, though, because who knows what the kid's up to out in the truck. When Mr. Caldwell stops talking for a second to thumb the tears from behind his glasses, I suggest we carry the dog on the blanket, me taking one end, him the other. He stalls, offers me a drink. "I'm driving, but you go ahead," I tell him. He pulls a pint of something from between the cushions of the couch and has a swig. I wonder if he'll find another dog to keep him company, or whether he's decided, no, this is it, never again, as old men sometimes do.

The dog doesn't even stir on the way to the truck. We lift it up and over the tailgate and set it gently down. Mr. Caldwell leans in and arranges the blanket so that just the dog's head is sticking out. He kisses his fingers and touches them to its nose. I almost tell him to keep his money when he opens his wallet, but that would be stupid. Shelly didn't speak to me for a week once after she saw me give a bum a dollar at the supermarket. As we're driving away, the kid stands on the seat to look out the back window at the dog.

"He's dying," I say. "We're taking him to the doctor."

"Did that man kill him?"

"No, that man was his friend."

I'm prepared to answer the harder questions, the ones I would have asked at four years old, about angels and heaven and death in general, but the kid's already turned his attention to the truck's radio. He punches the buttons, jumping from station to station, never holding on one for more than a few seconds. It's something his mother would do in the same situation, not giving a damn about anybody but herself.

SHELLY WOULD HAVE you believe she's on a first-name basis with half the famous people in Hollywood. According to her, all kinds of stars are always coming into the coffee shop where she waitresses. They ask if she's an actress and invite her to parties and nightclubs, which is why she rarely makes it home before dawn, even though her shift ends at one. Of course it bothers me. I've even given up watching TV with her, because we can't go fifteen seconds without her saying, "I know him," or, "Look at Jimmy there. I've been to his house," as if I was some stranger she was trying to impress.

She swears she's been faithful, but what's that hickey about, then? And the bastard in the Escalade who dropped her off that other time, the one I saw through the curtains with his hands all up in her shirt, what about that? In her book these questions reveal my jealousy, paranoia, and lack of trust. In her book they're an excuse to gut our checking account and disappear for three days. "How could you do that to your son?" I asked her after that episode. "Three days never killed anyone," she said.

If I was anything like my dad, I'd knock her on her ass, and that would be that. But my dad only used his fists to shape the world to his liking because he was too stupid and impatient to wait for things to fall into place on their own. Shelly and I loved each other before, and we will love each other again, I'm sure of it. We can only, all of us, run so far before what we really are and what is meant to be catch up to us. She'll slip into the apartment one morning just as the sun is beginning to peep into the dark corners and unroll itself across the floor, just after the sprinklers in the courtyard have shut off, leaving each blade of grass crowned with a ghostly drop of water. She'll be tired and ashamed but happy at the same time, as anyone is who suddenly comes to their senses. "What was I thinking?" she'll say, or something like, "I've been so foolish." And there I'll be at the kitchen table with a fresh pot of coffee and a full pack of cigarettes, as cheerful and steadfast as one of those birthday candles you blow and blow on but just can't blow out, no matter how hard you try.

SHELLY TURNS ON her side to make room for the kid on the couch. "Who's this?" she asks every time another video starts on MTV, and the kid names the band. If he misses one, she goes over and over it with him until he gets it right.

"See how smart he is?" she says.

"So when's he going to learn to tie his shoes?" I reply, and believe me, unless you've ever been the person who has to bring up these kinds of things, you don't know how mean it can make you feel. That's why I decide to leave them to their fun. I go into the bedroom with the calculator to figure out how we're doing at sticking to our budget. Turns out, not half bad. With the fifty from Mr. Caldwell and the tips I finally talked Shelly into kicking in, we have twenty-five extra this week to save or spend as we please.

It's not even noon yet, but I lie down on the bed with the intention of taking a short nap and starting the day over with a better attitude. I roll onto my stomach and grab a pillow and think how nice it would be if Shelly joined me. I've been doing without for a long time now, one of those things where she's always tired and I'll be damned if I'll beg. It's still her who comes swimming into my head, though, when the TV fades and gravity gives way — on all fours, smiling over her shoulder, astride me, bounce, bounce, bouncing, a pale nipple grazing my lips, long blond hair taut across my knuckles, the backs of her knees sliding sweaty into the crooks of my arms. I kiss her feet, I kiss her stomach, I kiss the perfect swell of the young actor's perfect ass while the older one tugs at me, insistent.

My eyelids ache from the strain of being forced open so suddenly. Sour and sweaty and mortified, I fling myself toward Shelly's purse and upend it, but those goddamn Polaroids are not part of the mess that spills onto the carpet. Drawer by drawer, the dresser gives up nothing, and the nightstand is a bust. I'm sliding my hand between the mattress and box spring when Shelly opens the door.

"Tell me where they are," I say.

"They're mine. I found them."

"Stole them, you mean. I'm getting rid of them."

"Yeah, right."

"Come on, Shell, this isn't our style, selling what isn't yours. We're not that desperate, are we? We're not hurting that bad."

This stops her for a second, cools the fire in her eyes, and I think, *Damn, I've done it!* But then she says, "I hid them better than you know how to look, so just leave my shit alone," and slams the door so hard the pictures she's hung on the walls jump and rattle, all those ballerinas and kittens and vases of flowers. I sense she's bluffing, so I go through her purse once more, unzipping every pocket. Way down at the bottom I come across a rubber, a silly glow-in-the-dark number that makes me wonder what kind of clowns she's fucking. I'm afraid I'll kill her if my hands don't get busy doing something else, so I gather all the clothes tossed around during my search, pile them on the bed, and take my time folding them, doing my best to put everything back exactly where it belongs.

THE PIZZA PLACE in the minimall closes early. The sun hasn't even set, but the owner's already drawn the steel grate across the windows, which gives us a really pleasant perspective on the parking lot. Shelly puts her foot down when he starts to mop the floor, saying, "Do you mind? We're eating here." Her tone always riles me these days.

"Give the guy a break."

"He should learn how to treat his customers," she says.

"He just wants to get out of here at a decent hour."

"You're such a dick."

The kid climbs from under the table and grabs another slice, then worms his way back out of sight. Shelly picks at her pizza, eating the pepperoni, and after that the cheese, bit by bit, until only the crust is left, freshly skinned and gory with sauce. It pains me to see food wasted, but I bite my tongue when she pushes the crust aside and starts on another piece. I'm trying not to make her mad, because I want her to spend the rest of her night off with us, instead of going to the party I overheard her talking to her friend about on the phone. I plan to buy her a lottery ticket after dinner and let her rent whatever DVD she wants.

A fire truck passes outside, and we turn at the same time to watch. When it's gone, I catch her eye, and she shoots me a cute little pout. I'm thrilled to discover something we share that she hasn't forgotten, even if it is only the chills sirens give us.

While I'm paying the owner, his wife is cleaning out the display case. She removes a pizza with a couple of slices missing and carries it toward the kitchen but stumbles on the way. The pizza slides off the pan and lands on the floor. Her husband barks at her in a language I don't understand, and she snaps right back at him. Whatever he says next makes her glance at me and shrug. He follows me to the door and locks it behind me.

Shelly has seen the pizza fall, too. She pulls me down to her mouth and whispers, "You know what they're up to, don't you? As soon as we're gone, they're gonna scoop that thing off the floor so they can serve it tomorrow."

"Oh, please," I say.

"Bet you a million."

I look inside at the two of them standing behind the counter, watching us.

"You're wrong."

"Like you know. Like you've spent any time working in restaurants."

"They're good people."

Shelly snorts and shakes her head. "I swear to God." She's already walking away, dragging the kid after her. What exactly was it, I wonder, that destroyed her faith in me and everything else? This city hasn't kept its promises, but its lies were no worse than those we left behind. I wave to the owner of the pizza place and his wife. They wave back. An ambulance screams down Venice in the same direction as the fire truck, and I shiver alone this time and picture myself dying that way.

THEY CAME IN through the front door, I suspect. One strong yank on a crowbar is all it took to bend the bolt of the flimsy lock and splinter the jamb. The apartment looks like someone has picked it up and shaken it, everything upside down and across the room from where it was when we left. Shelly waits outside with the kid while I make a quick circuit. I throw open closets and fling aside the shower curtain, but whoever it was is gone.

The TV lies faceup against the overturned couch, too heavy for them maybe, but then I notice the DVD player in the corner, and the boom box. It hits Shelly at the same time it hits me. She rushes into the bedroom and comes out crying a few seconds later.

"They found them," she sobs. "They took them back."

My anger at her for not getting rid of the Polaroids when I told her to is a weak spark against the happiness swelling inside me. I was so right about those pictures being nothing but trouble, I don't even have to say it. I wrap my arms around Shelly, and she really cuts loose. Not even by pressing her face into my shoulder can she muffle the wails that climb out of her. I hold her tight to let her know that I forgive her. I kiss the top of her head.

"I was fucking out of here," she gasps.

"It's okay."

"Those fuckers."

A neighbor pushes open the useless door and gapes at the mess.

"You call the cops?" he asks.

"We'll handle it," I say. "Thanks."

Everything that was in the refrigerator is slopped together on the kitchen floor with everything that was in the cupboards. The kid slides around in the mess, laughing and smearing his face with flour and ketchup. I laugh, too, because now that it's all been wrecked, we're free to build something new out of the pieces, and I'm the man with the plan; Shelly will surely have to grant me that.

She's stopped crying but looks like she could start again any second. I think back to Texas, to me and a cousin parked outside a liquor store a couple towns down the highway from ours, egging each other on, pistols cocked, and how the only thing that saved us was a cop car rolling into the next space at the instant we'd decided to make our move. I remember how we tore out of there and drove straight to a reservoir and sank our guns in the muddy water. I remember bawling because I couldn't believe how stupid I'd been, and I remember praying that I never got that stupid again. I have an idea Shelly's feeling a lot like that now.

I right the couch and sit her down, and when I put the TV back on its stand and plug it in, it works fine. I tell her to relax, I'll whip the place into shape in no time. The kid pitches in as best he can, and we heave and ho and sweep and straighten, singing silly songs and sharing cans of root beer. He looks so much like his momma when he's happy. Every so often I lean over the back of the couch and touch Shelly somewhere. She actually manages a smile, and not once does she push my hands away.

THE LIVING ROOM is dark when I wake up, except for the hissing glare of the empty TV screen that silhouettes the kid asleep on the floor in front of it. Shelly is gone from where she was, on the couch beside me, and I rise and walk to the bedroom, already knowing that she won't be there either. The room is still sweet with the smell of her perfume, and I'm able to follow the scent all the way down the hall and into the courtyard before the night gobbles it up. From there laughter and a revving engine lead me to the parking lot, where I watch the Escalade that dropped her off that time bounce over the speed bumps in the driveway as it carries her away from me.

Back in the apartment, I sit at the kitchen table and smoke a couple of cigarettes. The people in the next unit are arguing about money, and the guy upstairs flushes the toilet and turns on the shower. It's something I'm usually able to ignore, the dreary murmur of these other lives at the edges of my own, but not tonight. The kid screams himself awake when I pick him up. I quiet him and wrap him in a blanket. There's no way to lock the ruined front door, so I just pull it shut and leave it.

IT'S EASIER TO think out on the bright, straight streets, behind the wheel of the truck. With half of me busy watching for stop signs and keeping to the speed limit, the ringing in my ears fades, and I try to put this latest disappointment into perspective. I let my hopefulness get the better of me again, which is just the kind of lamebrain leap I'm always making. The women at the coffee shop know where Shelly is, and I could get it out of them by saying the kid is sick. I could drive right up to so-and-so's fancy house and barge right into his party and tell Little

Miss Starfucker exactly what I think of her sneakiness, but what good would that do? She'd laugh in my face and call me an asshole. We wouldn't talk for a few days, until I apologized for embarrassing her in front of her friends, and then we'd be right back where we started. I've been running in circles like that for years now, with her just one step ahead of me, and not once did I consider the possibility that I might never catch up. I was always sure she'd wear out before I did.

THE KID IS hysterical again. He struggles to open the door of the truck, and I almost kill us both, veering into oncoming traffic as I try to stop him. I pull into the minimall to calm him down, but he's tired and cranky and won't let me touch him. The lights are still on in the doughnut shop, and I tell him that if he'll be a big boy, he can have whatever he wants. He allows me to take his hand and lead him inside.

I don't say anything when he orders more than he can possibly eat, I just have the clerk add on a coffee and pay for it all. We sit across from each other at a little plastic table. When I ask for a bite of one of his maple bars, he shoves it back into the bag and hugs the bag to his chest. Sad music is playing on the radio, and the beginning of a thick fog smears the lights shining down on the empty parking lot. I'm reminded that there's an ocean nearby, that we've come about as far as there is to go in this direction.

THE SUN IS rising when the kid awakens. He sits up next to me on the seat of the truck and sleepily watches the breakers fold into the shore as we zip along beside them, headed north. A guy once told me Oregon was a nice place to raise children. Said the trees there were older than anything we know. It sounded like something to see. Our clothes are in back, a few other things. We don't need much. Shelly can have the rest.

She should be getting home right about now, drunk probably, a fresh hickey on her neck. The note I left was pretty basic.

Dead Boys

When it was time to put everything on paper, there wasn't much to say. Still, I imagine her crying as she reads it. Or maybe she'll be angry and tear it into little pieces. Not that it matters.

"I've got to pee-pee," the kid says.

I pull off the freeway and swing back under it to a parking lot on the beach.

"Want to wear my sunglasses?" I ask, and the kid smiles at me with his momma's smile as I set them on his face. We get out, and I unbutton his pants so he can do his business. There are seagulls here, surfers, a few fishermen. I walk to the crumbling edge of the asphalt, pick up a handful of sand, and fling it at the waves. The breeze blows right through me.

Love Lifted Me

===

A SHOTGUN BLAST AT DAWN SEPARATES NIGHT AND DAY. I come awake awash in adrenaline before the echo has faded and roll off the bed to sprawl on the nappy motel shag, where I hope I'll be safe if war has broken out between the crackheads in the next room and the pimp downstairs. The carpet reeks of cigarette smoke and spilled perfume. I press my face into it and wait for another explosion, but there's only this dog somewhere, putting together long and short barks into combinations reminiscent of Morse code. I imagine that I'm able to decipher the gruff pronouncements: *He who feeds me is a liar and a thief. His hand upon me is a curse. God sees all and does nothing.*

The parking lot is quiet when I finally muster the guts to crawl to the window and peek between the drapes. The other rooms are shut up tight, and a perfect mirror image of the neon vacancy sign shivers in the placid, black water of the swimming pool. So I guess I dreamed the gunshot, or maybe it's Simone again, my dead wife, trying to drive me crazy.

Linda is still sound asleep, too, but that doesn't prove anything. A stone speed freak, her standard routine is seventy-two hours up and twenty-four down, and when she crashes, she crashes hard. Right now she looks as serene as an angel or a sweet, dead baby. A blanket hides most of the damage: the tracks; the scabs that keep her nervous fingers busy; the bruised skin stretched thin over her ribs and spine, elbows and knees. She's sixteen years old and has been raped three times, and I'm like an uncle to her, like a big brother, she says, because I let her stay in my room when it's cold outside. No, I'm not fucking her. I'd like to, but then Simone would kill me for sure.

I rejoin her on the bed, careful to keep to my side, and watch the walls go from blue to pink to white, until the river of grief twisting through me unexpectedly swells and jumps its banks. At the first rush of tears, I get up and shut myself in the bathroom, and it's as rough as it's been in a while, but by the time the liquor stores open, I'm showered and shaved and empty enough to bob like a cork on the surface of another day.

THE LISTLESS WINTER sun doesn't do much to warm the chinky concrete of the pool deck, where I sit sipping beer and tomato juice, my feet dangling in the frigid water. The pool is the heart of this place. From here I can keep an eye on all of the doors and windows. I can see everything coming at me. I work on a letter I've been meaning to write. *Dear Simone, please leave me alone.* Relaxing my neck by degrees, I let my head fall back until I'm staring up at the sky, which is crawling with choppers and blimps and spectral silver jets. The wind steals half of every cigarette I light.

The bad guys sleep at this time of day, so the kids who live here are running wild, making the most of the few hours when it's safe for them to be out of their rooms. While their mothers cluster around the Coke machine, as vigilant as nursing cats, they play hide-and-seek among the cars in the parking lot and pedal tricycles in sloppy circles. I ignore them as best I can. They make me nervous. I'm afraid that at any moment they'll go off like a string of firecrackers and disintegrate into acrid smoke and drifts of shredded newspaper.

A couple of them, little boys, rattle the gate of the fence that surrounds the pool and beg in Spanish to be let in.

"Vamoose," I say. "Adios."

Undaunted, they snake their skinny arms through the bars and strain to reach the lock. I scoop some ice from my cup and fling it at them, and they fall back laughing as a police car eases into the lot, no lights or sirens. Before it has come to a stop, the boys' mother is herding them back to the family's room, and the other mothers, too, gather their children. Within seconds the parking lot is empty. The sudden silence makes my palms itch. Mrs. Cho, the owner of the motel, leads the cops up the stairs, and I lift my feet out of the pool and stomp some feeling into them in case things get ugly and I have to run for cover.

When the eviction party reaches the second floor, it's round and round she goes, where she stops, nobody knows. Room 210: old guy, Mexican, Cuban, something. Wears a cowboy hat and plays the radio loud late at night to drown out the whores' comings and goings. The kids and their mothers watch from behind half-closed doors as one of the officers knocks with his baton. His partner cups his eyes to peer in the window, but the glass has been covered over with tinfoil. Mrs. Cho dials her cell, and the phone in the room rings and rings and rings. After a bit of discussion, she unlocks the door with her passkey and moves off down the walkway so the cops can do their stuff.

"Police!" they shout in unison as the door swings open. Guns drawn, they roll into the room, one high, one low. Such caution is unnecessary, however — the guy has been dead for a while, judging by the stench that billows out and settles over the motel like another coat of stucco. Mrs. Cho backs away, covering her nose and mouth. She bumps into the railing and slides along it toward the steps. Then the cops reappear on the walkway. One of them says something snide to the other and both laugh, but they're not happy, and neither am I. I'll be smelling death for days.

Are you happy now? I promise I'll take the blame for what happened to you if you'll just let me be.

My shadow lies beside me, a wan and shapeless stain in the gutter. I drag it into the liquor store, to the beer cooler, the register, and out again. The effort leaves me winded. Twisting the cap off my forty, I drop onto a bus bench, but I'm barely settled when a passing car's backfire sends my heart wheeling with the pigeons from the telephone wire overhead.

Eightball rolls up on his bicycle with Linda perched on the handlebars. Eightball, because that's how black he is. He doesn't care for the name, but so what, the little dope fiend, the little thief. I don't care for how he professes to love Linda one minute and pimps her the next. She's welcome in my room, but he is not allowed.

"S'up," he says. He feigns interest in a billboard across the street, a giant hot dog adorned with a bolt of yellow mustard. He can't look me in the eye.

Linda slides off the handlebars and sits beside me on the bench, then immediately pops up again like something has stung her. She stands on one foot, using the other to scratch the back of her leg. She's tweaking, every hair of her platinum crewcut in frenzied motion, her nostrils rimed with dried snot.

"Fuckin' that dude killed himself," she blurts through clenched teeth. "We saw'm carryin'm out. Smelled like fuckin' I don't know. Like shit. You see it? Hung himself in the closet. C'n I have a hit of your beer?"

I give her one, and she tries to sit again, but is soon back on her feet, rocking from side to side like a metronome marking loony time.

"They took'm away in an ambulance. What they do with guys like him, with no family and shit, is they take'm to the hospital and give'm to the students there. They're learnin' to be doctors, and it's a law they c'n do experiments and shit on your body if you're poor. That's why I made a will and left it with my mom. If I die, they got to burn me and spread my ashes over Hawaii."

A car sidles up to the curb, driven by a kid with a mustache that looks glued on. He rolls down the passenger window and calls out to Linda, "You for sale?"

"Yeah, she for sale, she for sale," Eightball says. He pedals to the window and practically climbs inside. "How much you got?"

The kid speeds away in a panic, tires squealing, and Eightball's lucky his head doesn't go with him.

"You fucker," Linda wails. "I can't believe you."

"What you mean? I's just joking."

Eightball drops the bike and hurries to put his arms around her. She hugs him back. Don't ask me why people do what they do. After Simone jumped off the freeway overpass, taking our baby girl with her, the cops brought me to the station and wondered aloud what drove her to it. I was her husband, they reasoned, I should know. I didn't, and I still don't, and I think that's what pissed her off.

"We gettin' married," Eightball says over Linda's shoulder. He grabs her wrist and forces her hand my way. I glimpse a ring. Linda's face ripples like the motel pool in a downpour, translucent and impenetrable all at once.

"My mom signed the paper," she says.

"And my daddy comin' to sign mine tomorrow," Eightball boasts.

"You can drive us to the place, can't you?" Linda asks. "If I give you gas money?"

"Sure," I say.

"First thing tomorrow morning."

"Whenever."

I won't hold my breath. We've been through this before.

Eightball slides his hand under Linda's thin white T-shirt, up under the black bra showing through it. He squeezes her tit and stares at me like, *What the fuck are you going to do?* This kid. This fucking kid. I pretend to doze off and picture him dead in the street.

"He all fucked up," Eightball snorts.

Linda climbs back onto the handlebars, and the two of them wobble their way down Van Nuys Boulevard. When they're good and gone, I open my eyes. Traffic whips past. There's a loose manhole in the street that bucks and clatters whenever a car passes over it, and it's bucking and clattering like crazy right now, as if to remind me that it's Tuesday, three p.m., and everybody has someplace to be except me.

Stop it, I say to Simone. *Please.*

I wish she'd just get it over with. Hiding in palm trees and broken-down taco trucks and stray cats, she haunts this whole city, lashing out at me, dismantling my life piece by piece. My job, the house—I can't even keep a decent pair of shoes. Two days after I buy any, they're gone. They disappear right out of the closet. She wants me to suffer, and I have obliged, but the price of peace remains a mystery. I've offered to take the blame for her death and for the death of our child, but that's not enough. I'm beginning to think she wants me to die, too.

THE BAR STILL reeks of Pine-Sol or whatever they swab it out with before opening. The TV's off, and Cecil is the only other customer, at the far end, intent on the newspaper crossword puzzle.

"The hell's Jimmy?" I ask.

"In the can."

I slip behind the bar and draw myself a Bud.

"What a ruckus at your place today," Cecil murmurs.

"Somebody said suicide."

"Sounds about right. I smelled it way the hell down the block. Must have been a loner, to get that ripe."

"I don't know. I try to keep to myself with those people. They have problems."

Jimmy returns from the bathroom, collects for the beer. Nobody has much to say after that. I sit listening to ice melt somewhere for as long as I can, until I think I might start talking to myself. Then, feeling as brittle as improperly tempered steel, I get up and walk to the pool table.

The balls drop with a thud, and I arrange them in the rack, stripes, solids, bury the eight. Circling the table, I ignore the easy shots and try for miracles, and I'm on, I can't miss. The incontrovertible laws of physics have been declared invalid. Balls smack into other balls and assume impossible trajectories that always end in corner pockets. What goes up doesn't necessarily come down.

And if Simone had been given a moment like this? I wonder. Why, she'd have flown when she jumped, instead of falling. She and our baby would have sailed off that overpass and glided toward Pasadena, traffic glittering and roaring beneath them like a swift, shallow river in the evening sun. Oh, shit. Here I go again. I've also dreamed that I was there to catch them, and other times I've been able to talk her down from the guardrail; I've convinced her to give me the baby, then to take my hand herself. Next I'll be Superman or something. That's how stupid it's getting. I'll build a time machine or rub them down with Flubber. Whatever it takes to keep them alive. Whatever it takes to make things different from what they are.

EIGHT A.M., AND someone's knocking at the door. I shake myself the rest of the way awake and pull on a pair of pants.

Most likely it's one of the girls from down the hall, wanting to bum a cigarette. If so, she's out of luck. Those whores never have a kind word for me. It's always faggot this and chickenhawk that just because I'm not interested in buying what they're selling. I check the peephole to be sure.

A black guy wearing a purple suit leans forward to knock again.

"Wrong room," I shout through the door.

"I'm lookin' for Deshawn. Goes by Little D. He with a white girl, Linda, and they gettin' married today."

Deshawn is Eightball's real name.

"So?" I say.

"I'm Deshawn's daddy. He give me this number to meet him at."

"They aren't here."

"But Deshawn give me this number."

Something in his voice makes me want to help him. He sounds civilized. I open the door and step outside, join him on the walkway. The sun is high enough to catch the second floor, where we're standing, but the first floor and the pool remain in shadow. It'll be a while before it warms up enough for me to move down there.

"They said they'd be by, but not when," I inform Eightball's dad.

"You know where they stay?"

I shake my head. In addition to the purple suit, he's wearing purple leather shoes and purple socks. By the way he keeps tugging at his clothes, constantly adjusting and straightening, it's obvious he's not used to being so dressed up.

"Well, then, how about where to get some coffee?" he asks.

"There's a doughnut place. Hold on and I'll show you."

I have him wait outside while I put on my flip-flops and a T-shirt. It'll be my good deed for the day, walking him over there. He's whistling something. I press my ear to the door and catch a bit of "The Wedding March."

EIGHTBALL'S DAD DUMPS a packet of sugar into his coffee and stirs it with his finger. The coffee is hot, but he doesn't flinch. He raises his finger to his lips, licks it clean, and asks if I've accepted the Lord Jesus Christ as my personal savior. I swear I've never heard as much Jesus talk in my life as I've heard since I hit bottom. For the sake of my daughter, I've held on to heaven, because I like to picture her snug among the clouds when I close my eyes at night. But that's as far as it goes, that's all I need of it.

"What's it to you?" I ask Eightball's dad.

"I just want to share the good news with you about God's plan for your salvation," he replies.

"Forget that, man. That's all right."

Eightball's dad chuckles and taps his tie clasp, a gold crucifix. "Oh, so you that rough and tough, huh? I got you. Just let me reassure you, though, you are loved."

I pick up a newspaper someone has dropped on the floor and pretend to read.

One of the fluorescent tubes in the ceiling has burned out, and the Cambodian who owns the shop stands on the counter to replace it. He slides the cover of the fixture out of its frame and passes it down to his teenage son, but the tube itself is jammed. His son hisses instructions at him while he struggles to remove it.

"Deshawn's girl, she saved?" Eightball's dad asks.

"I couldn't say."

"Deshawn saved. He was raised in the church."

The owner finally gives up. His son takes his place on the counter. The kid jiggles the tube and twists it. His baggy pants slip down to his knees, revealing Harley-Davidson boxer shorts. His father tries to pull the pants up, but the boy slaps his hand away. While he's distracted, the tube comes loose on its own and falls in slow motion, like a bomb dropped from an airplane. It hits the floor and shatters with a glassy pop, but none of this fazes Eightball's dad. He's deep into something about the Israelites. Saliva thickens in the corners of his mouth, and he grips the little red table between us like it might try to run away. I interrupt with a question.

"How long's it been since you've seen Deshawn?"

"Deshawn? Four, five years. Five years it must be. His momma brought him up to Bakersfield to visit."

"And what was the last time before that?"

The guy's smile goes mushy at the edges. It's the kind of reaction I was looking for. I'm fucked that way.

"All right then," he says. "Enough of that."

The Cambodian brings out a broom and begins to sweep the milky shards of the broken tube into a pile. Eightball's dad suddenly turns to him and crows, "Jesus loves you, you know that, brother?"

"Okay, okay, good," the Cambodian replies. He sounds like he's had a bellyful of that shit, too.

"What's your name?" I ask Eightball's dad.

"Reggie."

"You drink beer, Reggie?"

THE SUN IS useless for warmth at this time of year, but I like the feel of the light on my skin. Its gentle pressure keeps me from thinning into nothing like a drop of blood lost to the sea. Reggie thanks me for mixing him another beer and tomato juice, then reclines again on the webbed chaise and goes back to humming complicated tunes under his breath. He seems content to lie here and drink and watch the kids hard at their morning games on the other side of the fence. They don't make him nervous at all.

Room 210 has been cordoned off with yellow police tape. Mrs. Cho can't get in to clean up until the coroner certifies that the death was a suicide, so we live with the stink, which lingers one tiny step behind everything else. You fool yourself that it's gone, but then the wind shifts and you get a snootful and almost puke.

A syringe floats in the pool, spinning in slow circles whenever the breeze ruffles the water. After a while, it strikes me how disgusting this is. Someone has stolen the long-handled net Mrs. Cho uses to scoop trash out of the water, so I have to strain and stretch and splash to force the syringe to the side of the pool where I can reach it.

"What you got?" Reggie asks.

"Nothing. A bug."

There's blood caked inside the cylinder, and the needle's bent. I slip it into an empty beer can and toss the can into the Dumpster. Reggie pipes up again while I'm washing my hands in the pool.

"Deshawn should be here by now. I could of taken a later bus if I'd known. Been up since three a.m."

I don't tell him about the last time Eightball and Linda were supposed to get married, or the time before that. He's removed his purple jacket, hung it on the back of his chair, and loosened his tie. Now he untucks his shirt and unbuttons it. He has a big old belly, and a dull pink scar puckers the center of his chest from the top of his breastbone to right below his rib cage. None of my business.

I slide into the chair next to his and pick up my drink. The children screech like wounded rabbits, and the beetle-browed motel that surrounds us declares with a groan and a fresh set of cracks that it can't take much more of this. A junkie steps out of a room on the second floor. He flings his arms up before his eyes to protect them from the light and staggers along the walkway to the room next to mine, where it seems they've been expecting him. The door opens onto blackness, and he's sucked inside.

Dear Simone. Dear Simone. Dear Simone.

Reggie reaches over and shakes my chair. I flinch so hard something in my neck pops.

"What you need to get for out here is a radio, put on some

good gospel for these children. Some of that 'Love lifted me, love lifted me.'"

Linda and Eightball slink out of the same room the junkie disappeared into. They know we're here. Linda waves as they walk toward the stairs, but Reggie doesn't notice. I don't say anything. Let him be surprised. I light another cigarette and open another beer.

Eightball rattles the gate and shouts, "Yo, old man, you drunk already?"

"Little D. Lord, my lord."

Reggie pads over to let them in, buttoning his shirt on the way. It looks like the wedding is still on. They've even gone so far as to dress for it this time, Eightball wearing a white turtle-neck and an old suit coat, Linda a pale green minidress.

Reggie embraces Eightball. "Look at you," he says. "My little man." Then he turns to Linda and holds out his arms. "Come on, girl, we all in this together." She moves forward and lets him hug her, too.

He drags more chairs over, arranges everything in a circle, and Eightball and Linda sit reluctantly. It's too much for them, as high as they are. Eightball fidgets and Linda gnaws her lips. They lie shamelessly in response to Reggie's questions. At first I'm impressed that they even make the effort, but then it becomes ridiculous. I laugh out loud when Linda claims she's been offered a job as a nanny to some rich doctor's kids.

Reggie wants to say a prayer. Linda bows her head, and I can see right down the front of her dress. The crack and speed have gobbled up most of what was there, but what's left is right out in the open. Eightball catches me looking and drops his hand to the inside of his thigh to flip me off where his daddy can't see, and I close my eyes and grin like that peek at his girl's titties was the biggest thrill I've had in ages.

A flock of gulls descends upon the motel from out of no-where. Some strut stiff-legged across the parking lot, running to avoid the kids, while others eddy overhead like trash caught in a whirlwind. They say this means a storm is coming, when they travel so far inland. Or maybe it's the smell that's drawn them, Room 210. It's a fact they'll eat just about anything. I knew a kid once who fed them bread wrapped around fishhooks. The hooks were tied to fifty or so feet of monofilament, which the kid staked into the ground. It was a neat little trick, practically turned those birds inside out. And the sounds they made. My fucking God! It's like I used to tell Simone: You want nightmares, honey? I'll give you nightmares.

I SAID I'D take them to the county clerk's office, so I do. Reggie rides in front with me, and the happy couple slouches in the backseat. It's good to be away from the motel. The freeway sweeps up out of the Valley and swings us past Hollywood, and the traffic zipping along in all four lanes makes me feel like I'm actually part of something that works. Reggie fiddles with the radio and tunes in an oldies station. "Rockin' Robin," stuff like that.

Eightball has the window open. He holds his hand out, palm down, fingers together. The hand banks and swerves like a jet fighter in the air rushing past. "Red Team Leader to Red Team One," Eightball says, "prepare to engage." He purses his lips and makes machine gun sounds, tapping his tongue against the roof of his mouth.

Linda watches, irritated, then finally says, "You're trippin', boy." She imitates his make-believe plane, exaggerates it into ridiculousness, until Eightball yanks his hand back inside the car and rolls up the window.

We pass over the four-level interchange where the Hollywood, Harbor, and Pasadena cross, the very one Simone jumped from. It's the first time I've been here since it happened, but, *Okay,* I think, *I can handle this.* I keep my foot on the gas and my eyes forward, away from the guardrail. I treat it like any other stretch of road. Simone's not going to let me off that easy, though. We haven't gone a hundred yards further when the car begins to shimmy and grind. I manage to pull over to the side of the freeway before it dies completely.

"I said I'd give you money for gas," Linda whines.

"That's not it, I don't think," I reply.

I pop the hood, and Reggie gets out with me to see what's wrong. I'm lost looking down at the smoking engine. I was a salesman, for fuck's sake, stereos, TVs, etc. Cars are not my thing. Reggie pulls out the dipstick, wipes it on his handkerchief. When he reinserts it and removes it again, it comes out clean.

"When's the last time you put oil in here?" he asks.

I admit that I can't remember, and the way Reggie looks at me, almost wincing, it's obvious that he's finally figured me out, and I'm filled with shame. I try to explain in a whisper. "It's my wife," I say, but right then Eightball pokes his head out of the window and yells, "So what we gonna do?"

Reggie turns away from me to reply. "We're going to get us some lunch."

It's just as well. He wouldn't have understood anyway. That this was the car she rode in, and my baby, too, and that now she's ruined it and left me nothing from our time together. *But it isn't over yet, is it?* I ask her. No, it isn't.

The four of us walk to the next exit and come up off it on the edge of Chinatown. That sounds fine to Reggie, a little chow mein, some egg rolls. To get there we have to cross the freeway on an overpass, and they pause in the middle to watch the cars gurgling by beneath them, but not me. It's all I can do to keep from running.

THERE'S A FOUNTAIN in the main square of Chinatown, tucked in among the empty restaurants and the stores crammed full of dusty souvenirs. Dirty water trickles down a rocky hillside studded with small gold bowls labeled LOVE, LUCK, MONEY, and the like. The coins people have thrown at them glimmer so hopefully, I almost have to turn away.

Reggie passes out pennies and dimes, and he and Eightball and Linda line up at the rail and take turns tossing.

"Ooooh, yeah," Eightball crows when he hits his mark. He raises his hands over his head and does a victory dance.

"You cheated," Linda insists. "You leaned."

"Bullshit, woman. Ain't no leanin' involved."

I sit on a bench a short distance away and watch the red paper lanterns strung overhead twist in the stiffening breeze. The gulls were right, a storm is coming. I can feel it in the air.

"Hey," Linda calls to me. "Thanks for screwing everything up."

"Come on, now," Reggie says. He takes Linda by the shoulders and turns her to face him. "We'll figure something out. Don't you worry. You'll have your wedding yet."

I let my eyes drift to one of the store windows, and I swear I catch a glimpse of Simone reflected in it. It's the first time she's revealed herself, and a leathery strap of panic jerks tight around my chest. When I blink and look again, she's gone, but I know what I saw. The day takes on a dead, gray quality, like someone's thrown a shovelful of ashes on the sun.

Linda and Eightball and Reggie approach me. They're talking and laughing, but I can't understand them anymore, and I don't feel anything when Reggie lays his hand on me. I'm as numb as a tooth. I gurgle some kind of nonsense and pull away, and the next thing I know, I'm running down an alley and all the signs are in Chinese and the buildings are Chinese and everything smells like rotting meat. The wind in my ears is a woman screaming, and the clouds are boulders rolling in to crush me.

"Why?" I yell. "Why now?"

Dizzy with fear I stumble upon a pagoda with a neon beer can in its window. They're churches over there, aren't they? Temples or something. The door swings open before my hand even touches it, and, sure enough, Buddha smiles down from a shelf above a dark and quiet bar. I take a stool and order whiskey. Its heat spreads through me, resoldering all the connections. The bartender lights some incense, and my heart slows to normal. I've got fingers now, I've got toes, and that makes me okay, I think. I wipe away the tears on my face and take a deep breath. It's close enough to hallowed ground that she can't set foot in here, and there's twenty dollars in my wallet. I'll just wait her out.

A woman wearing a mail carrier's uniform goes to the jukebox, and soon the music starts. She motions to the bartender, who picks up her drink and carries it over and places it on a fresh napkin next to mine.

"Is this too weird?" she says.

Ha ha ha!

WE'VE CUT THROUGH the crap by the time Reggie comes in. We're laughing and telling jokes, and I'm resting my hand on her thigh.

"I need you outside," Reggie says. "It's an emergency."

I have every right to ignore him. Number one, there's nothing between us—no money has changed hands, no vows of friendship. He merely showed up at my door this morning and by nightfall will be on a bus back to Barstow or Bakersfield or wherever he's tumbled in from. And number two, I haven't forgiven him, and won't, that moment back there on the side of the freeway, when, struck suddenly by the truth of me, his eyes showed nothing but scorn and disappointment. I don't demand understanding, but I do believe we're all entitled to a little tact.

So I hesitate. I sip my drink and let him dangle until he sucks in his bottom lip, rubs his open hand over his face from forehead to chin, and squeezes out a "Please." Only then do I say to my new drinking buddy, "Don't move a muscle," and motion him to the door.

The clouds have thickened and swallowed up the sun, and

the first fat drops of the storm splat onto the asphalt of the alley. Eightball is sitting on the ground, his back against the pagoda. His eyes are closed, and he clutches his stomach. Reggie kneels beside him, reaches out to touch him, but hesitates as he's about to make contact.

"The girl stabbed him," he says.

"Who?" I ask. "Linda?"

"They was fussing in the restaurant, and she up and took a knife off the table and stabbed him."

The shakes begin in my knees, and I worry that I'm about to lose it again. I need to get back inside where Simone can't see me. All I can think to say is, "So he's dead?" and as soon as I do, Eightball scrambles to his feet and rushes me, furious.

"I ain't dead, you stupid motherfucker, and I ain't gonna die."

Reggie tries to hold him back, but he breaks away and gets right in my face.

"And you best tell that little ho she better watch her motherfuckin' back, 'cause I'm goin' to fuck her shit up when I catch her. I'm goin' to cut her a new pussy."

"Deshawn!" Reggie shouts.

Eightball pushes me and turns to him. Spit flies from his mouth as he shouts, "And you can step off, jack. I still owe you a fucking up for runnin' off and leavin' my momma all alone."

Pain finally gets the best of him. He grits his teeth and bends at the waist, his hand going to the flower of deep black blood on his shirt. A jet screeches somewhere above the clouds, and the rain comes down harder.

Reggie stands slump-shouldered, staring at nothing. Where are the hymns now? I don't know why I didn't see from the beginning that he's just as undone as I am. I head back to the safety of the bar, but he stops me with a hand on my shoulder and a beseeching look. What more can he want? I brought his goddamn son back to life.

"I got to get him to a hospital," he says.

"Try Union Station over on Alameda. You can find a taxi there. Or call 911."

"Could you help me?"

It's cold in the alley, and wet. Greasy puddles have begun to form where the rain splashes off the eaves of the buildings. Very faintly, I can hear the jukebox playing inside the bar, and I'm glad I don't believe in anything anymore, because that means I won't go to hell for saying, "No, I can't."

"Fuck all y'all," Eightball hisses. He lurches away like some wronged and wounded hero, and I think how funny it is that he gets to play that part.

"Deshawn," Reggie cries. "Son." He hurries after him, but I don't wait to see what happens. I've had it up to here with tragedy.

When I've finished off my twenty, Gina takes up the slack. She came right over from the post office to get blasted after a particularly nerve-racking shift.

"Do you think they'd hire me there?" I ask.

"Sure. I'll tell them you're a good guy."

"But am I?"

"Sure you are."

We drink for hours, through the quitting-time crowd and the before-dinner crowd and the after-dinner stragglers. It's so nice to be warm and full of beer and whiskey, to watch the people come in out of the rain and shake off their umbrellas. In a little while I've forgotten all about Reggie and Eightball and my dead wife's vengefulness. Buddha smiles down on me, and I smile back.

Gina and I move to a booth, where it's easier to kiss and cuddle. She keeps making me put my mouth on a certain spot on her neck — her G spot, she calls it — and bite down hard. When I do, she rolls her eyes and moans "Oh, yeaaah." I get confused a couple of times coming back from the bathroom, because of her uniform. Once I think she's a cop, and another time a sailor.

"Anchors aweigh!" I shout, and she laughs so hard, she spills her drink, but then the song playing on the jukebox makes me cry, and I lay my head down on the table and bawl like a baby.

"Do you love me?" I ask Gina.

"Sure," she says.

"Can I live with you?"

"No problem, no problem."

She gets up to go to the bar for some napkins so I can blow my nose. When I open my eyes again, she's gone. I sit and wait for her until the bar closes and the bartender tells me to leave.

THINGS HAVE GONE to shit in the last few hours. The buildings that line the alley are crumbling, the mortar between their bricks eaten away by the rain, their nails rusted. They lean into each other, forming a dripping black tunnel that is the only way out, and I know what Simone is up to, but what else can I do? I throw my arms over my head and make a run for it. I say, "Okay, fuck it," and enter her trap. I just want it to be over with.

There's a grating sound, metal on metal, and the heavy crash of collapsing masonry in the darkness all around me. Louder still is the slap slap of footsteps approaching. Simone, broken-boned and wormy, cracked and oozing like a rotten egg, pursues me with awful puposefulness. Her dirty fingernails clutch at my hair, and her graveyard perfume brings bile to my throat. My screams echo off the concrete that closes in as I rush deeper into the slippery blackness.

The tunnel narrows and the ceiling descends. I hit my head and drop to my hands and knees, and still she jerks and slides toward me. Scrambling over broken glass, I cut myself to ribbons, and the passage squeezes tighter, so that I'm forced to squirm on my belly with my arms pinned to my sides as Simone giggles and licks my heels. Down and down I go, my blood slicking the way, until the rubble finally clenches around me like a fist and forces the last bit of air from my lungs. I gasp once, twice, but it's no use. Simone's teeth work at my calf. She tears loose a mouthful of flesh and gobbles it down. Utter darkness descends over me like a condemned man's hood as I dig my toes in and give one final push, as I wedge myself even further into the tomb.

And then there's the rain again, cold on my naked body, its drops spreading across my eyeballs like spiderwebs. I lie on my back and run my fingers lovingly over the sidewalk beneath me, ignoring the police cruiser that jabs me with its spotlight.

A cop pulls himself out of the car and steps up onto the curb. He nudges me with his boot and asks, "Do you know where you are?"

"Chinatown," I reply.

"And your clothes?"

I point to the drainpipe I spurted out of, the one that now dribbles bloody water and the sound of Simone's frustrated weeping.

"My wife took them," I say.

He doesn't get it, and I really didn't expect him to. Trying not to laugh, he turns to his partner and says, "Pat, better dig that blanket out of the trunk."

So everything's okay for now, but I don't kid myself that I've beaten her. I'm not that crazy.

I OPEN THE bottle of pills they gave me upon my release from County General and shake a few of them into my hand. They're as blue as the sky is sometimes. The psychiatrist I talked to during my stay was a very busy woman. She ran quickly down a list of questions only a lunatic would give the wrong answers to and then asked if there was anything I wanted to discuss. I said no, not really, that I'd been under a lot of stress lately, thinking about my wife's suicide, and maybe that and the booze had led to what she referred to as my episode. She nodded understandingly and scribbled something in my file, and after seventy-two hours they cut me loose.

I swallow the pills without water. Linda is looking at herself in the mirror. She moans and falls on the bed and starts to cry. Two black eyes, her nose probably broken—Eightball's revenge. He caught up to her this afternoon over at crackhead park and beat the piss out of her, and not one person stepped in to help her.

"They said they was my friends," she wails.

I dip my cup into the cooler to fill it with ice and pour whiskey over that. I'm living it up, because this is my last week in the motel. I've run out of money, and the welfare checks I'm due to start receiving won't cover the rent here. Things are finally going to get worse.

Something crawling on the carpet gets my attention. I walk over and step on it. When I bend down, I see that it's a false eyelash. Where the fuck did that come from?

"Want to watch TV?" I ask Linda.

She rolls over and reaches out her arms, and here it is again, a chance to get it over with once and for all. *Kill me,* I tell Simone as I move toward the bed. *Kill me.*

I lie down next to Linda. The pills have turned my brain into a cotton ball. She winces when I hug her and says, "Careful." My fingers stroke the dead leaves between her legs, and I position myself on top of her. She draws the sheet over her ruined face.

"Could you give me some money when we're through?" she asks. "I want to go back to my mom's."

"Sure," I reply, but I won't, because I don't have any to give, and she knows it. She's just setting things up so later she can yell at me and call me a liar, and that's fine. Whatever it takes to make her feel better about this.

Before I can get inside her the bed begins to shake. A low rumble fills the room, and the TV skips off the dresser and crashes to the floor. Every board in the building creaks with the strain of the wave swelling beneath it. Linda rolls away from me. She scurries to the bathroom and crouches there in the doorway as the toilet cracks behind her.

"It's okay," I say, and stand up to prove it. The carpet writhes beneath my feet like the back of some great galloping beast. A chunk of plaster falls from the ceiling, and Linda screams.

"It's okay," I say again as the window rattles, desperate to be free of its frame.

I'm ready to die. I stand with my arms outstretched, a smile on my face, but we drop back to earth after a final jolt. The rumble fades away, replaced by the wails and chirps of a thousand species of car alarms, and my disappointment almost sends me to my knees. Really, her viciousness is astounding.

"It's just my wife," I explain to Linda.

"What the fuck're you talking about?"

"She gets jealous."

Linda looks at me like Reggie did on the side of the freeway when my car broke down, like I'm not the same person I was a few seconds ago. While I'm making myself another drink to replace the one Simone spilled, she slips her dress over her head, grabs her shoes, and runs away.

I step out onto the walkway a few minutes later, but she's nowhere to be seen. There's a commotion in the courtyard. Someone panicked during the quake and jumped over the second-floor railing. The body is lying in the parking lot, as still as a perfect summer night in the desert, and the blood that's leaked out of it looks like a big red pillow. My throat tightens and tears come to my eyes, and I almost cry out, "Simone!" until I see that it's one of the junkies from the room next door, a guy with long, dark hair. *Some joke, baby.* All of the tenants have gathered around him, the poor families and the whores and pimps and dopers. They're all standing together, staring down at him, while Mrs. Cho calls for an ambulance on her cell phone.

The sun is hidden behind a thick brown haze, which means that either the whole Valley's on fire or summer is just around the corner. A thin trickle of blood slithers away from the dead junkie's head, across the asphalt and under the fence to the cracked white concrete of the pool deck. It picks up speed there and spills over into the water, turning the deep end pink.

So now that's ruined, too. Are you happy?

No, she's not. Not yet.

Loss Prevention

———

Every junkie i've ever known has had a thing for Neil Young. Be he a punk, a metalhead, or just your garden-variety handlebar-mustachioed dirtbag, if he hauls around a monkey, he's going to have *Decade* in his collection, and he's bound to ruin more than a few parties by insisting that you play at least some of it, no matter that the prettiest girl in the room is begging for something she can dance to. Even if he gets off dope, he sticks with Neil, because by then Neil's become the soundtrack to his outlaw past. Let him hear "Old Man" or "Sugar Mountain" years after the fact, and everything in him will hum like a just-struck tuning fork as mind and body and blood harmonize in mutual longing for a time when desire was an easy itch to scratch.

So this is why, when the deejay announces that a rock block of Neil is coming up next, three classic cuts in a row, I know there's no hope of Jim budging until the last song ends. We're sitting in the parking lot of the Busy B market, where Jim's been working security for the past few months. He's training me for the night shift, but it's already two minutes past the time we were supposed to have punched in. I want to make a good impression on my first night on the job, but Jim just laughs at me and, sure enough, turns up the radio of his mom's old Lincoln. His latest thing is that I'm too full of myself, and he says it again now. "Does the sun care what kind of impression it makes?" he asks. "Does a bird?" He picked this up in rehab, the idea that all the world's problems stem from a surfeit of ego. My immediate inclination is to tell him to stuff the Intro to Eastern Thought bullshit, but because he's convinced the owner of the store to hire me, and because he's now sort of my boss, I have to humor him.

He pushes the button on the door that reclines the driver's seat so that he'll be closer to the rear speakers, the only ones that still work. The seat's smooth electric descent reminds me of those machines that scan your body and produce color pictures of all the cancer in it, and this is funny to me in a sick way, because Jim actually had cancer when we were in college. He got over it, but only after they removed his testicles and replaced them with plastic ones. Guys who lose their arms or legs, you see them on TV, playing wheelchair basketball and using their hooks to hurl shotputs and shit, but what do you do to prove you're as much of a man as you ever were if you lose your balls? Big, fucking stupid skinhead that he was, Jim chose heroin. His claim to fame was that he could shoot three times as much as anyone and still beat you at chess. Then he got pulled over in a stolen car and did a year in County, got popped dealing, and drew another year. His dad died during this stretch, and they wouldn't release him to attend the funeral. Something about the shame of that straightened him right out. He rid himself of his addiction and his ego, had his swastika tattoo covered over with the yin/yang symbol, and metamorphosed into a true-blue, eight-buck-an-hour crime fighter. When anybody asks, he says he's a loss-prevention specialist, and somewhere on his person is a gun he's not licensed to carry, bought from a drunken off-duty cop at a barbecue in Simi Valley.

The rain comes down so hard it cracks the night into a million pieces. All I can see through the windshield is glistening shards of cars and blacktop and the kaleidoscopic whorl of a woman skedaddling across the parking lot. I roll my window down a bit and stick my fingers out, and licking them afterward is like running my tongue along a galvanized nail. Old Neil's whining about four dead in Ohio when Scarlett Johansson suddenly pops into my head stark naked. This has been happening a lot lately, and, frankly, it's starting to piss me off. I mean, I've seen some of her movies, and she once strolled through a bar I was drinking in, but I'm not exactly a fan. I don't tell Scarlett this, of course, not when I'm lying on top of her on a bed veiled by mosquito netting, syrupy waves kissing the sand outside our super-deluxe grass shack. Her pale, pale skin soaks up so much moonlight, she gleams icy blue, but her thigh throbs hot beneath mine, and sweat beads along the thin trail of hair that runs from her navel down the flat plane of her stomach to the balmy darkness between her legs. I snap at her nipples and growl like a dog, which makes her laugh and laugh. She places a hand under my chin and pulls my face to hers, the insistent prodding of her heels against my ass urging me to go to it. "Not so fast, Scarlett baby," I say. "I didn't ask for this, but I'll damn sure make it mine."

The rain has eased into a lacy drizzle. Small drops are overtaken and swallowed by bigger drops that slide down the fenders of the cars like great glowing tears as I follow Jim across the parking lot, holding up my pants to keep my cuffs from dragging in the puddles. His extra uniform doesn't fit me too well, not even with all the safety pins and duct tape we used to take it in, and the gaudy tin badge hanging over my heart, SPECIAL OF- FICER, is a surplus-store joke. Jim assures me that it won't matter. He says most of the customers are Central American refugees who were so terrorized by their armies and police back home, they're afraid to look a Cub Scout in the eye.

I want to trust him on this. I want to believe that for once we're seeing the world through the same prescription, because it's a rough neighborhood, graffiti twisting like angry black vines up the sides of the buildings, half the streetlights shot out. On the way down from the freeway we passed under a pair of Nikes dangling from a telephone line—a gang signal, I've heard, drugs for sale or something. The market itself is a windowless bunker that's been tarted up with a thin coat of hot pink paint. A high cinder-block wall protects the loading dock and Dump- sters out back, topped by coiled razor wire that looks, if you squint, like the skeleton of some nightmare snake chewing on its own tail.

The automatic doors are on the fritz, propped open with cof- fee cans filled with cement. Mr. Ho, the owner, wobbles on a stool at the front of the store, behind a high desk surrounded on three sides by thick Plexiglas. He has skinny little legs and a big potbelly, and his forehead is shiny with the pomade he uses to slick back his thinning hair.

He says, "You late, Jim. What I gonna do with you?"

"I don't know, boss. Shanghai me and sell me into white slavery?"

Mr. Ho spits out the coffee he's drinking, he laughs so hard. He shakes my hand and welcomes me aboard and presents me with my very own time card. The three checkstands are manned by glum Chinese clerks in red aprons and bow ties—Mr. Ho's sons and daughters—and during a quick tour of the store Jim intro- duces me to the butcher—Mr. Ho's brother—and the produce man—Mr. Ho's nephew. The way it's going to work is, Jim and I will take turns walking the aisles for half an hour at a time, on the lookout for cereal swipers and Beanee Weenee thieves. The guy who isn't making the rounds will stand beside Mr. Ho's desk and cover the front of the store. Jim suggests that I go out first, to learn the lay of the land and such. I leave him and Mr. Ho talking about Rush Limbaugh. Mr. Ho loves Rush.

Because of the rain, customers are scarce. Whenever I pass any in the course of my patrol, I nod without smiling, friendly but stern. It's families mostly, and none of them seem like they're here to pull off the Great Kraft Dinner Heist, so after my third circuit I relax a bit, get into playing name that tune with the Muzak. Pig snouts are on special, seventy-nine cents a pound, mountains of them on display behind the greasy glass of the meat counter. Also pig feet, pig ears, and curly little pig tails oozing watery pink blood that pools in the corners of the trays. A fly that's succumbed to the cold lies belly-up on the hamburger. I point it out to Mr. Ho's brother. He reaches into the case, grabs the bug, and pretends to pop it into his mouth. Then he offers it to me.

"No thanks," I say, and we're both startled when the fly suddenly twitches back to life and zooms up to bounce against the jittery fluorescent tubes mounted on the ceiling.

Mr. Ho's brother laughs and says, "Jesus fly. Easter fly."

Two carts can't pass in the narrow aisles without one pulling over. The glass in the doors of the frozen food cases is cracked, and the milk is warm. There's a single brand of mustard on the shelf, two of toilet paper, and something somewhere really fucking stinks. Dented cans, stripped of their labels, are stacked under a sign, YOUR CHOICE 50 CENTS. I pick one up and shake it. Whatever's inside squishes back and forth. My first official act as a Special Officer is to tell a little boy to stop running. His dad grabs him by the arm and thumps his head. Over the kid's sobs, he asks where the beer is.

Then Jim and I trade places. Hands clasped behind my back,

chest puffed, I try to compensate for my baggy uniform with a hawkish demeanor as I stand beside Mr. Ho's desk. When he asks me to carry a round of change to one of the registers, I practically march there, and I know I'm in trouble, that this job isn't going to last any longer than the others, because I almost burst out laughing at myself. After a while Mr. Ho starts in with the kind of questions only an idiot or an asshole asks someone in my position.

"Jim say you went to college?"

"Once upon a time."

"So what you study?"

"English." I designed my own major, actually, a scramble of cinema, literature, and anthropology that culminated in a multimedia senior thesis exploring Charles Manson's influence on popular culture, but I've been lying about it since the day after graduation.

"English!" Mr. Ho clucks his tongue and shakes his head. "Oh, man, that no good. What you gonna be, a teacher? You see my kids." He sweeps his arm over the checkers, one of whom is absentmindedly picking at a patch of acne on his face, then smelling his fingers. "Business, chemistry, business. They gonna be rich when they finish school."

Scarlett overhears this. Her mouth tightens, and her eyebrows collide over her nose. She rams a shopping cart into Mr. Ho's desk and flips him off through the Plexiglas.

"Hey," he says. "You that girl in that movie."

She ignores him, throwing her arms around my neck to pull me down for a kiss.

"Don't you get a coffee break or something like that?" she asks.

"Go, go," says Mr. Ho. "Take five."

What can I do? She's come all this way.

Scarlett wants me to quit working and move in with her, and

loves me because I won't. She brags to her friends about my shitty jobs, tells them I'm a genius, and compared to the pretty-boy wake-and-bakers she usually dates, I guess I am. Hermann Hesse was her idol when I met her. *Steppenwolf,* blah, blah, *Siddhartha.* I turned her on to Kerouac and Bukowski, stuff I'd long since gotten over, but that I knew she'd fall for. The problem is that now I have to accompany her and her annoying friends to the worst skid row dives, and we always end up fucking in some piss-smelling alley or cheap motel room with bars on the windows, which bores me to death, because I already played the same part for too many USC sorority girls way back when.

As I'm showing her around the store, she takes my hand and slides it up the back of her leg, up under her dress, to let me know she's not wearing any panties. It's the saddest thing that's happened to me in a while. She thinks she's the first woman to ever pull this one on me, and I wish she was, I really do. The impossibility of us almost kills me, but I haul up the proper response. I moan low in my throat and cup her ass cheeks, which, to be honest, are somewhat larger and less firm than they appear on the screen, and then I lift her onto a shelf, where we grind away, boxes of laundry detergent toppling to the floor around us.

On my third patrol of the evening, I'm reading a recipe for shepherd's pie on the back of a box of instant mashed potatoes. A skinny black woman wearing four or five sweaters shuffles past in slippers that used to be pink and fluffy but now resemble dirty drowned kittens. She takes a can of tuna from the shelf and drops it into the big purse she's carrying, and when I crane my neck, I see bologna in there, too, and tampons. With me following close enough to touch her, she continues down the aisle to the deli case, where she adds some cheese and a pack of hot dogs.

"Still raining?" I ask, making sure my badge is visible.

She squints at me like I'm someone she can't quite place, then turns and walks away. Duty-bound, I jog to the front of the store to alert Jim, and we find her in the produce section. Jim crouches behind a tortilla chip display and hisses for me to join him. Instead I walk over and stand next to the woman as she tosses a few mushy bananas into her purse.

"How's life on Mars?" I ask, loud enough that Jim can hear. "I take it the invasion is proceeding according to plan."

She doesn't even react this time, just wanders off to get some carrots. Jim's waiting for me with his arms crossed. All his Buddha-boy cool disappears as he lectures me about protocol and arrest procedures and blowing the bust.

"It's a question of professionalism," he says.

We used to call him Ping Pong because of his balls, but never to his face. I shrug and say fuck it.

"You see," he says, disgusted.

"What?"

"I'm trying to help you."

He knows how broke I am. He knows he's got me over a barrel.

"Okay," I say. "Ten-four, good buddy." Ping Pong. Mother-fucker.

We go up front to wait for the woman to make her next move. A few minutes later she steps over the chain blocking off a checkstand that's been shut down for the night and scuffs past us, hugging a box of Cocoa Puffs. Everybody's watching her — Mr. Ho, his kids, all the box boys — but it isn't shoplifting until she's actually out the door. When she steps over the threshold, we're on her.

"Excuse me, ma'am," Jim says.

She keeps walking, off the curb and into a fresh downpour, each drop flaring like a match as it hurtles through the abrasive orange glare of the mercury vapor lamps that ring the parking lot. She's skinny and pitiful, and her cereal's getting soaked. We're getting soaked, too. The rain stings my eyes and burrows through my hair to chill my scalp, and I'm just about to tell Jim that it's over, I'm through, when he steps in front of the woman and turns to face her.

"You're under arrest," he says.

She doesn't break her shuffling stride, so Jim grabs her wrist, but he isn't ready for the fight she puts up. All her limbs go at once, kicking, punching, scratching, and Jim barely manages to disentangle himself. He backs off a bit, then lunges, catching her in the throat with his elbow. They both fall splashing to the ground, and in an instant Jim's kneeling between her shoulder blades, immobilizing the upper half of her body while the bottom tries to crawl away. He tosses his handcuffs to me, and I kneel and cinch the stainless steel around her wrists, careful to avoid her grasping fingers with their ragged, septic nails.

She comes easy to the break room with us, crying some, and Jim sits her in a folding chair and secures her to a pipe on the wall with another pair of cuffs. His sopping wet shirt is missing two buttons, and a scratch puckers his face from the corner of his eye to the bottom of his jaw. Me, I'm shaking so bad, I'm sure he can see it. I can't help thinking I could have stopped what happened, but I don't know how, which is the way I feel about most things in my life these days. Just to be doing something, I buy two cups of coffee from the vending machine and pass one to Jim. The Muzak's loud in here, that Carpenters song about birds suddenly appearing.

The woman has lost her slippers. Her bare feet look sad and strange tapping on the linoleum. She hums to herself and rocks back and forth in the chair, head down. Jim turns away to tuck in his shirt. He's still breathing hard and sways a little when he asks the woman for ID. She doesn't have anything to say to him.

"Fine," Jim continues. "Let the Man deal with your shit, then. I don't need it. I just want you to know I'd have given you the money to pay for that stuff if you'd asked, okay. Think about that when you're doing your time, how close you came to the good side of this world."

I can't decide whether he's trying to teach her something or make her miserable. Not that it's relevant, because she's still rocking, still humming, oblivious. Jim and I step into the hallway, and he gives me the keys to the cuffs.

"Walk her out to the parking lot and let her go," he says.

"After all that?"

"The bitch is crazy. A couple days in jail isn't going to change it."

He's going guru on me again, smiling enigmatically.

"Stop fucking around," I say. "I know you, and you know me, and this is bullshit."

"Exactly, grasshopper. Maya, the grand illusion. Now cut her loose." He leaves me dangling with a little bow, and I have to say, philosophically speaking, I think I liked him better as a junkie.

I pull the woman up off the chair and practically have to drag her through the store. Outside, she doesn't react when I free her from the cuffs, just stands stock-still at the edge of the parking lot.

"Fly away home," I say. "Get along little dogie."

She takes one or two stuttering steps that rev up into a run. When she's halfway to the street, she turns back and yells, "Motherfucking Hitler!" and I fake like I'm coming after her until she runs again, disappearing into the rain. I light a cigarette and squeeze into a dry spot next to the pay phone.

Scarlett's hair is wet and smells like peaches. She opens her coat and lets me crawl inside. I should be nicer to her than I am. She's a good girl, and I don't think I've ever felt anything quite as right as her warm body against my cold one. I tell her what Jim said, the illusion crap, and she laughs and rests her chin on my chest and gazes up at me with a look I've done nothing to earn, a look so full of love that it shames me, because I don't even know what color her eyes are. Just as I'm squinting to find out, a flash of lightning erases everything. She holds on tight in anticipation of the thunder, and when it comes, it forces a tiny sob out of her.

"It's not fair that God hates us so much when we don't even believe in him," she says.

"You know what," I reply. "I think it's time we end this," and she cries even harder.

At eleven p.m., I take my last break. With only ten dollars to see me through the week, I skipped dinner, but now I splurge on a Snickers and a Coke to keep me awake until closing. The one checker still on duty grudgingly leaves his textbook and calculator to ring me up. There are no customers in the store at this hour, and I imagine them hunkered down for the night behind triple dead bolts and steel doors. They pay a price for that kind of security, sometimes burning to death because they can't get out of their houses fast enough when fires start in the rotten wiring.

Cases of dog food and creamed corn and paper towels are stacked to the ceiling in the cavernous back room of the market. I've been in museums that have the same musty, dusty smell, and churches. Rain ticks against the roof as I arrange a few boxes into a kind of couch and stretch out on them. The wind keens in the rafters, and the candy hurts my teeth. I try to think a thought I've never thought before, a daily challenge designed to keep my brain from softening. Nothing comes.

The box boy who enters a few minutes later doesn't see me lying in the shadows. He swipes an apple from a crate near the freezer and bites into it. I rise from my bier like Dracula and bark, "Hey!" making him jump and sag against the wall. Then I take an apple for myself.

"That wasn't cool, homes," the kid says, his hand pressed to his fluttering heart. "That was fucked-up." He's a little Mexican guy whose short hair grows in a swirl that resembles one of those crop circles in England that everyone thought were made by UFOs until they turned out to be a hoax. I apologize for scaring him, and he says, "You didn't scare me, you just caught me off guard."

I take out my Swiss Army knife and help him break down some of the empty cartons piled up in back, in preparation for feeding them to the trash compactor. It's not one of my jobs, but the kid's funny and has a sweet way with a story. He shows me pictures of a trip his family took to Yosemite.

When he claims he can throw my knife more accurately than I can, I bet him that he can't, even though I've never thrown my knife before. There's a calendar with a picture of Jesus on it hanging on the wall, but the kid frowns at my suggestion that we use that as our target. He finds a Magic Marker and draws three concentric circles on a box of toilet paper instead, filling in the smallest, the bull's-eye. We agree on five throws apiece. A broom handle serves as the foul line. I go first, and the knife bounces off the wall two feet from the target and clatters to the concrete floor.

The kid laughs and laughs and then all of a sudden he's not laughing anymore. He goggles at something in the doorway behind me. The devil looms there, a red ski mask pulled down over his face, the snout of his sawed-off shotgun sucking all the air out of the room. I should apologize to the kid, as I'm defi-nitely to blame for conjuring up this horror, having seen him before in countless nightmares and casual morbid thoughts — the Raiders jacket, the ratty Jordans — but before I can, the devil says, "You best move your fucking asses."

We proceed wordlessly on watery legs into the market. The devil floats at our backs, reeking of sweat and chemicals. Mr. Ho is lying facedown in front of the meat counter with his brother and son and nephew. A second devil stands guard over them, bouncing on the balls of his feet. His shotgun swings up to wink at us, and he yells, "On the motherfucking floor."

I'm thinking, *Not here, not in these clothes,* as I lower my cheek to the gritty linoleum. The box boy pauses on his knees, hands clasped, a prayer burbling out of him, until the first devil kicks him the rest of the way down and tells him to shut the fuck up.

Mr. Ho says, "I take you to safe. No problem. Don't hurt nobody," and the devils let him stand. One of them twists his arm behind his back and jams a gun into his neck. He pushes Mr. Ho toward the office so fast, Mr. Ho stumbles and almost falls. They round the end of the aisle, the squeaking of their sneakers fading quickly. The pin that fastens my badge to my shirt is sticking me in the chest. I hear a hiss and smell something funny and see that the devil left to guard us is hitting a pipe. This is a bad sign, what with the trigger of his gun curled so comfortingly around his finger. It's made to be pulled, it's begging to be pulled, and the last thing anyone wants to do when he's high is say no to a friend.

The box boy's watch is close to my ear, and I count the seconds thudding by to keep from screaming when the devil pulls a roll of duct tape from his pocket. He kicks the bottom of my foot, tells me to get up. The tape screeches off the roll, and I use my teeth to tear it as the devil hovers over me, tapping me with his gun. The tape fouls in my shaking hands. It twists and curls and sticks to itself, and I have to toss aside the first few strips. The devil taps me harder, in a new spot each time, and says, "Somebody's fixing to die."

I start with Mr. Ho's brother, his wrists, then his ankles. When I get to Mr. Ho's son, he begs me not to cover his eyes like I have the others'. He makes me feel awful for doing the devil's bidding, for not even contemplating a refusal. They'll die hating me for this, I think, and then I realize I'll be dead, too. Mr. Ho and his devil return just as I'm finishing up. I'm shouted to the floor again, but I'm barely on my knees when Jim charges out into the aisle from behind the beer cooler. His little pistol clicks once, twice, then discharges, and the shots are like hammer blows on concrete, sending up sparks that set the air ablaze.

I scrabble through the conflagration, past the blind men wriggling and screaming behind their gags, to the meat counter. Up and over is the plan, and I make it up but not over before a thousand steel bees swarm and shatter the glass of the case and dig their white-hot stingers into me. I fall back to the floor in an avalanche of pig parts. Will I taste the blast that takes off my head?

Scarlett glides through the rising smoke to crouch beside me, and the mess I've made flattens and recedes and turns into television. Her nose crinkles at the stink of gunpowder, and I can tell she's worried about ruining her new shoes, but that doesn't stop her from crouching beside me. As the echoes of the last shots carom up and down the empty aisles of the store, she takes a tissue from her purse and wipes the drool from my chin.

"Aren't you pretty," she says.

"You didn't leave."

"Don't be mad."

"I'm not," I say, and I'm not.

My shoulder is a gory snarl of meat and muscle and yellow fat, but it doesn't hurt much unless I look at it, and the only time it really pumps blood is when I curl my fingers to see if they still work. Some of them do.

One of the devils is sprawled on the floor. Scarlett and I watch as he jerks himself into a ball and dies. The other sits with his head between his knees until Jim nudges him and he flops onto his side, his ski mask flushing a deeper shade of red. Mr. Ho is busy untaping his relatives and the box boy, who, as soon as he's loose, begins to pray again. The Chinese stand together like football players in a huddle, crying into each other's hair.

Jim comes over to check on me.

"I'm sorry," I say. "I didn't even notice you weren't around."

"I was watching the whole time, my brother. I wasn't going to let them take you out."

He examines my wound with a grimace, then begins clearing away the pig parts.

"It's okay," he says. "I think it's okay. Just be cool."

Scarlett snuggles closer. She asks if I want a piece of gum.

The cops arrive, and Jim rushes toward them, yelling, "What took you so long? My partner's fucking dying." They order him to shut up. He hurls his gun deep into the store and presses his palms to his temples. I guess it's sinking in now, what he had to do. The floor is wet with the devils' blood, twin lakes of it that the cops tiptoe through to yank off their masks. Jim tries to stop them, but they ignore him. The devils turn out to be a couple of kids, sixteen, seventeen. Crazy fucking kids. Jim moves off to sit by himself, folding his body in half like his stomach hurts.

"Jim," I say. "Buddy."

He looks over at me.

"Listen." An awful Muzak version of "Heart of Gold" is blasting over the store's speakers. Scarlett and I watch as Jim begins to mouth the words, and I promise myself I will never laugh behind his back again.

"He seems nice," Scarlett says.

She sits with me until the paramedics arrive and walks beside the gurney, holding my hand, as they wheel me out to the ambulance. Just before they load me up, she gives me a quick kiss, which is soured by the rain on her lips.

"Well, bye," she says.

"Could you stay?" I ask. "I know this isn't your life or anything, but it's starting to hurt a little."

She looks away like she's thinking it over, then turns back to me and nods. She climbs into the ambulance and slides in next to me, and I begin to believe I just might see morning.

Whatever wonderfulness the paramedics have doped me up with has me smelling incense and hearing hymns. I feel as if I've been lanced and drained, and I don't hate anyone anymore. I cough up a mouthful of blood, but big fucking deal. There exist certain wildflowers that must be burned in order to bloom, and who's to say I'm not one of them?

The siren bawls, announcing my departure, and I wave out the windows, flashing everyone the thumbs-up, all the strangers who have lined the rainy streets to see me off, at last, at last, the gracious Grand Marshal of my very own parade.

The Hero Shot

WHEN DID EVERYONE GET MARRIED? WHEN DID THEY
all have kids? Suddenly there's no room for me. I spend an hour
on the pay phone trying to wrangle a couch to crash on, and all
I get is "Sorry," "Sorry," and "Really sorry."

Fan-fucking-tastic. In-fucking-credible. The cops show up to
put me out of the apartment, and it starts to rain. I can't hold a
thought in my head. My unemployment has been used up, and
I've sold everything but my television.

The bartender gives me a look when I come dripping in with
my suitcase, the Zenith twelve-inch tucked under my arm. I put
the set on the floor next to my stool. It's just past noon, and I'm
down to my last fifty bucks.

"Bring it on," I say.

For every three drinks I pay for, the bartender slips me a free-bie. I buy him a few, too. He warms to me when he realizes I'm not a bum. The day passes at a slow trot. I'm up, then I'm down. A good idea, a fresh start. Something. Anything. Please.

I drink through happy hour, the shift change, the after-work rush. Nobody knows me here. I go to put a dollar in the jukebox, but one of the regulars reaches out and grabs my arm and pleads, "No, man, not now," and what can I do? It's his hideout.

A stranger listens to my troubles. Antonio Alfredo Blah Blah Blah. Not to worry, he says, I can sleep in his toolshed. We seal the deal with decent tequila, but he's nowhere to be found at closing time.

I spend the rest of the night cradling my TV in the doorway of a beauty supply store. The rain is still coming down. There's thunder and lightning, and big black bugs emerge from the cracks in the sidewalk and scurry for dry ground. Even with all the booze in me, I can't sleep. Right before dawn I see bats cir-cling the streetlights.

I'm waiting for the bartender when he opens at six. The first drink warms me up, the second makes me puke. By noon I have just enough money left for bus fare and a phone call to Riverside. "Mom," I say — the receiver shakes — "I'm coming for a visit." I change my shirt in the bathroom, and the bartender treats me to one for the road. I'm teetering, I'm teetering, I fall.

I'm not going to fight the old fights this time. We're a family; that's all there is to it. It takes her a while to unlock the door. Her hands are hurting her again. I had a key, but I lost it. She hugs me around the neck, trying to smell my breath.

"You know the rule," she says. "Not in my house."

What did she do to her hair? Something funny. "It looks good," I tell her. She's put clean sheets on one of the beds, but my brother's high school golf trophies are frosted with cobwebs. He and I shared this room forever. Mom hasn't changed anything. It's as if we died, and she's honoring our memories.

I open a drawer filled with comic books, grab a few, and sit at the desk where I did my homework and built model cars. I swore it wouldn't happen, but here I am again. My mouth is dry, my head throbs. The first twenty-four hours will be the worst. It takes time to get used to having a body again. I turn the pages. The Incredible Hulk bounds across the desert, covering miles with each leap, a soaring green cannonball.

EVERYTHING ABOUT THIS place makes me sick. It struck me when I was twelve, and from then on I was miserable. I don't know what it was—the dust, the crowded church parking lots, the way any kind of decent plan fell apart. The one teacher I could stand in high school said that everybody hated their hometown when they were my age and that I'd grow out of it. But not me. Never. I left for the first time at seventeen, and I left running.

Hollywood, baby. I slept on the floor of a guy who had moved from Riverside a year earlier to start a band. He got me a job busing tables at the restaurant where he worked, and within a month they made me a server. I blew my tips on beer and ecstasy and dated a rich girl who lived in the Hills.

It's hard to recall how happy I was. I don't let myself get that excited anymore. Everyone I knew was on the verge of something big. And me, too—why not? You could see it in the double takes we got when we walked into the clubs. "It's you," said the music. "It's you," said the lights. "It's you."

MOM MAKES ME lunch. Tomato soup, grilled cheese, and a tall glass of milk. She washes dishes while I eat. The TV is blaring in the living room, one of those court shows people love so much. Mom's robe is pink silk. Her toenails are pink, too. She

173

keeps herself up, that's what everyone says. I think she's sixty, sixty-one. My brain can't do the math right now. She was a schoolteacher for thirty years.

"So, the whole world's against you, huh?" she says.

"That's one way of looking at it."

"How do you look at it?"

"That way. Sometimes."

Mom laughs, but if she wants trouble, she's out of luck. I'm fading fast. I count the crumbs on the table, gathering them with a moistened fingertip. My headache has sharp spines that gouge me when I swallow. The tile is cracked, the wallpaper moldy. Mom spends all her money on clothes.

"Tell me again how it's not your fault you were evicted," she says.

I can't even hear her. I'm too busy trying to keep my food down. She's not being cruel; she thinks she's funny. All her friends tell her she's funny. All those friends of hers. She wasn't around much when we were growing up. I feel so heavy, I have to use both hands on the tabletop to lift myself off the chair.

THE SHEETS BURN. I curl my fingers and toes, and my breath roars in and out. The shadows of the trees outside stroke the ceiling. I put all my faith in them. It's not right for a grown man to be back in the bed that he wet until he was ten. Part of me wants to work on a plan, but the rest of me shuts down and bows again to the leafy shadows. We need sleep. A bird sings, and the sun slides lower in the sky. I'm losing another day.

I LOADED TRUCKS, I tended bar. I got my head shots done. Nothing happened the first year or the year after, but I still believed. People gave up and moved away, and new people arrived to replace them. There was always someone hopeful to talk to.

"You're dreaming," Mom would say when I called, but what was wrong with that? It was a good life for a young man. The big thing wasn't money, the big thing wasn't cars or clothes.

And then — wow! One of the regulars at the club I was working at in those days was a half-assed agent named Rusty, who was always mouthing off about who he knew. I finally got fed up and said, "Rusty, you're so full of shit. Why don't you send me out on some auditions?" He did, and I got the second thing I was up for, two lines in a straight-to-video quickie.

We shot on the patio of a mansion in Malibu. The guy playing our boss paced back and forth, reminding us of the insults, the lies. He wanted us to make things right. He wanted us to go to war for him. "Can I trust you, Frankie?" he asked. "Absolutely, Vito," I replied. The lights were hot on my face. The camera dollied toward me, and the assistant director pointed. "It would be an honor to die in your service," I said. One take. One. The other actors said I was a natural. They had all been on TV and drove new cars. I felt like I'd finally turned a corner.

The glow lasted months. I took acting classes and went on dozens of calls. I spent hours at the gym — me and everyone else. Nothing came of it. Then Rusty went to jail, and I couldn't get another agent to see me. Extra work didn't pay the bills. I began to doubt myself, which is deadly in that business.

HULK IS IN love with a shapely green girl who's just as strong as he is. Together, they defeat the bad guy. I'm missing the next issue, but in the one after that the green girl is dead, and Hulk is alone again. Mom busts in and whips open the curtains and the window. She wrinkles her nose at the smell. I've been lying here for days, but I think I'm over the hump now.

"I need help with the groceries," Mom says.

It's windy outside. Fallen leaves school like fish in the street, following each other from gutter to gutter. The mailman passes by, keys jingling. I carry the bags into the kitchen. Mom's on the porch, all bundled up in a hat and scarf. She smiles at the bare trees.

"The most beautiful time of year," she says.

We're deep into fall. Nights are cold, and everything that dies is dead. I'm a summer man, myself.

SpaghettiOs, bologna, pot pies — all my childhood favorites. Mom's proud that she remembered, but I haven't eaten this shit in years. We put it all away, then watch TV. There's a car chase on every channel. The driver makes a big loop, the police right on his tail, from the Hollywood to the Harbor to the Century to the San Diego. People crowd the overpasses to cheer him on. He waves and honks his horn. Mom and I split a box of macaroni and cheese.

"Your dad used to do that, the way you chew with your hand over your mouth. Do you remember?" she says.

"I was maybe six, Mom."

"I remember things from when I was six."

"You think you do."

"The neighbor boy did magic tricks. He could make bottle caps disappear."

Dad died of cancer. He smelled like medicine. From pictures Mom has, I know he played golf and rode a motorcycle. The car on TV spins out, and the driver makes a run for it. I want a drink. Not desperately, but a beer would be nice, and if I had a twelve-pack, I could bullshit with Mom all day long. She changes to a talk show, and I go to my room and read more comics.

MY BROTHER'S HOUSE is about a mile away. Paul. I walk over. He's in his garage when I get there, working on his truck. I'm three years older. We've never been particularly close. He's surprised to see me.

"Mom didn't call?" I say.

He shrugs. We stand side by side, looking down at the engine. The fan belt is loose. All the men in the neighborhood took him under their wings when we were kids. He could catch a ball, swing a hammer. They loved him more than they loved their own sons.

His wife, Kelly, comes out. We've only met once before. Her dad owns the plumbing company Paul works for. I didn't know she was pregnant. She asks the questions Paul won't. I like that.

"How long are you staying with her?"

"It's kind of open-ended."

"Are you working?"

"Nah, taking some time off."

"She must be so jazzed. She talks about you constantly, wondering why you don't come see her more often."

"She's lucky she has you guys so close."

This is a dig. Mom's already told me they never visit. Kelly gives me a dirty look and goes back inside. I hold a flashlight for Paul while he tightens the belt. All his screws are sorted by size and stored in baby food jars. His tools hang on the wall above his workbench, each outlined in Magic Marker. I think he's happy. He seems happy.

"Is that how you're going to play it this time, that you're visiting?" he asks.

"There's some stuff to do. The house is in bad shape."

"Good a place as any to dry out, I guess."

I can take it; I'm a man. I ask him for some weed, a little something to smooth the rough patches. He still smokes—I know he does—so what's with the disgust on his face? What's with the sigh? He wipes his hands on a bright red rag before walking into the house. Growing up, I tried to be a big brother to him, but he wouldn't have it. He scorned my advice, denied my wisdom. I never trusted him, either. We turned on each other all the time.

I'm playing with a vise mounted on the workbench when he returns. I put my finger in it and tighten it until it hurts. He passes me a film canister containing a fat green bud.

"Atta boy," I say.

I STAYED AWAY those first few years, made all kinds of excuses not to come home. Acting in the movie finally gave me something to talk about, though, so I told Mom she'd see me on Christmas Eve. I don't know why; we were never any good at holidays, Mom, Paul, and I. All the things you were supposed to say and do—one of us would invariably crack under the pressure.

Dinner went fine. Paul had a girlfriend over, and the three of us used her to keep our distance from one another. She was delighted by the attention. I'd stashed a bottle in the mailbox, and Paul and I took turns sneaking out to hit it.

Cheap whiskey makes me boastful; it always has. By the time we sat down to unwrap presents, I couldn't shut up about myself. I said I was close to getting a TV series. I said I could see dolphins from the balcony of my apartment, when the truth was I'd been sleeping in my car for a week.

For gifts, I gave both of them one of my head shots, framed, and a funny little IOU I'd drawn up that promised something more when my money situation improved. They were unimpressed.

"Next time you're going to cheap out, let me know," Paul huffed. His present to me had been a beautiful leather wallet and silver wallet chain.

"Maybe next year we'll get the Cadillacs," Mom said with a smirk.

I snatched the photos away from them. I tore up the IOUs. "This family is fucked," I announced.

Paul went off, and the tree got knocked over. Mom threw me out. I drove a few blocks, parked in a cul-de-sac and finished the whiskey, then fell asleep listening to carols on the radio. In the morning my battery was dead.

I START WITH the gate. It's falling off its hinges. Mom has a hammer and nails, so I straighten that out and then tack up a few boards that have come loose from the fence. The backyard has been invaded by the kinds of plants that creep in when your guard is down. Ivy spills over the retaining wall, and morning glory climbs the trees and chokes the rosebushes, flashing sickly purple blossoms. I wade in with hoe and pruning shears, and by noon the flower beds have been liberated.

Mom brings me a sandwich and a Pepsi. I eat at the picnic table. The neighbor's orange cat watches from under a bush. I dangle a shred of bologna and make kissing sounds, but he's not buying it. There's dried blood on my knuckle. I lick it off and reopen a little cut. A thorn must have hooked me. The birds are going crazy, talk, talk, talking among themselves.

"Hey, stranger," Boots yells out the sliding glass door. Her rings catch the sun when she waves. Boots is Mom's oldest friend. She taught me to sing "Folsom Prison Blues." She and Mom are going to the movies. Every Wednesday it's that and a cheeseburger at Carl's Jr. "Don't let her work you too hard," Boots says. "Lincoln freed the slaves."

I mow the lawn and edge it. I prune the skeletal peach trees and grapevines. The trimmings fill the trash can. Used to be you could burn this stuff. I remember flames snapping and smoke in my eyes. Was it Dad who lit the match? Two Mexican kids watch from across the street as I sweep the sidewalk, the driveway, the gutter. The fat one wrestles the little one to the ground, letting him up when he screams. The sun is setting by the time I uncoil the hose and wet everything down.

THE SHOWER NEEDS to be caulked and the faucet leaks. I should start a list. I dry off, then wipe the fog from the mirror with the edge of my hand. A good shave isn't in the cards, though — my razor's for shit. I wouldn't say I'm vain, but the web of tiny wrinkles around my eyes depresses me. At least my gut's holding up.

Pork chops for dinner. Milk gravy. Mom tells me about the movie. "It was sad, but good sad. He loved her so much. Boots cried and cried." I'm doing calculations in my head, tearing down walls. I could turn this house into something sweet. Mom agrees to give me the money for paint and linoleum to fix up the bathroom. She grabs my hand and presses it to her chest. "You've been sad, too, haven't you?" she says.

I'm embarrassed. I pull away. "I'm fine," I say. "Don't get all worked up."

REED AND SUE Richards of the Fantastic Four have a son named Franklin. Dr. Doom steals the kid, and they go to war. My mind wanders. I toss the comic and close my eyes. Someone once taught me a Buddhist chant to calm myself, but I forgot it a long time ago. I slide my hand down my pants. That's a bust, too.

Mom's asleep in front of the TV when I sneak out the door. I wait until I'm around the corner to light the joint. It's been a while since I smoked. By the second hit, I could tell you everything you need to know about the neighbors simply by analyzing the cars in their driveways. It's so obvious. The high intensifies, though, and turns creepy. A dog snarls at me. A Toyota makes a questionable left. And my heart. Man! It's racing like a sonofabitch.

THE KICK CAME out of nowhere, catching me square in the mouth. I almost swallowed my teeth. That's what you get for fighting in bars. A few years had passed since that Christmas mess. Mom gave me a little attitude but finally said I could stay with her awhile. I had to get out of Hollywood; I didn't want anyone to see me like that.

It shocked her. My nose was broken, too. She sent me to her doctor and her dentist. She was still teaching, so I had the house to myself for most of the day during my recuperation. I'd take fistfuls of pain pills and watch TV, drifting in and out. Commercials made me cry, and I'd see old friends gasping and clapping in studio audiences. I couldn't stop running my tongue over my new front teeth.

Mom tried to lay down the law when she found my stash. I was ready to go anyway. A buddy had called with a remodeling job in Brentwood, and they were holding auditions for some reality show. I left a note on the kitchen table, not thanking her for anything, but promising repayment. I was always hopeful on my way out.

Mom, Boots, and some of their friends enjoy helping those less fortunate than they are. Once a month they volunteer to chaperone a dance for the mentally retarded at the community center. Mom thinks it would be good for me to come along. I'm not so sure, but she won't take no for an answer.

"Look nice," she says. I put on a dress shirt and my black shoes. Boots drives us. There are two other women in the car. Everybody picks up where they left off last time. The conversations have been going on for years. I taste perfume and hair spray.

The woman who runs the thing is all business. She doesn't even thank us for coming. Mom helps with the last-minute decorations, and I'm assigned to the refreshment table. I arrange my Styrofoam cups in neat rows. I stack my cookies. They have a deejay and everything. The lights go down, and the music starts. The kids arrive all at once.

They're teenagers, I think. It's a big deal for them. Most of the girls wear dresses, and the guys have on ties. The parents and chaperones have to pull them out on the dance floor and start them moving, but after a while they get the hang of it. The deejay yells, "Whoo whoo!" and all of them repeat it, lifting their hands in the air and jumping up and down.

One kid keeps coming over for punch every five minutes. Little bitty eyes, great big head. "I hope you're not driving," I say.

He purses his lips and wrinkles his nose. "Do you want to dance?" he asks.

"We're not allowed to date customers," I reply.

He laughs, but who knows why. A retarded girl moved into the neighborhood while I was growing up. Leah Leah Diarrhea. She used to French-kiss her dog. We conned her into taking off her clothes once. Her mother caught us in the alley. We were just boys, stupid boys, but the look on her mother's face has never left me.

When it's time for my break, I lock myself in a bathroom stall and suck on a roach I brought just in case. I can't hear the music, but when I lean my head against the wall, the bass jiggles my eyeballs. I'm confused about what kind of person I am. Good or evil doesn't get to the heart of it. Someone has carved a big squirting cock into the toilet paper dispenser. They've tried to paint it over, but I can still see it.

PAUL KNOWS HIS way around Home Depot. We're in and out in half an hour. I can't even pause to look at a plumbing display or the circular saw on sale without him saying, "Focus, dude, focus." I don't let it bug me, though; I'm used to being hurried along. It's like I get hypnotized sometimes, by the bustle, by the crush.

There's money left after paying for the stuff to fix up the bathroom. I make Paul stop at the hot dog cart in the parking lot. I want to treat him to lunch for bringing me here in his truck. Two cars get into a honk fight over a prime space, and I watch a girl smoke a cigarette and stare at the endless empty sky. The peppers I put on my dog burn my tongue.

"You like that, huh?" Paul says, talking about the girl.

"It's her eyes. The shape, the color."

"Right."

Paul is going bald; I'm not. Funny. I wish he'd stand up straight. He eats with his hand over his mouth, too, like Mom says our father did.

"Hey, I might have found a car for you," he says. "Can you scrape together eight hundred dollars?"

I loved that Honda they repoed. Leather seats, sun roof. It's just as well they took it back, though. It was dragging me down. To make the payments I had to tap the till at the shoe store where I was working.

THE BATHROOM KEEPS me busy for a week. I rip up the old linoleum and lay down new stuff. I paint the walls pale pink. I even replace the shower curtain. It tires me out. There's no time for cravings or regret. I dream about drinking once but wake up feeling guilty.

THE LAST TIME I was here, Mom wasn't around. I made sure of that. I climbed in through a window I knew about that wouldn't latch. A bad guy was after me because of some money he claimed I owed him, and I was behind on rent. The idea was to make it look like a stranger had done it.

I went through her jewelry box, her dresser, her closet. I looked under her mattress. The house creaked and groaned in protest. Everything made me jump. I unplugged the TV and the microwave. There was also a clock radio by her bed. Sweat ran down my face and dripped on the floor, and I wondered if that's how the cops would catch me.

And then I put everything back. Every bit of it. I crawled out the window empty-handed and got in my car and drove away. We were in the midst of a heat wave. As usual, poor people and animals suffered most. I passed sweaty families playing minigolf and crazy bastards crouched in the shadows of telephone poles.

The sun beat down on all of us like it had a monstrous grudge. Riverside, California.

MOM LOANS ME her car to drive to a comic book store that I find in the phone book. It's in a strip mall past the railroad tracks. The kid behind the counter perks up when he starts looking through my box. He pulls out a price guide and says it's going to take a while.

There's a doughnut shop next door. I order coffee and sit by the window. I used to envy guys like me, relaxing in the middle of the day, reading the paper. *And me busting my ass,* I'd think. Christ, things get away from you.

The kid tries to hide his excitement when I return to the store. He has the comics stacked on the counter in various piles. His T-shirt has a picture of a fist on it and the name of a band. I thought metal died out years ago.

"I can give you six hundred dollars for everything," he says. "There's good stuff here."

"Like what, for instance?"

He points. "*Amazing Spider-Man* 129. The Punisher's first appearance. It's near mint, so we'll go one hundred."

I pick it up, thumb through it. One hundred dollars! My lucky charm. "I'll hang on to this one," I say. "The rest are yours."

I stop by Paul's place and give him the money. He agrees to float me a loan for the three hundred more it'll take to buy the car. Maybe we could have been friends, if we hadn't been brothers. I hug him when I leave, just to watch him flinch.

WE HAVE A party to celebrate the new bathroom. Mom makes cupcakes for it. Boots stops by, but Paul and Kelly have other plans. The fixtures sparkle, the tile shines. Boots wants to know how much I'd charge to remodel her kitchen. We drink hot chocolate and play hearts. Mom loves cards. Poker, canasta, bridge. "It takes a certain kind of mind," she says. I don't have it. I lose every time.

The storm they've been talking about for days is fast approaching. A black roil of clouds bears down on us, and the trees twist in the wind, as if they want to run away. Boots cuts the game short. She doesn't like to drive in the rain. Mom and I step out onto the porch to wave. The first fat drops whisper in the grass.

We get ready for the news, Mom in her recliner, me on the couch. Her constant sniping is getting on my nerves—the dead girl was stupid for hitchhiking; the corrupt politician looks like a rat fink. I go into the kitchen for a glass of Pepsi.

Dad drank. That's why Mom can't stand drinkers now. He hit her once, when I was a baby. Divorce never came up, though. She says they were made for each other. What do you call that? Love? It's pouring outside. The wind flings rain against the window. I rinse my glass, dry it, and put it in the cupboard.

Mom is staring at the TV. There's a magazine in her lap, *People*. She runs her finger over the face of the movie star on the cover and says, "I actually believed I'd see you here someday."

"Don't count me out yet."

"Come on, kiddo."

I shrug. Who knows? What I can say for certain is that whatever needs to happen next isn't going to happen here.

LET'S JUST SAY a woman was involved. She wasn't the only reason I pissed everything away this time, but she was there at the start and not at the end, and it killed me that I couldn't keep her. Jenny Pool, Jenny Pool, Jenny Pool. We did our best, right?

I'd pulled myself together and was doing the job thing and the exercise thing and the early to bed, early to rise thing. I got a callback for a play—a small role, but a good one—and went out to celebrate. Jenny was the hostess at the restaurant. My buddy knew the owner, and we closed the place. The staff joined us at the bar. Jenny told me a joke I didn't get. She danced with a lonely Guatemalan dishwasher and brought tears to my eyes. By morning I was convinced that she was the missing piece of the puzzle.

Her dad was an actor, so she swore she'd never date one. Of course that's all she dated. We both went into it like it was our last chance. It was a moony, miserable teenage kind of whirl. I said things like, "I wish I could crawl inside you," and, "How many lives did it take us to get here?" She bought me a puppy that my landlord wouldn't let me keep. I snuck it to the pound and told her it ran away.

I got the part, but the play fizzled in rehearsals. This made me a little introspective. Jenny took it as something else. She had abandonment issues, whatever that means. All of a sudden we didn't see eye to eye on anything. Picking out fruit at the supermarket was a goddamn prizefight. Someone said she's in Sedona now. The love of my life, quite possibly.

THE ROUTE TO Paul's house passes by my high school and the burger stand where I got my first job. Mom says a Korean family owns it now. Change upsets her, but I couldn't care less. Last night's storm has left the street a mess. I step over fallen palm fronds that resemble dried sea creatures. The clouds have blown away, and the sky is as blue as it gets.

Paul's at work. On a Saturday? An emergency call. Kelly asks if I want to come in. I sit on the couch. A picture of them on their wedding day hangs over the fireplace.

"Where'd you guys get married?" I ask.

"Maui."

"I've got to get over there someday."

She stands in the doorway to the kitchen, holding the phone. The baby is coming soon. Every little twinge inside probably stops her in her tracks. Her friends have told her how much it's going to hurt. She's waiting for me to explain why I'm here.

"I need to ask you a favor," I say. "I want you to make sure Paul visits our mom more often."

"Shouldn't you talk to him about that?"

"I need you to work on him, too. She had that party the other day, and it was nothing, but you guys didn't even stop by."

"We had things to do," she says. "We've invited her here plenty of times, you don't know."

"She's getting old. Look in on her once a week or so. No biggie."

"You should hear her. She's not exactly nice to me."

I raise my hand. "Once a week or so."

Kelly has more to say, but I'm done. No need to go in circles about it. She gives up and walks into the kitchen. I watch HBO until Paul gets home. His face is dirty, and he seems tired. I don't have the heart to start in on him. I pretend I dropped by to see what's up with the car.

THE BACK DOOR sticks. I fix that and clean out the rain gutters. Mom is angry with me. She thinks my leaving so soon is a mistake. I tell her she can come visit when I get settled, make sure I'm on the straight and narrow. We eat a silent dinner. I notice she's having trouble with her fingers, uncurling them, but she won't answer my questions about it.

I lie awake in the dark, trying to see the future. I'll find a job, get an apartment. Something good will finally happen. The silence is broken by sobs. I pull on some pants and hurry to Mom's room. She sits up at the sound of my voice but looks right through me. Tears shine on her cheeks.

"Please don't die in the ice," she cries.

"Mom," I say. "Mom."

Her eyes begin to focus. The fear drains from her face, leaving it gray and devoid of expression. *You poor woman,* I think, as if she were a stranger.

"I'm fine," she says, coming back to herself. "Let me be."

THE CAR IS a real beater, an old Sentra, but the engine is in good shape. Paul gives me the keys, and the title is in the glove box. I can live with the dents and dings for now. Mom and Kelly are standing on the porch. Paul watches them, ignoring what I'm saying. Mom reaches out and touches Kelly's stomach. The baby is kicking.

We sit together at the kitchen table and eat lunch. It's been a long time. Mom is nervous. Her hands shake when she passes the coleslaw, and she laughs at anything even vaguely funny. Paul shows us a scar on his leg, where he was burned by a motorcycle muffler. Conversation goes here and there, just like it should. We help each other along. I'm antsy, though. I don't know where I'll be sleeping tonight, and I'd like to get a move on.

Paul wants to see what I did in the bathroom. The bead on my caulking is a little crooked, and I also didn't do the greatest job matching the pattern on the linoleum in a couple spots. He tries to be funny when he points these things out. I turn on the shower, and the pipes rattle and groan.

"There's a project for you," I say.

"Don't worry about it," he replies. "Don't worry about anything."

"Oh, so you're the big daddy now."

"What do you mean 'now.'"

I pretend to swing at him, and he pretends to block my punch.

Everyone walks me to the curb. I put my TV in the trunk. The lock is broken, but it shuts tight. Mom presses some money on me. I take it without counting it. She tells me again I'm making a mistake. That's fine. That's her part in this thing. I promise

Dead Boys

Paul I'll pay him back. The three of them are waving as I drive off. My people.

YOU PICK YOURSELF up and go on. That's what you do. Over and over and over. The big drunk Limey wants to know where the movie star footprints are. Three blocks west, I tell him. Across the street. Can't miss them. I draw him another Guinness.

Martin's drinking rum. He's a director. Videos, I think. A nice kid. I show him the Spider-Man comic, my good luck charm. I keep it in a Ziploc bag behind the bar. "Ever seen one of these?" I say.

When my shift is over, I walk the Boulevard. I'm still not drinking, so I try to keep myself occupied. It's Friday night, and the tourists are out. I offer to take a picture of a German family crouched around Clint Eastwood's star. Music blasts out of a souvenir shop, and there are so many lights my eyes hurt. Dizzy, dreamy, I flop down on a bus bench and smile at the passing cars. Sometimes happiness sneaks up on you like a piece of a song on the wind. Just that random, just that rare. Jenny Pool, Jenny Pool, Jenny Pool. Hollywood sends its love.

Blind-Made Products

—

Dee dee's moving again, for the third time this year. She doesn't feel safe anymore, not since she asked the Mexican guy down the hall if he would fix her leaky faucet and his wife called her a *puta* and threatened to kill her. She says her life has taken a dangerous turn, and she's always on the run from one assassin or another. That's just the speed talking. Her green hair bugs me, too, and the haughty tone she adopts with waitresses and 7-Eleven clerks. But Grady's God-knows-why sweet on her, and he's my only friend, so here I am, watching her have a nervous breakdown and wishing I was somewhere else.

Grady promised she'd be packed and ready to roll by the time we arrived with the truck, but it's been an hour already and the boxes are still empty, and now Dee Dee has collapsed on the living room floor, crying because she can't decide where to stick what. My advice would be to drag it all out to the sidewalk and burn it. The dirty stuffed animals, the torn paperbacks. The thrift-store ball gowns and ancient punk rock records. All of it. Because there's something morbid about hauling around so many mementos of your worthless past. Something morbid and resigned.

"Why won't you help?" Dee Dee wails, and Grady leaves me sitting alone on the couch to kneel beside her. He lights her cigarette, cracks a few jokes, and pretty soon she's laughing. I could join in when they begin filling boxes, I guess, but I don't. I don't feel like it. The hot wind that's been blowing off the desert for days rattles the screen in the window frame and snatches up a blackened match from the coffee table. I stick my finger into the hole in my beer can and wonder how hard I would have to twist it to cut myself to the bone.

Don't get me wrong. I used to do pretty well with the ladies. I don't know what it was, but for a while there I had it. The way some retarded people can play piano or memorize baseball stats, I could pick up girls. Black, white, brown. Twins once, at the same time; a mother and daughter separately. A veterinarian with too many dogs, a welfare queen who used her government check to buy me quaaludes, a former Sea World mermaid, a blind girl. A beautiful blind girl.

I spent years jumping from woman to woman. It was fun and all, but you get caught up in a grind like that, and you fall behind in other areas. That's why I was glad when it ended, when the magic finally faded. Suddenly everyone saw right through me, and I couldn't have been happier. Really.

Being alone took some getting used to, of course. I had my booze and pills and whatnot, but some nights I just wanted to die. I kept telling myself there had to be more to life than breaking hearts. I pressed on. I let the years pass. And now I'm doing fine.

*   *   *

MORE PEOPLE WERE supposed to be here to help Dee Dee move. Grady said it was going to be like a party. We'd have a couple beers, everyone would carry down a box or a piece of furniture, we'd follow the truck to the new place, unload, and have a few more beers. It didn't work out that way, though. Grady and I are the only suckers who showed, and Dee Dee's idea of a festive spread is a bag of stale Doritos and a warm six-pack of Bud.

Grady does his best to keep me entertained as he and I wrangle the futon and kitchen table down the narrow stairway. He just got back from Vegas, where he hit a royal on video poker. A thousand and change. He goes through every hand the machine dealt him leading up to the jackpot, and I don't have the heart to tell him that other people's gambling stories bore the shit out of me. He's going to use the money to get Dee Dee some new head shots — she's taking acting classes again — and he wants to buy another gun.

We break for cigarettes after carrying down what seems like a hundred milk crates full of junk. Grady stretches out on the U-Haul's ramp, I sit on the curb. There's a hot spot on my left foot from my new steel-toes. I unlace the boot and pull it off and roll down my sock to see how close I am to blistering.

"Think she's got any Band-Aids?" I ask.

"Somewhere, man, I'm sure," Grady replies. He reaches into one of the boxes and pulls out a grinning ceramic monkey on a surfboard. "This won't help?"

The battered ice-cream truck parked down the street is playing "It's a Small World." A bunch of Mexican kids have gathered at its door. They hop up and down and spin in circles and kung fu their buddies. One little girl stands apart from the rest, waving a dollar bill over her head. I don't have any children. Nobody I know has any children. And nobody wants any. I squash an ant with my thumb. Then another. Then another.

Grady flicks away his half-smoked cigarette. "As of now, I'm quitting these," he announces.

The wind picks up. It's like a sick old man breathing in my face. I lie down and watch the shaggy crowns of the palm trees toss back and forth high overhead. The dry fronds crack and rustle and hiss.

"She wants me to torch her car," Grady says. He's running his hands over his crewcut, a nervous habit he's picked up lately.

"What do you mean?" I ask.

"Like for the insurance. You take it out somewhere and set it on fire, so she can collect."

"I know you're not that stupid."

He shoots me a fuck-you look. "I said she wants me to, that's all."

Grady loans me money. He steals CDs for me from the record store where he works. When I got my DUI, he bitched at the cops until they cuffed him and put him in the backseat of the cruiser, too, because he didn't want me to go to jail by myself. You can see why I worry about him.

WHILE HE AND Dee Dee are carrying down more boxes, I'm left alone in her bedroom. I pick up one of her pillows and press it to my nose, then move to the dresser, where I finger her hairbrush, her makeup sponges, her lipstick.

The top drawer of the dresser is full of panties arrayed like the lustrous black and blue and red pelts of small exotic creatures. I slide my hand across them, then wriggle my fist deep into their silky depths and stand there buried to the forearm, listening to the wind slam a tree against the side of the building. My car insurance is due and I'm completely broke again. A mother lode of G-strings, and this is where my mind goes. My, how things have changed. Grady and Dee Dee come tromping up the stairs, and I grab a box of comic books to take to the truck.

THE BLIND GIRL's name was Mercedes. She was a Filipina who attended the Braille Institute, which was down the street from where I lived at the time. It was a funny neighborhood. The traffic signals chirped like birds to alert the students when to cross, and there was a small factory a few blocks away, Blind-Made Products, where many of them worked. In the morning they gathered in the doughnut shop, some in dark glasses, the bolder ones with their dead eyes bared. I loved to watch them prepare their coffee. Their hands seemed to have an intelligence all their own as they tore open sugar packets and tapped about in search of cream.

I met Mercedes at the liquor store. She'd asked for gummi bears, but the Korean clerk kept leading her to the chewing gum display.

"No," she said after running her fingers over the racks for the third time. "Gummi *bears.*"

I stepped in and took her arm, steering her to what she wanted, and we ended up spending the rest of the day together. She lived with her parents out in Palms somewhere and rode the bus east every morning to the institute. At first we rendezvoused in the doughnut shop when her classes were over and walked together to my place, but after two weeks she'd memorized the route, so I'd wait in the apartment, listening for the zipping sound her cane made against the sidewalk as she worked her way up the block.

She was one of those who preferred to wear dark glasses, and even when she took them off, she kept her eyes closed. We'd smoke dope and listen to music, and when we fucked, those incredible hands of hers would roam my body like soft, warm spiders. She liked to talk about religion—silly shit. Once she told me that she believed God was blind.

She was the most beautiful girl I'd ever been with, but since she couldn't see me, I wasn't sure if it counted.

GRADY'S GOING TO drive the U-Haul to Dee Dee's new place, and he asks me to ride over with her in her Malibu. It's been sputtering at stoplights lately—the fuel pump, he suspects—and he'd feel better if she had someone with her in case it conks out. When I seem a bit hesitant, he gives me twenty dollars to pick up a twelve-pack on the way and tells me I can keep the change.

Dee Dee's a complete idiot behind the wheel, nosing right up to slower cars in front of us and laying on the horn, a cigarette in one hand, an open beer between her legs. I roll down my window and try to relax. Most of the signs are in Korean on this stretch of Western. We pass a building I remember seeing on TV during the riots. They interviewed the owner as he stood in front with a rifle, holding off looters. About all he could say in English was "Why?"

We get stuck behind a bus, and the exhaust makes me light-headed. I watch the eight-ball air fresheners hanging over the rearview mirror swing back and forth and pretend I'm being hypnotized. A Jeep full of vatos pulls up beside us, and one of the guys points at Dee Dee's hair and laughs.

"Fuck you!" she yells, flipping him off. The gob he spits lands on the hood, and the next thing I know she's halfway out the door. I yank her back inside, but the vatos are in a fighting mood. They spill into the street waving baseball bats and tire irons, and I realize I've died this way before, in dreams.

The first of them reaches the car just as the light changes and traffic begins to move. A passing police cruiser slows for a look, and the driver of the Jeep whistles a warning. The vatos break off their attack and return to the Jeep, which speeds away while the black-and-white screeches through a U-turn to follow, one of the cops already calling in the plates.

My voice is shaking as bad as my hands when I shout at Dee Dee, "If you ever do that again, I swear I'll leave you to the fucking lions."

"I spilled my beer," she sobs. Big, black mascara tears crawl down her cheeks.

I screwed her once, eight or ten years ago, back in my heyday.

A quickie car date in the parking lot of some goth club off Melrose. She went by Trixie then, something like that, and what attracted me to her was her blue eyes, maybe, or the rings she wore on every finger, little screaming skulls. Anyway, I never saw her again until Grady brought her around a couple of months ago, and if she remembers me, she hasn't let on.

She cleans her face with a fast-food napkin from under the seat and goes right back to swearing and swerving.

"You know what that motherfucker said to me?" she asks out of nowhere as we're passing over the Hollywood freeway.

"Who?" I ask.

"Grady. He said, 'I can rebuild you, baby. I have the technology.'"

I see the sheet of black plastic coming from a hundred yards away. It flaps and billows in the wind like an angry ghost. Pursing my lips, I empty my lungs in a quick puff, as if to ward it off, but this wayward shred of night has its heart set upon devouring us. It swoops low over the road and skips across two lanes before whipping up to flatten itself against the windshield with a loud slap. We can't see anything ahead of us, yet Dee Dee doesn't ease up on the accelerator one bit. I sit back and grit my teeth and wait for her to lose her nerve.

She finally screams, "Do something!" and I stick my arm out the window, but the plastic slithers from my touch and launches itself again into the air, where it shoots straight up into the sky, up and up and up, to join the satellites and space junk. Dee Dee and I laugh and fiddle with the radio and keep on driving, any righteous wonder the moment warrants swept away by the cheap high of shared relief.

DEE DEE'S NEW apartment is a block north of Hollywood Boulevard, in a scabby, has-been building that's supposedly haunted by Sal Mineo. Luckily a few of her friends are waiting, because the elevator is out of order, and everything will have to be carried up to the fourth floor. After Dee Dee jump-starts the late arrivals with a line or two of her stash, they're raring to go. "Beep beep," they shout as they squeeze past me, competing among themselves to see who can haul the biggest loads. I take up a position in the back of the truck and spend the next hour sliding boxes and furniture down the ramp to Dee Dee's buddies. They make a couple of remarks about me not doing my share, but fuck it, I've got nothing to prove to these boneheads.

More and more people straggle in, and it actually begins to resemble a party. The unloading goes quickly, and when it's done, Dee Dee takes everyone up to the roof of the building to cool off. It's just an expanse of gravel with a few potted palms scattered about and some rusty patio furniture, but the wind has lost its burn now that the sun is setting, and the Hollywood sign glows a pretty pink. Soon reggae is snaking out of a boom box, and a girl with a pierced eyebrow hands me another beer before I've finished the one I'm drinking. Someone discovers a barbecue grill, and a contingent is dispatched to buy hot dogs and veggie burgers.

I drag a lawn chair to the edge of the roof. The sky out this way is a map of hell — blood and fire and gristly bruised clouds. I stare at it until I think I have it memorized, then lower my eyes to an open window in the next building, through which I can see a fat man lying on his couch, watching television. There is an empty birdcage in the apartment, a treadmill. He scratches his belly and coughs. These lives, these lives.

The girl with the eyebrow ring approaches tentatively. She's playing with a yo-yo. She stands with her back to me for a few seconds, taking in the sunset, but I can tell she has something prepared.

"You went out with my sister," she says when she finally turns to face me.

"What was her name?"

"Christina. About five years ago."

197

The aromatherapist, with all her little vials and potions. She thought she could help me, but my sense of smell was shot. Too many cigarettes. Christina's sister walks the dog, then jerks the yo-yo out of its stall into a cat's cradle. She's hot, in a black nail polish kind of way.

"How is Christina?" I ask.

"Married. Pregnant."

"Good for her."

"Like you give a shit," she says.

The yo-yo zips out and stops about an inch from my face before racing back up the string to her hand. She wraps it in her fist like she's going to clock me with it.

"Are you mad at me?" I ask.

"Yeah, I am. I'm fucking pissed."

I get up from my chair and walk back to where everybody's hanging out. A couple of guys I know are there now, Charlie and Nick. We talk about their band for a while, drink a few more beers.

MERCEDES' BLINDNESS BROUGHT out the best in most people. Strangers were always grabbing her arm, trying to help her. We'd be eating breakfast at Denny's and old women would come up to our table and say, "God bless you, dear," and shove a few dollars into her hand. The neighborhood where the Braille Institute was located was a little rough—I heard gunshots almost every night—but Mercedes never had a problem. In fact, the only time she was robbed, the thief apologized. "I'm a drug addict," he confessed before snatching her purse, which she later told her parents she'd left on the bus, because her getting mugged would have been just the excuse they needed to keep her locked up at home.

She planned to go to college someday. She wanted to work with children. She also wanted to visit France. "Why?" I asked. It was a legitimate question. I mean, she was blind. That was the only time I saw her cry. She had a cat named Lilly and a brother named José. Once when we were high in my apartment, she got confused and walked into the kitchen, thinking it was the bathroom. "It's okay to laugh," she said, so I did.

Saturdays we'd go places together—Griffith Park, the rose garden down by USC. She'd ask me to describe the flowers, the trees, the carousel, but this was beyond me. I couldn't find the words. She said I was lazy, that if I cared about her I'd try. So I practiced. *The moon looks like a drop of milk,* I'd say to myself in the mirror, *like a pearl, like a peephole into heaven.* I never worked up the nerve to repeat any of it to her, though. She bought me a shirt for my birthday, the ugliest shirt I'd ever seen.

THE PARTY MOVES back down to Dee Dee's new apartment, and Grady pulls me into the bathroom and offers me one of the lines of speed he's laid out on the plastic case of a Motörhead CD. I've been trying to stay away from that shit, but I'm drunk already, and I want to drink more. The speed sears the inside of my nose and drives tears into my eyes.

"Katy got busted," Grady says.

I nod like I know who he's talking about. The bathroom is painted light green, hospital-gown green, and there's wall-to-wall shag carpeting on the floor. I don't even want to think about that carpet.

Back in the living room they're playing a Greatest Disco Hits record, and a few people are dancing to it in that exaggerated way that lets everyone know they're only kidding. We're all on something or other now. A forest of beer bottles has sprouted on the coffee table. Everywhere I look, I see a guy chewing the inside of his cheek or a girl bouncing her knee and laughing too loud. Great secrets are revealed to strangers who will forget them by morning, and the smoke of a thousand cigarettes rises like scum off boiling meat and tries to find a way out through the earthquake cracks in the ceiling.

A space opens up on the couch, and I take it, settling into the thick of things. The speed is tickling the back of my neck, where my skull joins my spine, and my earlier drunkenness fades into a taut chemical clarity. I open myself up as wide as I can, so wide that all of the goodness inside me sparkles like diamonds there for the taking, and sure enough, the guy to my left, the white boy with dreads, asks my name.

My tongue can hardly move fast enough to push out the words my brain drops onto it. I've got so much to say to my new acquaintance, a whole life to explain. Twenty minutes or so into it, he excuses himself to fetch another beer, but that's okay, someone else takes his place. And so on, and so on, for what seems like hours. One by one people get their fill of me and slip away. I don't even try to keep track of the changing faces, because I've got this idea that if I stop talking before I'm all talked out, I'll seize up and die.

I reminisce about Christmas when I was a kid and reel off the names of every dog I've ever owned. I discuss the themes of *Moby Dick* and explain how to make perfect scrambled eggs. I tell them about Mercedes and what finally happened between us and toss out every other miserable and degrading memory that comes to mind. Dee Dee finally jumps on me, pinning me to the couch. She's laughing so hard she's crying as she puts her hand over my mouth and squeezes my lips together.

"Shut up," she gasps. "Shut up, shut up, shut up."

I GET A grip on the reins after another beer or two, jerk myself back into a trot. Everything's sort of whirling around me, slightly distorted, like I'm watching from inside a fishbowl, which is fine: I enjoy the distance.

Some joker comes prancing down the hallway wearing one of Dee Dee's dresses and sends the party into hysterics. I'm swept up by the unruly stampede to the bedroom, where all of the men are soon tearing through the boxes of clothes and pulling on whatever fits. Mine's a frilly blue thing that reminds me of the toilet-paper covers in my grandmother's bathroom. A seam rips when I bend over to roll my jeans above my knees. Dee Dee's makeup case is unearthed, and we go to work on each other with lipstick and eye shadow.

"This is pretty fucking gay," I say as I draw a bright red whore's smile on Grady's face.

He takes a hit off a joint that's going around the room, then passes it to me, and it looks like it's been dipped in blood. I realize that I'm sweating, have been for hours. I stink.

There's some kind of contest. One by one we're to exit the bedroom and let the girls judge us. I stomp out and do a couple of pirouettes and some half-assed pop-locking. A flash goes off in my face and a Polaroid whirs. My performance draws a few claps and hoots, but nothing like what the next guy gets when he raises his skirt to reveal that he's not wearing underwear and shakes his gear in time to the music. The winner, instantly, and his prize is that he can kiss whichever of the girls he wants. He chooses a guy, though, and everybody loses it when they tongue each other right there in the middle of the living room.

"Cheater," I keep yelling, "no fair," until someone tells me to grow up.

When nobody's looking, I sneak over and steal my picture out of the stack of photos on the couch.

I should have told Mercedes when I began to date Pam, the barfly nurse. Instead I kept my mouth shut and pulled double duty, waiting for an easy way out. One day Mercedes showed up with all her hair cut off. She started to talk about getting a tattoo, a small one on her butt. The institute called her parents and let them know she'd been missing classes, and her mother sent her to a priest, who made her swear on the Bible that she was still a virgin. Mercedes could smell Pam on my sheets. "That's another girl, I know it is," she said.

In the midst of all this, I got a little strung out. My dealer, a fat pig named Alberto, had seen me around the neighborhood with Mercedes and was fascinated by our relationship. When I wound up in over my head to him, he suggested I could clear my debt by letting him fuck her. I told him he was crazy. "Let me watch, then," he said. "She'll never know." He stood in the kitchen, and I turned up the music and got it over with quickly. He was right—she never suspected a thing.

Eventually I stopped answering the buzzer when Mercedes showed up. The tapping of her cane as she walked away made me want to puke. I felt creepy and weak and my blood burned like poison. I'd see her sometimes, headed for the bus stop or doughnut shop, and pass within feet of her without saying a word. "You are such a fucker," Pam would tell me—Pam, who lasted less than a month. I wound up getting loaded on Percodan and driving my car into a Taco Bell. That was as close as I came to asking for help.

I BREAK THE surface somewhere between dead and alive in the backseat of a car speeding through the desert. It's still night, and Dee Dee's driving, and I've got my hand down Christina's sister's pants. She shoves a stick of gum into my mouth and pulls my face to hers. My lips are raw and slimy. We've been kissing for hours. I touch the ring in her brow, think about yanking it out to see if she'll explode like a grenade, but she slaps my hand away.

Grady's Cadillac is behind us. His headlights flash, and Dee Dee pulls over. I leap from the Malibu and cross the dirt road to piss against a Joshua tree. I'm still wearing the dress. I have to pull it up around my hips to get at the buttons of my jeans. The massive sand dune swelling on the horizon glows like a pile of lost, old bones, and the wind howls in my ears. It's a lonely and truthful place, and it scares me. Grady and Dee Dee and Christina's sister are standing around the Caddy, washing down little white doughnuts with beer. I see that Grady is still wearing his dress, too, so it must be something we agreed upon.

He tosses me a Bud, and we walk to the Malibu. He has me hold a flashlight on him while he uses a screwdriver to pry the CD player from the dash.

Who are these people, I wonder, *and what happened to my cigarettes?* I can't stop looking at the stars swarming overhead, preparing to attack. Christina's sister comes up behind me and wraps her arms around my waist. Her breath against my spine makes me want to scream.

When Grady's done, he tosses the stereo into the Caddy, then hops in and backs the car farther away from the Malibu.

"Let me pour," I say, just to say something, just to get away from Christina's sister.

Grady hands me the gas can. Following his shouted instructions, I douse the interior of the Malibu, the tires, the engine. The fumes sting my eyes, my swollen lips. I want to be the one to put the spark to it, too, but Grady won't allow that. He tells the girls to move across the road, to the Joshua tree. I stay where I am, beside him.

He strikes a road flare. It sputters and catches, giving off a rosy glow. With a smooth underhand toss, he sends it through the open window of the Malibu. There's a loud roar, and the sun rises inside the car, finds itself trapped by the roof, and so forces itself out wherever it can. A fiery arm reaches for us. Grady runs, but I don't see the point. The air begins to crackle around me, and hot fingers caress my cheeks, my nose, plunge into my eyes. My tongue crumbles into ash when I laugh, my teeth are nubbins of coal.

Grady yanks me backward by my collar. He rolls me in the sand to put out the fire. I sit next to the Joshua tree in the mud my piss made and stroke the remnants of the dress that still cling to me. The clothes I'm wearing beneath it are untouched.

Across the road, the Malibu pops and whistles, a musical inferno. Birds chirp in the false dawn, jackrabbits awaken confused. Black smoke billows up to obscure the marauding stars.

"You okay?" Grady asks. The girls await my answer, hands over their mouths.

"I'm fine," I say.

We use the rest of the beer to wash the soot off my face. And I *am* fine, except that when I close my eyes there are flames dancing on the backs of the lids.

WE'LL STOP IN Barstow for booze and cigarettes. Back in L.A., Christina's sister will crash at my apartment for a few days, and it will be fun and all, but we'll finally come to our senses. I'll tell her to leave, and she'll try to stab me with a broken tequila bottle. After that I'll be lonely for a good long while, but then things will get better. I'll find a job, lose it, find another. A few years from now I'll come into enough money to take a trip to Hawaii. I will not enjoy it. There will be birds there, flowers red as candy, and waves just like in the brochure, but they'll all remind me of Mercedes. I'll stand on the shore and scream descriptions of everything into the night, descriptions that will tremble and falter and fall, and be gobbled up by a black, buzzing sea.

Everything Beautiful
Is Far Away

———

I'M NOT SUPPOSED TO BE WITHIN FIVE HUNDRED YARDS of the house, but rumor has it she's hired a gang of Vietnamese hard cases to get rid of me, so order of protection or no order of protection, I'm going in. The back door is unlocked, and her mom and dad are just sitting down to dinner. They look like a couple of ghosts; I could put my fist right through them.

We had Christmas together at that table, Valentine's Day. Her dad once complimented me on how clean I kept my car. I tell them not to mind, go ahead and eat. I lean against the kitchen counter to wait for them to finish. The sun pushes red through the window, and the refrigerator and Crock-Pot and microwave are hot to the touch.

"What's this about?" her dad asks.

"Does a gang of Vietnamese hard cases ring a bell?"

"Lana moved to Chicago six months ago," her mom says.

"Nice try."

Her dad wipes his mouth with a napkin, then stands and walks out of the room.

"It's true," her mom continues. "You remember all the phone calls you made here afterward."

"My finger slipped," I explain.

Her dad reappears, carrying a shotgun. I try to grab something out of the dish rack to defend myself, but my knees give way, and I end up scrambling out the back door on all fours.

I've always thought their yard was special, the fruit trees and the fishpond. Concrete deer graze in the bushes and something is always blooming. I hop over the fence just as her dad appears on the patio. He points the gun at me, the same man who admired the shine on my chrome that time.

"That isn't necessary," I yell.

A couple of cop cars howl past as I drive out of the neighborhood. It's not even dark yet, but already the gas stations and grocery stores are all lit up. There's no such thing as a hiding place. Through a window I can see people waiting in line at McDonald's. They comb their hair and smile at their own reflections.

In order to shake any tails I go home via a new route, cutting corners, doubling back, and running a few reds. After a while even I don't know where I am. It seems impossible that I could get so lost in the city I grew up in.

MARTY BLAMES HIS worthlessness on one awful season of Little League. When he starts in on it sometimes, the whole bar yells at him to have another drink. You have to wonder about a guy who can trace thirty years of failure back to a grounder he bobbled when he was eight. You also have to wonder about the people who call themselves his friends but won't let him get it off his chest.

Dead Boys

In crowded places I sometimes have trouble with conversations. Here at the bar, for example, a dude can be talking right to me, but I can just as clearly hear the person sitting next to him, and the person sitting next to that person, which leads to confusion. It's a filtering problem, I guess. Like drowning in words.

Marty's sitting near the TV with three packs of Camels stacked in front of him. He smiles and points hopefully at his glass.

"Jennifer, honey," I say, "get Marty another on me, okay?"

I help when I can.

Marty inherited a chimp named John Wayne from an uncle who had something to do with the rodeo. Marty thought he might put the chimp in the movies, but all John Wayne did was drink beer and smoke cigars. He got loaded one night and set Marty's apartment on fire, and then a few days later he bit off the tip of Marty's nose. When the cops showed up, John Wayne charged them. They had no choice but to shoot. Marty still carries the newspaper clipping in his wallet.

I'M CAREFUL COMING up the stairs into my building. One of the kids who lives here is riding his tricycle in the hall. I ask him if he's seen anyone strange snooping around, and he stares at me with the blankest face.

My place is what they call a bachelor. It doesn't have a kitchen, just a room to sleep in and a bathroom. It's against the rules, but I snuck in a hot plate so when I get tired of fast food I can heat a can of soup or spaghetti. As soon as I find one cheap, I'm buying a little refrigerator. Then I'll be able to cook bacon and eggs some mornings.

I sit in my recliner, which faces the only window in the room. The window looks out onto the brick wall of the apartment building next door. I don't have a regular TV schedule other than the eleven o'clock news. A man who comes by the newsstand gets the listings out of the Sunday paper and underlines everything he's going to watch for the entire week. That's a little much.

At times like these I wish I still smoked.

They've got us on some kind of flight path here. All night long helicopters clatter back and forth, rattling the windows and the loose change on the coffee table. I tried to organize the tenants in the building to make a complaint to the city. I typed up a letter at the library, xeroxed it at my own expense, and slipped it under every door. The only response came from a squirrely guy on the first floor who calls himself an actor but who I know sells office supplies over the phone. He stopped me in the lobby and asked to borrow twenty dollars.

JAMES TELLS ME some people from a magazine are coming by to take pictures. They have his permission. They show up before noon, while I'm straightening the out-of-state papers. A bee has been hovering around the stand all morning, making me nervous. I try to swat it a few times, but it reads my mind.

The photographer thinks he's a badass. He's got muscles and tattoos and calls his assistant dickweed. A closet case, for sure. He drops a can of Red Bull on the sidewalk, and it spills all over everywhere. He doesn't say a word.

"Hey," I yell. "Do something with that."

The models arrive later, after the camera and lights are set up. I figure out ways to stare without anybody catching on. The blonde looks like she'd break if you spooked her. Her face when she's not posing is wiped clean of expression; she doesn't give anything away for free. I used to drive myself crazy dreaming about banging girls like her.

The photographer wants me in some of the shots. I pretend to sell the girls a magazine. I stand between them with my back to the camera. In one I am looking over their shoulders as they read a newspaper. That pesky bee lands on the blonde's throat, and I swear I see its stinger pierce her skin. She screams and crumples to the sidewalk.

"What is it?" the photographer shouts. "What the fuck's wrong?"

She lies there bawling like someone died. The photographer, the assistant, the makeup girl—everyone gathers round.

"Are you allergic, Tina? Tina, listen."

Tina's face is bright red. She gurgles and wails, and snot drips off her chin. I watch from the register, not realizing I'm smiling until the photographer notices.

"This is funny?" he shouts. "This is funny?"

I CAN'T SLEEP, the helicopters and all, so I gather my dirty clothes and drive to the twenty-four-hour Laundromat on La Brea. Tricky shit goes on late at night. He-shes and burglar alarms. Moonlight. Elaborate detours pop up out of nowhere and disappear by morning. Men with long poles change the names of movies and the price of gas.

An old Armenian is asleep on the bench in the Laundromat. He snores loudly, and it looks like he's pissed himself—there's a puddle, anyway. Over by the sink a Mexican woman folds towels while her kid plays with a toy car on the floor.

Half of the fluorescent tubes in the ceiling fixtures are burned out, which makes for some dark corners and jagged shadows. The change machine is on the fritz, too. I ask the Mexican lady to break a dollar, but she pulls the no-speakee-English bit, so I have to go next door to the liquor store. It all makes sense when I see that Ho Chi Minh himself is behind the counter. I get the feeling he's been waiting for me.

No CHANGE warns a sign on the register. I give him a dollar for a twenty-five-cent pack of gum, scoop up the three quarters he slaps on the counter, then lay down another pack of gum and another dollar.

"Got you," I say as he slides over three more quarters. "They sure didn't teach you much about customer service in Saigon."

He goes back to the newspaper spread out in front of him. It's written in his language, I guess. The letters look like bugs.

"You and your boys better watch yourselves," I continue. "I don't like being followed. My dad fought over there, get it? My Lai, motherfucker."

"I'm Korean," Uncle Ho says.

"What?"

"I'm Korean."

I see myself on the security monitor hanging from the ceiling. Lana's got me so wound up, I can't tell if I'm coming or going.

All my clothes fit in one machine. I don't worry about separating whites and colors. I wash everything in cold. The Armenian is quiet now, and it is piss; I can smell it. When I close my eyes, I see bombs going off. The Mexican kid won't listen to me. I just want to tell him a joke.

AFTER THE MORNING rush I sketch my idea on the back of an old invoice. The bar has a ladder they let me borrow, so my only expense is paint.

The narrow passageway that runs between my building and the one next to it is filled with garbage. When everything finally quiets down at night, you can hear the rats down there, hustling and bustling and doing business. High fences topped with razor wire seal off both ends of the passage, but that doesn't stop me; I go out my window.

The sky is first. I draw the brush back and forth, laying down a patch of palest blue on the bricks I've grown to hate over the past few months. While that bit dries, I swing the ladder around and climb back into my apartment. From my recliner, I admire the beginning of my new view.

A splash of ocean dotted with whitecaps, a crescent beach, a bright yellow sun. Piece by piece it comes together. My only screwup is the hula girl. I can't get her face right, so I turn her into a palm tree instead.

I gaze at the scene for an hour after I finish. If I squint, it looks almost real. Everybody has the right to something nice. It's not against the rules to prime the pump now and then. A stray sunbeam hits the paint, and the colors glow. I open a beer and put my feet up on the windowsill. If it weren't for my recliner's funny smell, I could be somewhere else.

THE PARKING LOT attendant from the pizza place comes over on his breaks. I never bug him about browsing in the adult section, because once my horn started honking and wouldn't stop, and he showed me what wire to pull. He has a baby daughter who was born with her heart outside her body. Down in Mexico, where he's from, the cops and dope dealers get away with murder. He's funny the way he opens the centerfolds then shakes his head and whistles.

"Have you seen anybody strange hanging around?" I ask him.

"No, boss. Nobody. Who do you mean?"

"Like some Vietnamese dudes. Gangster types."

A car pulls up to the curb, and the driver yells at me to bring him a *New York Times*. I hate guys like that, I don't care if they do let me keep the change.

When my shift is done, I count out the till. It balances for the ninety-eighth straight time. The night clerk takes over, but I linger for a while. He's new on the job, so I warn him about the kids from the high school always trying to swipe cigarettes. His shoulder-length black hair is parted in the middle, and he's reading a book about vampires. He hems and haws when I ask if he believes in that shit. I don't know what James was thinking, hiring this one. The little old ladies will be scared to death.

AS A PRECAUTION, I park two streets from the one I live on and hoof it the rest of the way. The shadows of a flock of birds passing overhead swarm across the sidewalk like vermin. I hear things breaking behind me, but you couldn't pay me enough to turn around.

The actor, the office supply salesman who says he's an actor, is eating grapes on the steps of the building. He's not wearing a shirt, and I catch a glimpse of a gold ring in one of his nipples.

"Hey," he says as I pass by, then gets up and follows me inside. "I saw you painting the other day."

"It's personal," I reply. My mailbox is packed with sweepstakes applications. I think someone is giving out my address.

"Not to get all woo woo, but what sign are you?" the salesman asks.

His lips, his hands—something about him makes my skin crawl. Can't he understand my situation? I don't have time for his silliness. Pushing past him, I hurry up the stairs.

THERE'S NO LISTING for Lana in Chicago. I try ten different times with ten different operators to make sure. Then I check other cities: New York, Miami, Dallas. The operator in Paris, France, barely speaks English.

"Bonjour," I say. "What time is it there?"

"Six in zee morning," she replies.

"Dawn, huh. And the weather?"

"Zee numbair you want?"

"It must be gorgeous. Tell me about it."

"Zee numbair, sir?"

I met Lana at the mall. I saw her shoplifting mascara, and she saw me see her. Later she approached me at the food court to find out why I hadn't turned her in. "Because you're hot," I said. I was doing great then, processing work orders for the phone company. We went out to dinner all the time. I bought her a diamond tennis bracelet I'm still making payments on. She never told me she loved me, but she'd never told anyone else that, either. We were easing toward something special. I was allowed to tongue-kiss her and put my hands on her tits, and she once rubbed my cock through my sweats.

She was younger than me. Barely legal. Eight years' difference doesn't sound like much, but you'd be surprised. I don't remember ever being as silly as she sometimes was. She got drunk and puked in my car after I warned and warned her. She wrote letters to rock stars and got depressed when they didn't respond. Her parents thought I was great. Looking back, they were probably happy to have someone take her off their hands. We dated for three months and twenty-two days.

DOWN AT THE bar, Marty passes around a bottle of pills he found on the floor at Arby's. The prescription label has been peeled off, and he's hoping someone might know what they are. Jennifer says antibiotics, but her boyfriend, Bob the snob, smells one and thinks Valium. I drop a tablet on my tongue and wash it down with beer. They all swear I'm crazy.

Someone's seen a movie that gets us on the subject of time travel. I can tell you this: My dream is not to go back and lay a bunch of money on the Derby or the Super Bowl. I also wouldn't save Lincoln or Kennedy or Martin Luther King. Invisibility interests me more, but nobody wants to talk about that. "Figures, you skeev," is how they put it. This place is a pigsty.

Some Fridays women come in, two or three together. Usually they're too old for me. I don't go for the druggies, either. They giggle and flirt and sing along to the jukebox and get all the wet fart regulars squirming on their stools. Marty's the worst. I once saw him spend half his paycheck on a couple of grannies who bugged their eyes at each other and laughed up their sleeves every time he turned his back on them. I'm so lucky I have Lana to keep that part of my brain busy.

The place is dead tonight, though. The end of the line. Marty follows me out to my car, parked in front of the pet store. While we're standing there talking about nothing, every animal in the place starts screeching at once, like they all have knives at their throats. It gets louder and louder, but Marty won't shut up. "I mean, the damn world does its thing," he hollers over the din.

At Denny's, where I stop to eat, I get this idea stuck in my head that I can see through everyone's clothes.

"THE POLICE WERE here looking for you," my mom says first thing when I walk in the door.

"You don't know the half of it," I reply.

"Leave that girl's family alone. They're serious."

She sets her wineglass on the kitchen table and goes back to cracking walnuts. Shells fly all over the place. It's like she doesn't even care where they end up. This makes me angry right off the bat, because I'm reminded of how utterly incapable she is of putting two and fucking two together.

Dad is in the living room. There's something on TV. He raises his fingers in a wave but doesn't say anything. I walk over and look at the family portrait from Christmas 1995 hanging on the wall. My brother before he became an accountant, my sister before she became a housewife, and me. I know what I was thinking back then, and it didn't have anything to do with this.

When the commercials start, my dad sits up. He's wearing a neck brace as a precaution after some kind of operation on his back.

"Come here where I can see you," he says. "I can't turn around."

I join him on the couch. He pats me on the shoulder. They've redecorated twice since I moved. I'd have to scratch through two layers of paint to get to a color I remember. The latest thing is the vertical blinds on the sliding glass door that cast prisony shadows across the carpet.

"I quit smoking," I tell my dad.

"That's fantastic. I'm proud of you."

Dead Boys

Three weeks ago I was sitting at the bar, turning a pack of cigarettes over in my hands, and all of a sudden the surgeon general's warning leaped out at me like I was seeing it for the first time: SMOKING CAUSES LUNG CANCER, HEART DISEASE, EMPHYSEMA, AND MAY COMPLICATE PREGNANCY. What an idiot I'd been. What a victim. I went right into the bathroom and crumbled the rest of the cigarettes in the pack into the toilet and flushed them down. For once I was absolutely sure I'd done the right thing, and it felt great.

My mom comes in and hands my dad and me beers. She needs to know what kind of pizza I want, because she's calling Domino's. Then we have to be quiet. Dad's program is back on, a documentary on the secrets of ancient Egypt. When he thinks I'm caught up in it, I feel him staring at me. During the next commercials I ask, "Has Lana called here for me? Any hangups maybe?" and a tear races down his cheek.

I USED TO cut school and smoke weed with the older brother of the cop who cuffs me for the ride to the station. He and his partner show up at the end of my shift. I think about making a run for it, but James tells me to be cool and get it over with. He went through the same thing with his ex. To this day he's not allowed to speak to her except via her attorney.

The world looks different from the backseat of the cruiser. Everything suddenly assumes a new preciousness. If I get out of this, I promise myself, I'm going to buy a camera and start taking pictures. I also want to spend some time at the beach. It's twenty minutes away, and I haven't been there in years. Up front they're talking about a hooker they busted in front of an elementary school. She was so messed up, she was propositioning fifthgraders. We stop at a red light, and there are palm trees wherever I turn, and big white clouds that inch toward the horizon. *Click* —I snap a mental photo—*click click*.

The room they put me in has no windows. The drawers of the big metal desk are empty. I walk the perimeter looking for pinholes that might conceal lenses or microphones. A suit comes in and tells me to sit down. Detective something or other. "I know your dad," he says.

It's his duty to inform me that this is the last straw. If I violate the restraining order again, Lana's parents are insisting that I do time. I get the feeling there have been conversations about me going on behind my back. Nothing makes me more uncomfortable.

"I'm going to be blunt with you," the detective says. "If you're having mental trouble, we can get you help. Don't be ashamed to admit that you're in over your head."

"I'm fine," I reply.

"Your dad says this is about a girl who dumped you."

"Not dumped exactly. She moved away."

The detective brings the end of his tie up and brushes it against his nose, then suddenly drops it when he realizes what he's doing. I can just barely hear someone singing "Happy Birthday" over the station's PA system.

"I've been dumped; we've all been dumped," the detective continues. "It's fucked, but you'll get past it. Just tough it out. Not all that John Wayne stuff is bogus. He had balls, you know."

"Ha ha," I laugh. "Oh, yes, he did." I'm thinking of the monkey, not the man.

"Everything else okay?"

I tell him about the helicopters, but he says he can't do anything about that.

When they cut me loose I feel better in a strange way. Something like forgetting. There's one of those coffee machines in the hall, the kind where the paper cup drops down and the coffee dribbles in. I stand next to it and buy coffee for everyone who passes, good guys and bad. "Hey, thanks," they say, and, "You the man!" After a while I run out of money, though, and I have to walk all the way back to the newsstand to pick up my car.

JAMES GETS A nosebleed out of nowhere. He stands in the street so he doesn't drip on the magazines. One of the old lady customers says he must be low on iron. He leans his head back and pinches the bridge of his nose, and after a while that stops it. His blood turns black in the gutter as it dries.

We listen to opera on the radio. It's Friday, and everyone is in a good mood, getting ready for the weekend. The Witch Doctor stops by for the *Racing Form*. We ask him for a sure thing, but he just laughs at us. My lunch sandwich is especially tasty. "This must be made with love," I say to Agna behind the counter. She gives me a free refill on my Coke. Walking back across the street to the stand, I have a vision of how normal things could be.

I handle the register while James rearranges everything according to a plan he got out of a trade paper. The automobile section moves to where the do-it-yourself mags were, and they displace hair and beauty. It's all about guided focal points, he explains. Every month it's something new. The parking lot attendant comes over, and I point at James so that he knows what's up. He passes by the porno and buys a Mexican newspaper instead.

After work I go to a movie. It's something about teachers and high school kids. There's an actor in it I recognize from the stand. We have his picture over the register. Mostly, though, I watch the other people watch the movie. Lots of guys are there with their cute little girlfriends. I feel like I ought to warn them. The air-conditioning in the theater is cranked up so high I start to shiver, and I have to leave before the big showdown at the prom.

I BUY ONE of those disposable cameras on my day off. Twenty-four exposures.

1. The checkout girl at the drugstore, to see if the flash and everything works. "I have a cold," she says. "Leave me alone."

2. A police car speeding past with its lights and sirens on.

3. Pigeons on the steeple of a church.

4. The Hollywood sign, but I think I'm too far away.

5. A Mexican girl pushing a stroller. I tell her I work for a magazine and ask her name. "Maria," I say, "I'm gonna make you famous."

6, 7, 8. Two dogs humping in the alley behind Pep Boys.

9. A cactus with red flowers.

10. James at the register.

11. James again, because he says he had his eyes closed in the first one.

12. The parking lot attendant. He asks for a copy for his wife.

13. A stretch limo.

14. The sky.

15, 16, 17, 18. A girl who looks just like Lana. She won't stop, so I have to walk backward in front of her while snapping the pictures. She tries to grab the camera, and I almost get hit by a bus, running away.

19. Jennifer leaning over the bar to hug Marty.

20. Me and Marty pretending to kiss (taken by Jennifer).

21. My shoe (a mistake).

22. The first car that follows me home.

23. The second.

24. The third, close enough to see the Vietnamese guy behind the wheel.

The clerk at the one-hour photo place claims that the camera was defective and that none of the pictures turned out. Not believing a word of it, I tell him I want them anyway. A while later he hands me an envelope containing twenty-four black prints and twenty-four clear negatives. I spend half the night going over them with a magnifying glass, but nothing reveals itself.

SOMEONE AT THE bar has put a sign-up sheet for a day trip to Catalina on the bulletin board by the restrooms. There are only two names on it, and the deadline is tomorrow. They tried to start a softball team once, too. The mirror in the bathroom, which was broken last time I looked, has been replaced, and a fresh coat of paint covers the piss blisters pocking the metal divider between the urinals.

It's against the law to smoke in bars anymore, but the management here doesn't pay any attention. Everybody's puffing away, which is fucked, because the only time I crave one is when I'm drinking. I rest my forehead on the edge of the bar and stare down at my feet. Where was I last New Year's Eve? I can't remember.

"Don't you dare fall asleep here," Jennifer says, jabbing my arm with a long, red fingernail.

Any of these people would sell me out in a minute, and my suspicion is that one of them already has. Those gangsters are awfully familiar with my schedule. The door opens, and the setting sun roars in like a wildfire. A figure stands silhouetted on the threshold. Everyone turns to look, squinting and raising their hands to shield their eyes, and I think, *When they finally come for me, it will be something like this,* but today it's just Robo, taking his sweet time.

"Hurry up, asshole," Juanito yells. "All the dark's getting out."

"YOU'RE FUCKING WEIRD," Marty says. I've made a whole production out of unveiling my painting for him, the beach scene on the brick wall. I sat him in the recliner and replaced the white bulb in the floor lamp with a blue one for a cool nighttime effect.

I fixed him a rum and Coke and made sure everything was perfect before I raised the blinds, and "You're fucking weird" is what he comes out with, then, "I gotta go."

He's drunk and belligerent. They shut off his phone today.

"Wait," I urge. "Give it a minute. It looks almost real."

"I gotta go. Lemme use your bathroom."

Sympathy is like a gift, I know. You're supposed to give it without expecting anything in return. But this guy owes me, goddammit.

"Did you sell me out, you fucking Judas?" I yell.

I WAKE UP with a headache. The sound of my own footsteps makes me wince. Someone has scrawled WASH ME BITCH and a swastika in the dust on the hood of my car. It's Lana's handwriting. I usually stop at AMPM for coffee on the way to work, but today I drive right past, because there's a gas truck there, filling the underground tanks, and a spark could come from anywhere.

The night guy left a note asking me to restock the candy rack because he didn't have time. I get the boxes out of the storeroom and square things away between customers. It's a slow day. Everyone's eyes are puffy and red, and there's a haze that won't lift. This geezer buying *Variety* and the *Reporter* tells me it has something to do with the government putting viruses into jet exhaust. The viruses drift down and infect us and make us easier to control. Then the fucker tries to pay me with a counterfeit twenty.

James shows up about noon to spell me for lunch. I can't get anything down. When I swallow, I feel like I might choke. I sit in my car for a while, listen to the radio. Every song has the word *love, fire,* or *angel* in it. The headache is still there. It feels like somebody is kicking the backs of my eyeballs. I pull a rag from under the seat and press it over my mouth before I scream.

"Look, look, look," James says when I get back. He holds up the new issue of the magazine they were taking pictures for that day.

He opens it, and there's the stand, the models—Tina and what's-her-name—but something's wrong.

"At least you didn't break the camera," James says, pointing at the photos.

"That's not me," I reply, and I mean it. I've never seen that face before.

James ignores me, turning to show a customer. "Free publicity, right?"

The customer punches me in the arm. "Check you out."

"That's not me," I repeat, but they don't hear. I take a pack of Lucky Strikes from the cigarette display and step out to the curb to smoke. It was silly to quit in the first place, to torture myself like that, when waking up every day is painful enough.

I USED TO pick Lana up when she got off work at Jack in the Box because she hated riding the bus. She'd already wrecked two cars, her mom's and the Nissan they bought her for graduation. We disagreed about what color things were, smells. I heard her tell a friend that I was a pervert. That's what kind of bitch she could be.

I would have cut myself for her. I would have eaten shit. When she stopped answering the phone, I lost hope. The plans we'd made didn't mean anything. I finally tracked her down, but whoever brainwashed her did a fantastic job. "Get over it," she said. Suddenly I was the enemy. Her parents, the police. I backed off, but that wasn't enough. She had to get vicious, with the gangsters and all.

A KNOCK AT this hour can be nothing but trouble. I grab the knife off the coffee table and stand with my back to the wall in case they shoot through the door. But it's the actor, the phone salesman. Greg. He knocks again even after I tell him to go away.

"I've got something for you."

My stomach twists and gurgles, and I taste ammonia. I open

the door maybe three inches, stop it with my foot. Greg is alone. He's barefoot and hasn't shaved for days.

"Come on," he says, pushing with his shoulder. "Let me in."

I show him the knife. I stick it in his arm, just the tip.

He backs away and touches the blood.

"You make me sick," I say.

"You sure were singing a different tune last time, trick."

He throws an envelope at my face. The card it contains has a naked man on it. CHEER UP, Greg has written inside. I will kill him if I ever see him again.

THE PALM TREE appears first out of the darkness, then the ocean and the sand. An alarm clock beeps somewhere, and pretty soon it's noisy as hell as everyone in the building wakes up and starts to get ready for work. It used to give me a thrill to be part of it. I was convinced that I fit right in because I showered and dressed and ate breakfast like my neighbors. Anymore, though, all those radios tuned to all those different stations just sound messy to me. I get up from the stinking recliner where I've waited out the night and slam the window down.

There's a sign above the register that says ONE DAY AT A TIME, and I guess that's good advice, but I've got the creepy crawlies pretty bad this morning, and my left nostril is all stopped up. The night guy hasn't done the candy again, which means he takes me for a chump. I smoke half a pack of cigarettes before noon. A car slams on its brakes to avoid a wino, and the screech makes me bite my tongue. The sky seethes. I don't think I can handle rain.

A Vietnamese gangster sneaks up on me and buys a *Sports Illustrated,* then walks back across the street. He gets into a Jeep with another hard case, and they sit there, watching me. James keeps a starter pistol in a drawer under the register. He doesn't believe in real guns. When Lana's dad answers the phone, I lay it out for him: I'm on my way over, and I want Lana waiting in the front yard. The gangsters drive away. Message received. I call James and tell him I'm locking up.

The pistol rattles against the windshield if I lay it on the dash, so I move it to the passenger seat. It's green lights all the way over there, the first time that's happened. The sky is almost black now. People have their headlights on. The cops are in front of Lana's house with their guns already drawn. I pull over a block away and walk toward them. The television antennas are screaming at the telephone poles. In the clipping Marty carries, there's a picture of John Wayne sprawled dead on the floor. He looks ridiculous in his diaper and cowboy vest.

Here lies a man whose best wasn't good enough. I bequeath my car to the parking lot attendant. Everything else, you can burn to ashes.

Dead Boys

═══

HE NEEDS ME TO SAY YES. IT'S AN OLDIE BUT A GOODIE: keep the affirmatives coming. I read an article, an undercover, "Secrets of a Car Salesman" thing, that had a list of ten tricks to watch out for, and that was one of them. I held on to the magazine the article was in, putting it with a bunch of other magazines containing information that would someday be of use, but when the pile got to be about four feet high, Louise said, "This is ridiculous," and threw them all out. So now I'm at this guy's, this Rodrigo's, mercy.

"Do you like the color?" he asks.

"Yes," I reply.

"Red, right?"

"Red."

Rodrigo's hair is slicked straight back, and he has a goatee. There's a pack of Marlboros in the pocket of his shirt. He should stash them somewhere else, that's my advice. If he wants to look professional. A van from a Mexican radio station is parked on the lot. They're blasting music and handing out bumper stickers and T-shirts. I'm not sure about that either. It might scare away the white folks.

Rodrigo urges me aboard the SUV. The seat wraps itself around my body. "Special motors; they remember you," Rodrigo says. This model has enough chrome for three regular cars. Fog lights, leather interior, six-CD changer. The dashboard gauges glow purple when I turn the key. Way up here you'd see trouble before you got to it. No more sitting in traffic, wondering.

A few other salesmen stand together outside the showroom. They're smoking and watching two girls shake it to the music from the van. La Super Estrella. The boss comes out and says something, and the salesmen scatter. My fingertips are cold against my face when I adjust my glasses. The clouds look like skywriting that has just drifted into illegibility. I can't find the sun.

"Let me ask you something," Rodrigo says, putting one foot up on the running board. "If I could get you the price you wanted, would you write me a check today?"

"Come on, man," I scoff. "You'd have to be a pimp to drive this thing. A teenage pimp."

Rodrigo steps back and looks me over. Oh, he'd like to thump me. He's probably on straight commission. I read an article about that, too. I apologize for wasting his time. I can't afford a new car. Louise and I are saving for a house. I was just driving by and saw the balloons and heard the music. The Glendale Auto Mall. It seemed like a place where something was happening.

A PACK OF dogs trots through the intersection, all shapes and sizes, escapees and throwaways. The leader turns, a shaggy black beast, and gives me a look, flashing his teeth. I send him a mental message: *Car, dumbass. Me run you over.* The signal changes, and we continue toward LAX. Razor wire protects windowless bunkers and empty lots. It's six in the morning. Night tilts toward day.

Louise picked up this shortcut from a shuttle driver. It's useful at rush hour, but now — what's the point? The freeway's practically empty. You could keep it at seventy-five, no problem. Louise won't let me go that way, though. We have to take the same route every time. There are her rituals, and then there are her phobias. She's scared of birds, stairs, and electricity. No, really. She has a childhood memory of being struck by lightning. Her mother says it never happened, but Louise still uses her elbow to turn off the lights when nobody's looking.

She's okay with flying, though; a good thing, because her job involves a lot of it. She works for a company that publishes corporate training manuals, and two or three times a month she heads out to meet with clients in Chicago, Dallas, wherever. It's killing her, she says, so next year she plans to quit and have a baby. Ha ha ha.

We have to stop at the same McDonald's every time I drop her off, too. The sky is pearling as we walk across the parking lot. I recall a sunrise I saw on a beach in Hawaii. Something like that can save your life if you use it later, when you need it. A garbage truck pulls in, passing between us and the restaurant. It screams its guts out as it reaches for a Dumpster. Louise hurries into the restaurant, her hands pressed to her ears.

Everybody in line is wearing a uniform. There's a cop, two flight attendants, a nurse, some guys in orange vests and hard hats, and a postman. It's like a children's book. I go to the counter while Louise finds a table. That's how we always work it. I know her order by heart. The girl at the register has acne and a silver tooth. Her friend says something to her, and the girl asks, while handing me my change, "For real?" A button is missing from her shirt. I can see her belly.

Louise lifts the magazine she's reading so there's room for the tray on the table. It takes a minute to get everything arranged to her liking, and then she says, "There's a quiz in here that tells you how long you're going to live."

"I don't believe in that stuff," I reply, unwrapping my McMuffin.

"It's not a horoscope; it's a series of health-related questions. You can't not believe in it."

"Then what I mean is, I don't care."

"Do you smoke? No."

"I'm not cooperating."

"It's not like I can't answer them all for you. Do you exercise? If so, how often?"

"Louise, who says I'm *ever* going to die?"

She puts down the magazine and opens her juice. "Forget it," she says.

My coffee steams up my glasses. I wait for them to clear so I can read the newspaper. There's an article about an earthquake in India. They interview the guy in charge of burning the bodies. "There will be many more ghosts after this," he says. "But I won't be afraid. I have met ghosts so many times by now that I think I'm one of them."

Louise's cell phone rings. It's her boss, the one I think she's fucking. A UPS guy comes in, and a real, live sailor. The girl with the silver tooth takes a break. She walks outside and sits on the curb, poking at something with the toe of her shoe. I had a dream last night that they brought back an old TV show, and it made everybody happy.

You CAN SMELL the ocean at the airport, and seagulls plunder the trash. When you take off, you can look down and watch the waves crawl toward the shore. They seem like they're barely moving from up that high. Louise is jittery. Maybe it's the coffee. Her hand shakes when she twists the rearview mirror down to check her hair. She complains that my driving makes her nauseous. We fight the way people do in movies, always coming close but never landing a blow.

The streetlights go out as I pull up to the terminal. For an instant everything is hot pink. I pop the trunk and help Louise with her bag. She fits everything she needs into a single carry-on. That's one of the things I love about her: She's so practical despite her neuroses.

"Good-bye, husband," she says.

"Good-bye, wife."

A quick kiss, and she's off. I watch her until she's out of sight — my own ritual. I'm losing her. She slipped through my fingers somehow.

I TOOK MY cock out in the elevator once, coming back from lunch, just to do it. I unzipped my pants as soon as the doors closed and let it dangle until the bell rang for my floor. If the receptionist had looked up, she might have caught me getting myself together.

The corporate structure here is labyrinthian. They always reorganize when someone new gets to the top. My team is currently part of the production department. For the past two months we've been coordinating the development of a print campaign for a new brand of yogurt. There's the team leader, then me, then three facilitators. They used to be called assistants.

The facilitators sit in cubicles outside my office. There's talk that they're going to move everyone into cubicles, to improve communication. I'll quit if that happens. You can hear your neighbors sighing in those things, you can smell their perfume. If they catch a cold, you're going to get it. People sneak up on you.

The company leases the entire tenth floor. My window faces north, floor to ceiling. In the winter I close the door, turn my chair around, and watch the storms blow in. When Malibu burns, I can see that, too. I once hired a guy who quit after two weeks. "I don't know how you hack being in this box all day," he said. He left to spend more time painting. You can't rely on rich kids.

This morning I received a memo from the personnel department, regarding one of the VPs, Kress. His wife died, and he's been out of the office for a month. The memo relayed his request that nobody mention his loss when he returns. We are not to hug him, console him, or otherwise say or do anything out of the ordinary. He would appreciate this very much.

One of the facilitators pokes her head in, Heidi, a skinny girl with moles.

"Donna will be late."

"You're kidding," I reply, flatly.

Donna is our team leader. She's often late. Her children are her excuse. No one questions it. This one's sick, that one's got the shits.

"She asked me to tell you."

"Bless her heart."

"Can you initial these layouts?"

If Donna goes, I have a feeling they'll skip me and promote Heidi. She comes in early and stays past six; I air out my dick in the elevator. Her hair is a strange color, and I saw her crying in her car after the Christmas party. Someone said she's religious.

The phone rings. It's Adam, from accounting.

"What's up with that Kress memo? What a narcissist."

Adam keeps porno in his desk drawer. He smokes dope in the stairwell. We aren't exactly friends—I wouldn't loan him money, and he wouldn't ask—but we cut each other some slack.

"Let's go in on a wreath," I say. "Have it waiting for him."

"Know what I mean?"

"This place."

"Your old lady's gone, right? We'll have dinner."

Two years ago Adam ran over a jogger and killed her. The woman darted in front of his Explorer, and there was nothing he could do. Even the cops said so. This was before we met. Someone who knew him then told me he wasn't the same person afterward. One night while we were drinking, I asked Adam about that. "Of course it changed me," he said. "I'd been waiting all my life for an excuse to fuck up."

Louise shops off a list, but I like to freestyle. When she's out of town, I buy whatever I want: sardines, Ruffles and onion dip, pot pies, quarts of Olde English "800." They're getting ready for St. Patrick's Day at the store. Lots of cardboard shamrocks and leprechauns. If you believe the supermarket, we're always celebrating something.

Only two checkstands are open, and both have long lines. I pick up the *Enquirer*. The woman behind me bumps me with her cart. I ignore her. She bumps me again. "Listen," I say. She grimaces apologetically, all of her teeth showing. People often think I'm angry when I'm not. Something about me is too hard.

The days are getting longer. There's still an orange glow in the west when I leave the store. A hippie asks me to sign a petition. I refuse, but I try to be nice about it. Moths circle the lights in the parking lot, heroic in their single-mindedness.

A year or so ago I had a problem with earthquakes. The big one seemed to be imminent. I couldn't sleep, I couldn't swallow. My health insurance would have covered a shrink, but there was no way I wanted those kinds of claims floating around. I paid for it out of my own pocket.

She was nice enough, and I liked her office. The lighting or the furniture or something was very relaxing. Pretty good for a random pick out of the yellow pages. I told her that I felt something cataclysmic was about to happen, and this was keeping me awake nights.

"Do you see yourself as being in danger, or others?" she asked. "I just want to get rid of the insomnia," I said. "I have to work."

She set me up with weekly appointments and a prescription for Xanax. I never returned, though; I didn't want to answer any questions. Her receptionist called once or twice, but I pretended to be someone else and said I was out of the country. Louise was traveling a lot then. I went through the pills in a couple of weeks. Three of those and a beer—what a tremendous buzz. In the end there was no earthquake and nobody got hurt. That was good, I guess.

SOMEWHERE BETWEEN THE restaurant and the titty bar, Adam tells me he's going to kill himself. He's driving because he's less drunk than I am. First he gets quiet, then he says, "I'm never happy. I want to die." We're on Sunset Boulevard. Dreams have come true on this very street.

I take a deep breath and push it back out between my teeth. I didn't realize we were that kind of people. I thought we were tougher. Adam laughs when I don't say anything. He puts on his sunglasses. A song he likes comes on the radio, and he turns it up and yells, "This is my jam!" I have failed him.

Monday night is amateur night. Not really, but that's what the sign says. We're supposed to believe that there are all these horny housewives dying to take off their clothes for strangers. It's cute in a way. Old-fashioned. Another sign says DO NOT TALK ABOUT DRUGS OR YOU WILL BE ASKED TO LEAVE. There are nicer places, but we like this one.

We sit at the rail. The only other customer is a Mexican cowboy who spends more time staring at himself in the mirrors that cover the walls than at the strippers. He's got a beautiful pair of boots. The two girls dancing tonight take turns, three songs each. Whichever one's not onstage when we order fetches our beers from the bartender.

Adam's doing a thing now. Embarrassed about what happened

in the car, he's laying it on thick. He slaps me on the back, whistles and claps and throws too much money around. The dancers play along, illegally flashing their beavers and letting their nipples brush his face as he tucks bills into their G-strings and tells them he loves them. They lie, and we lie, and that's how it goes. The cowboy leaves. He spits on the floor on his way out.

One of the girls is named Danisha. Sometimes she speaks with an English accent, and sometimes she's Jamaican. She complains about the jukebox. "Too much 'eavy metal," she says. When she dances, she looks me right in the eye while grinding her pussy against the pole, and she sits beside me between sets. "Buy me a drink," she says. "The owner's watching." I'm having fun. This bar, this woman. It feels good to be in the middle of something.

I ask Danisha where she's from, and she draws little circles on the inside of my thigh with her long, red fingernail as she answers. "Baby, I been all over the world. London, New York." She keeps clicking the stud in her tongue against her teeth. Girls like her often wind up dead. Nobody claims their bodies. After an hour or so Adam gets tired of pretending. He twists his napkin into knots and frowns at his beer. "Let's go," he says. "Let's get the fuck out of here."

WINDOW WASHERS ARE working on the building next door. They stand on little platforms that lower from the roof like lifeboats. You couldn't pay me enough. I wonder if they ever see anything interesting—people fucking, people fighting. Heidi taps on my door with a pen to get my attention.

"I brought doughnuts. They're in the lunchroom if you want one."

It's not worth it. You never know who'll be in there.

Donna is out today. Something about chicken pox or flu shots or chaperoning a field trip. I take her calls and sit in for her at a meeting. On my break I go down to the little store in the basement of the building and buy a lottery ticket. The girl who sells it to me wishes me luck. "Thanks," I say, because that's what you say.

New e-mail. A couple of ads: "See your favorite movie and TV stars in hot XXX action." "Are you tired of working for someone else?" Adam has sent me a photo. I look over my shoulder before I open it, make sure nobody's around. It's a man who's been run over by a train. Half of him lies leaking on one side of the rail, half on the other. I hate the Internet.

There's also a letter from a girl I went to high school with. I didn't know her well back then, but she got my address from my sister and now writes me about once a month. She lives in Alaska with her husband and a bunch of kids. The usual thing is she complains about her life, and I tell her to keep her chin up. Lately, though, she's been fantasizing about having sex with me. Her letters make me blush. I asked her to send a picture, but she wouldn't. Adam says this means she's a pig.

Louise calls. She might be getting sick.

"Come home," I say. "I'll take care of you."

"Probably not till Friday. It's up in the air."

There's something cold in her voice. I play with the stapler on my desk, the paper clips. I don't want to love her more than she loves me. We've been married six years, and I hope we make it to seven. She tells me about a dinner she had with her clients. Tapas and sangria.

"Where are you again? Seattle?" I ask.

"Denver."

"Right, right."

Heidi is at my door. They need me in the art department. I rush the good-byes and hang up. There is nothing for me to do but stand and walk down the hall. I'm full to bursting and empty at the same time, like the universe on paper.

I OPEN THE window and lie on the couch. Our apartment overlooks a school. A sneaky breeze clinks and clanks the chains

233

on the swing set in the playground. It's warm for March. About now I would usually read one of the magazines that are always piling up, but not tonight. Tonight I'm not going to worry about what I'm missing. I turn off the TV. The moon climbs the palm tree across the street and sits there shining.

I'm thinking about my childhood. It used to be right there for me, but now there are so many blanks. A police helicopter flies low over the building, then circles, playing its spotlight over a house up the street. It makes a sound that I feel in my chest more than hear. I put on my flip-flops and go downstairs. One of my neighbors is standing on the porch, her hair in curlers. I didn't know women wore curlers anymore.

"See anything?" I ask.

"I think it's those Armenians."

I shuffle toward the commotion. Four or five squad cars are parked in the street, doors open, light bars flashing, abandoned in a hurry. The helicopter is right overhead. Its sun gun paints the house pale blue and makes the shadows wobble, like a whole day captured in a time-lapse movie. I'm surprised that I haven't been stopped yet. I start to cross the street to get even closer, but a cop steps out of the bushes and says, "Over here. Now!"

We are crouched behind a hedge: me, the cop, a bald-headed kid, and the kid's two Chihuahuas. The cop closes his eyes, listening to a sputtering radio. His shotgun is pointed at the ground. I've seen the kid walking the dogs before. He tells me it's a hostage situation. A man is holding a gun on his elderly parents. "They forgot his birthday," the kid says. "It's sad."

I reach down to pat the dogs, and they lick my fingers. There's some kind of flower smell in the air. The kid's leg is touching mine. He's shaking. Maybe he's scared and maybe it's crank. I'm not scared because I don't care anymore. It's a good feeling, like getting something over with.

Another cop joins us. He tells the first one to take us out of the area. I want something bad to happen; I dare it to. Electricity buzzes out of my balls and spirals up my throat. The Chihuahuas bounce at the ends of their leashes, pissing and sniffing, as we hurry away, bent double, and I glimpse the silhouette of someone standing in the doorway of the house with a gun to his head.

THE ALARM GOES off at seven-thirty. I spent half the night running up and down a beach, searching for a place to throw away a broken bottle. "Toss it in the water," said dream Adam, who looked nothing like the real one. The sand sucked at my feet, and there were bruised fish rolling in the surf. I find myself on Louise's side of the bed, my head resting on her special pillow, the only one she'll use. I once put the case on another pillow to test her, and she knew as soon as she lay down.

Some mornings I beat the guy in the next apartment to the shower, but not today, so the water pressure's for shit. Looking at myself in the mirror afterward, I decide to grow a mustache. I shave everything but my upper lip. There's not a word in the paper about the standoff. I go through it page by page at the kitchen table. If that didn't make it, what else was left out? I hate to start a day wondering.

Someone has slipped Jesus flyers under the windshield wipers of all the cars in the garage. Big black clouds are piling up on the mountains to the north, but the rest of the sky is clear. The radio says rain by noon, so the wind has a lot of work to do. I stop for gas, and a homeless man asks if he can pump it. He's not one of those funny ones. He stinks, and his pants are falling down. I give him a buck, but he can't figure out how to work the nozzle. I tell him not to worry about it, keep the money anyway.

Donna calls me into her office. She's wearing a denim shirt embroidered with Warner Brothers cartoon characters. Bugs

Bunny, Daffy Duck. "Did you sign off on this?" she asks, holding out the proof for an ad I okayed for her when she was out one afternoon.

There's an apostrophe missing in the copy: Yogurts finest hour. That's the kind of thing I'm supposed to be concerned about. It's difficult lately. I want to say, "Maybe you should do your own fucking job," but I don't. There are pictures of her children on her desk. I curse them instead.

The plaza is empty at lunch. The clouds have moved in, and the wind leans on the trees. I drop a potato chip bag, and it is carried off before I can get to it. The mirrored windows of the skyscrapers towering over me reflect the gray sky. Because of this, you almost forget the buildings are there. Birds sometimes smack right into them and fall to the ground, senseless.

I EAT SALTINES and Vienna sausages for dinner, sitting in front of the TV. I have a few drinks. The questions are difficult on the game shows tonight. The contestants sweat and lick their lips. We have surround sound. We have DVD. One day soon I'm going to bump us up to a plasma screen.

The phone rings. Someone says, "Sorry," and hangs up. The bathroom smells like cigarette smoke. It comes in through the air shaft from the apartment downstairs. The lady with the curlers lives there with her husband. I can never remember their names. He's on disability, and she's a part-time dog trainer. They keep odd hours. "The kike came by today," the husband says, his words drifting up the air shaft with the smoke. He's talking about our landlord. "How do you feel about wood floors?"

I pause to look at a picture hanging on the wall of Louise and me standing in the snow. What makes it funny is that we're in shorts and T-shirts. We're wearing sandals. You take the tram in Palm Springs, and they haul you up a cable from the desert to the top of a mountain in about five minutes flat. The right time of the year, it's eighty at the bottom and freezing on the summit.

Dead Boys

I had to beg Louise to accompany me. We were on a weekend getaway. She shut her eyes and clutched my arm as we swung out of the station. Now and then the gondola shuddered, drawing gasps from the other passengers and causing Louise to dig her nails into me. Going from rocks and sand to icicles and hissing pines with such startling suddenness was like a dream. I was a little unsure of myself. What other amazing shit would happen?

The snack bar on top was full of kids in some kind of uniforms. Their screeches rose up and were trapped in the rafters. Louise and I hurried out to a deck in back that overlooked a hilly area where people sledded and built snowmen. Everybody was dressed for the cold but us. The snow was dirty, and rocks showed through. Big black birds sat in leafless black trees. Louise had a headache. She thought she might pass out. I asked someone to take a picture of us. I put some snow in my mouth. Louise shivered and started to cry.

I wouldn't let her hang on to me on the way down. That was wrong. I told her it was time she got over herself. She closed her eyes and clung to the safety rail in the gondola, and I acted like I didn't know her.

Dear Robin,

How is Alaska? How is your husband? How are the kids?

You asked last time for a sexy story. Does this count?

"You again?" Danisha said when I showed up at the bar. She was a stripper. I had to wait for her to get off work. The lock on the door to her building was broken, and the lobby smelled like a toilet. I was worried about my car, parked out front, because I didn't want anything to happen that I'd have to explain. Danisha took my hand and pulled me up creaking stairs to her apartment. Her dress rode high on her ass, and she wasn't wearing panties.

"Help me with this," she said.

We worked together to turn the couch into a bed. The walls of the living room were papered with photos of rappers torn from magazines. I didn't know what to do with myself. I pulled the bottle of tequila that

I'd bought on the way over out of my pocket and took a drink. The lamp had a scarf draped over it, a piss-elegant touch. My eyelid twitched. My stomach fluttered.

"Want to get high?" *Danisha asked, examining her forehead in a mirror.*

I held up the bottle of tequila.

"Well, I'ma get high," *she said.*

She stepped through a door and closed it behind herself. I heard a TV and voices. This is where I get robbed, *I thought.* This is where I get killed. *I was too scared to sit down, so I walked to the window. The glass was broken. It was all over the floor.* What does she do when it rains? *I wondered. I tried to see my car but couldn't.*

"Where the fuck else am I suppose to take him?" *Danisha yelled.*

I couldn't hear the answer. She appeared again in the living room with a big smile on her face. I sat beside her on the dark green sheet, and she pushed play on a boom box. It was some woman with a gravelly voice. "Yeah, yeah, yeah," *she said. Danisha put a glass pipe to her lips. Her lighter had Tweety Bird on it. The smoke she exhaled wrapped around us and drew our bodies together. It tickled our noses. Danisha fell back on the mattress, and for a second I thought she'd fainted. Then she reached for me.*

While I was banging away, she coughed, and her pussy tightened around my cock. After half an hour, she pushed me off her and said, "That's it unless you got more money, honey." *I was all shriveled up anyway. I'd been faking it for a while. I walked to the window and cut my foot on the glass. I laughed, and she laughed. Then she told me I better leave. There was blood all over the place.*

Remember how you said it's dark there six months out of the year? Well, it's dark here all the time.

P.S. Don't write back.

KRESS RETURNS TO work. I see him walking down the hall. I see him at the Coke machine. People seem to be respecting his wishes; they stay out of his way. He's an old guy, with one of those comb-overs that you laugh at behind his back. Someone said that he and his wife were married for thirty years. I feel bad for joking with Adam about his loss. I don't know where we get off.

Adam's voice mail picks up when I try his desk. The receptionist says he didn't show up this morning and didn't call in. I dial his apartment, but there's no answer there either. I wave away the worry that flutters around my head. He's a flake. Everybody says so.

Donna and I proof some copy. She smells like sour milk. A cereal accident, I bet, while she was rushing to get her kids ready for school. What do I think of Heidi? she wants to know. I say she's doing a great job. "She is, isn't she?" Donna murmurs, bent over the table, squinting at a photo through a loupe. I get the feeling I've just cut my own throat.

It's drizzling outside. Little drops are swallowed by larger ones that race hungrily down the glass. I order a cheeseburger from the cafeteria in the basement. Louise calls. She won't be home until Sunday night. Things are crazy there. I can't prove she's lying, but I'll hire someone who can, I swear to God.

"You know that test you wanted to give me, the one that would tell me when I'm going to die?" I ask.

"What are you talking about?"

"In the magazine on the way to the airport."

"What about it?"

"I'm ready to take it now."

She pauses, then laughs. "I threw it away. It was stupid."

Later, I follow Kress into the bathroom. He locks himself into a stall, and I stand at a urinal. I wash my hands when I'm done. My new mustache looks funny in the mirror. It looks like a mistake. I open the bathroom door and close it, pretending to leave. Instead I wait, my breath stilled. Kress groans. He punches the wall. "Goddammit!" he screams.

This is grief. This, I understand.

*　　*　　*

THE TRASH SMELLS awful. There must be some chicken in there, some rotting meat. I grab the bag and carry it down to the Dumpster. It's dark outside. The streetlights have come on, a nightly miracle. I like it when things work like that. I like knowing that the garbage man will come on Tuesday. It's comforting.

The kid with the Chihuahuas passes by, hurrying them along before the rain starts again. He yanks their leashes when they try to drink from oily puddles.

"What happened to that guy down the street?" I ask.

He doesn't know. I walk with him to the house, and we pause in front. It's shut up tight. There's no car in the driveway, no flickering TV. I cross the lawn and climb the three stairs to the porch.

"Don't!" the kid hisses.

The welcome mat is red, white, and blue, like the flag, and a menu for a Thai place hangs from the doorknob. I peek in the window. I put my ear to the door. Nothing. I want to knock, but I don't. The kid and the dogs are gone when I turn around.

THE ARTICLE IS called "Hideouts: 10 Places You'll Never Want to Leave." I can't get through it. My eyes drift off the page every few minutes and wander around the living room. The apartment's pops and cracks make me flinch. I add the magazine to a new pile I've started so I'll know where it is when I need it.

It's late in Denver, but I call Louise's hotel anyway. The phone rings and rings. She never picks up. What happened to buying a house and having a baby? I want whatever she wants from now on.

The rain is really coming down. I stand at the window and watch it bounce off the street. My foot throbs. It's bleeding again. I must have ripped open the cut somehow. There are no Band-Aids big enough in the medicine chest.

Dead Boys

I try Adam again. I've been calling every hour all day long. Finally, he answers.

"Hello?" he says.

Tears well up in my eyes and get away from me before I can blink them back. "You're alive," I sob. "You're alive."

Acknowledgments

Thank you to everyone at Little, Brown, especially Asya Muchnick and Michael Pietsch, who took a big chance.

Thank you to my agent, Timothy Wager, who found me and stuck by me.

Thank you to everyone at the publications in which some of these stories were originally published. Without you, this book would not exist.

Thank you to T. C. Boyle and Jim Boyle, who encouraged me in the beginning.

And, finally, thank you to my family and friends, who make my life the good thing that it is.

About the Author

Richard Lange lives in Los Angeles. His stories have appeared in *StoryQuarterly, The Sun, The Iowa Review, The Southern Review,* and *The Best American Mystery Stories 2004.* His first novel, *This Wicked World,* will be published by Little, Brown and Company in June 2009.

Reading Group Guide

Dead Boys

Stories

RICHARD LANGE

A conversation with the author of *Dead Boys*

Richard Lange talks with John Kenyon for the Things I'd Rather Be Doing blog

Maybe I'm making too much of this, but I've been reading a lot of crime fiction this year, and reading a lot about crime fiction, and I've found that not everyone sees eye-to-eye on the genre. Most highbrow types — those who read literary magazines, for instance — dismiss it. Fans are understandably defensive, and seem content to spend most of their time reading only in that small subsection of the world. Both are clearly missing out.

So it was a pleasant surprise to come across Richard Lange. Most of the stories in his debut collection, Dead Boys, *were first published in those small literary journals, yet most of the blurbs he landed for the book come from some of my favorite crime writers, such as Michael Connelly and George Pelecanos. The other names under quotes on the dust jacket are perhaps most revelatory, because they come from people who, in my estimation anyway, have bridged the gap between those two worlds, weaving tales that are so well-written that few could sneer at the fact that crimes are committed and bad people do bad things: Chris Offutt, Daniel Woodrell, and others.*

What does all of this have to do with Lange? Simply that his book, no matter where you put it on the shelf, stands alongside the works of all of those mentioned above. There certainly are crime elements — one story, about a bank robber with a conscience, was selected for The Best American Mystery Stories 2004 *— but anyone who dismisses the book because of that is a fool, for this is one of the best books of 2007, regardless of genre.*

Lange is a graduate of the USC film school, but fiction classes with T. C. Boyle seem to have had a greater impact on him. His professional background is in edgy magazines and book editing,

3

pursuits that, as he says below, left him the time and the willingness to write.

The people who populate his books aren't people I'd want to spend much time with, but I'm glad Lange was willing to stick with them long enough to tell their stories. He also took the time recently to answer a few questions about his work. Do yourself a favor, read this interview, then head to the bookstore and get Dead Boys. *You won't be disappointed.*

These dozen protagonists are a pretty depressing bunch. How did you steel yourself to want to spend this much time with them? Did you get attached enough to any of them that you felt bad about the fate that befell them?

I actually enjoyed writing these characters quite a bit. They have extreme personalities and go through some pretty intense experiences, but at their cores they are all sensitive men trying to cope with the chaos that surrounds and permeates them. A trick of the light can elate them or throw them into deepest despair. A disapproving glance from a loved one can break their hearts for good. They walk through the world with raw nerves and wide-open eyes, furiously alive.

As for the second part of your question, it wasn't so much that I grew attached to the narrators as it was that I became them for a while. I had to embed myself in their minds in order to create them, and so I felt their dread when things weren't going well, and their joy when they were. A pretty intense emotional experience at times.

You're championed by some heavy hitters in the crime fiction world, though all of these stories were published in pretty traditional short story journals. Is genre a consideration for you? Do you identify with crime writers or mystery writers?

I didn't think about genre when writing these stories. That the book is considered by some to be a work of crime fiction is fine by me, but I wouldn't call it that. I do admit, however, to co-opting the language of crime fiction, particularly the hard-boiled stuff, and injecting it into stories that might have been fairly quiet "relationship" pieces without it in order to heighten the tension and describe the violence being done to the characters' psyches.

I don't read a ton of crime fiction — a lot of detective books have too many scenes of people talking in offices for my taste, or they're tough-talking iterations of Chandler or Ross Macdonald. I love Elmore Leonard, though, Charles Willeford, and Jim Thompson, and *Clockers* was great.

While short stories don't always have a tidy ending, many of those in Dead Boys *are very open-ended; much more so than most. Was that an organic development of these stories, a conscious choice to try something different, or perhaps a bit of both?*

One of my intentions with these stories was to see how little actual plot I could get away with and still make readers feel like they'd had some sort of experience with the narrators. People who consume media are such experts in narrative nowadays that it's possible to discard a lot of the old machinery and jump straight to the emotional core of a story, trusting that readers will be able to fill in the blanks. The open endings are an extension of that. Do you really need me to tell you what happened next? And does it even matter?

People often say that place is an important character in their work, but for you, to say Los Angeles is absolutely integral to the stories is no stretch. Have you written stories based elsewhere? Assuming you don't spend all your time in the city's seediest parts, do you explore areas in search of settings for your stories?

I haven't written any stories set elsewhere because there's still plenty to write about here. L.A. continues to fascinate me and provide me with a wealth of characters and images to fuel my fiction. I've lived here since I was seventeen, on the east side, the south side, and in Hollywood, so I know the turf pretty well. The stories in *Dead Boys* are all set on streets I've walked and in apartments and houses I've lived in or visited and establishments where I've worked or done business. I could point most of them out on a map or drive you past them. I used these various real sites as stage settings for the fictional events that transpire there.

Did you always have fiction writing in mind, or was that a detour while in film school? How did your work for magazines impact your writing, if at all?

Film school was the detour, I guess. Shortly after I started, I realized that I didn't enjoy the collaboration involved in the process. Too many cooks. I took some fiction writing classes from T. C. Boyle and found my niche. The screenwriting classes I took were helpful, however. They got me thinking about pace and structure and how to manipulate them. I learned a few important rules so I could break them later. I do love film, though. Certain movies have been as important in my artistic development as any book I ever read.

As for the magazine work, I never took a job that required me to write, preferring to save that energy for my stories. I worked as an editor for years, and the skills I developed definitely improved my fiction. I'm absolutely merciless about cutting out the fat.

The second book of your deal with Little, Brown is reported to be a novel. Anything you can share about that project? Beyond the obvious, how is the writing process different with a book-length work as opposed to crafting a short story?

I'm almost finished with the novel. This time I'm actually trying to write crime fiction, so it'll be interesting to see if I'm successful. It's called *This Wicked World*, and it's set in L.A.

The writing process for the novel has been much different than it was for the stories. I've found that I have to be much more direct and explain things a lot more than I'm used to. I also had to open up my style, because the kind of compression I used in the stories would exhaust a reader (and me) over the course of a novel. In a short story you only need the most important scenes. There's a lot more connective tissue in a novel.

The complete text of John Kenyon's interview with Richard Lange originally appeared on the Things I'd Rather Be Doing blog at www.tirbd.com. Reprinted with permission.

Questions and topics
for discussion

1. How does the collection's title, *Dead Boys*, help thematically link these stories? What do you think the author means to imply about the men in these stories from the title?

2. In "Long Lost," Spencer observes, "The streets down here are something else. The sun never quite reaches them over the tops of the buildings, and those who have chosen to live in this constant twilight collide with those who have no choice and those who are simply, in one way or another, lost" (page 80). How do you think this description of Los Angeles, and the city itself, shape the lives and hopes of the characters in *Dead Boys*? Is there something about the city that attracts characters like these, or something about it that creates them?

3. In "Loss Prevention," Jim says, "There exist certain wildflowers that must be burned in order to bloom, and who's to say I'm not one of them?" (page 169). To what degree do you believe this is true of Jim, and of other characters in *Dead Boys*?

4. Many of the men in these stories have trouble with the women in their lives. Is there something about these male characters that makes them prone to relationship issues? What about them do you think the women are attracted to?

5. Discuss what happens to the narrator at the end of "Everything Beautiful Is Far Away." Does his life end the way John Wayne the monkey's does, or is there still hope for him?

6. Do you agree with the narrator of "Bank of America" when he says, of robbing banks, that "I'd always imagined that when

you crossed the line, you saw it coming, but it turned out to be more like gliding over the equator on the open sea. Don't let them kid you, it's nothing momentous, going from that to this" (page 41). Do you think anyone is capable of crossing the line, given the right set of circumstances?

7. The narrator in "Blind-Made Products" betrays Mercedes's trust in more than one way. Which do think is the most damaging? How does the present-day story of his helping Dee Dee move relate to the flashback of his relationship with Mercedes?

8. In the story "Dead Boys," the narrator justifies going car shopping, despite not being able to afford a car, by telling us that "I was just driving by and saw the balloons and heard the music. The Glendale Auto Mall. It seemed like a place where something was happening" (page 225). What do you think he means by this? Can other actions he takes in the story be explained by this comment?

Richard Lange's playlist
for *Dead Boys*

The first album I bought was a battered copy of *The Ventures Play Telstar* from a swap meet in Bakersfield, California. It was all-instrumental, and I remember setting out to write a story for each song on the record. Like a lot of the big projects I started when I was eleven, this one didn't get finished.

The first record that really moved me was Springsteen's *Born to Run*. I listened to that thing over and over, and I maintain that it had as much influence on my artistic development as any book I ever read.

In fact, I learned a lot about writing from pop music. A good pop song conveys a wealth of emotion using a few well-chosen words, and good songwriters are masters of pacing and rhythm.

Below, I've chosen one song for each story in my collection, *Dead Boys*. (No, the book doesn't have anything to do with the late, great band.) These songs didn't inspire the stories, but they do strike some of the same emotional chords that I was going for. Coincidentally, a lot of them come from artists associated with L.A.

For an overture for the book, I chose "Los Angeles" by X. I love this band, and the songs on their first two albums give a great gutter-level view of L.A. that nobody has ever matched. I've always said that if I could write a story about Los Angeles that was as good as one of X's songs about the city, I could die happy.

Now, the stories:

"Fuzzyland" / "Georgia Lee" by Tom Waits

I've been a fan of his since I was fourteen, and when he starts braying one of his beautiful ballads, tears always spring into my eyes. This song is about a murdered child, but it conveys the overarching mood of the narrator of the story quite well.

"Bank of America" / "Sin City" by the Flying Burrito Brothers
My buddy George Edmondson turned me on to this classic many years ago. Financial ruin, sin and redemption, apocalyptic visions, and a stern warning to the rich and powerful—this one's loaded for bear.

"The Bogo-Indian Defense" / "Riches and Wonders" by the Mountain Goats
John Darnielle is another guy whose songs always get to me. This one's about doing your best to hold on to love in a world that isn't made for it.

"Long Lost" / "Ex-Con" by Smog
Smog is basically Bill Callahan, an exceedingly talented singer-songwriter. This song of his fits this story like a glove.

"Telephone Bird" / "What I See" by Black Flag
Had to put an old L.A. hardcore song on here because I've loved all those bands forever. I'm one of the few people who liked Black Flag more after Henry Rollins joined. There's a lot of inchoate rage floating through this collection, and nobody does inchoate rage like Black Flag.

"Culver City" / "You Can't Put Your Arms Around a Memory" by Johnny Thunders
Sad story, sad song.

"Love Lifted Me" / "I'm So Lonesome I Could Cry" by Hank Williams
I grew up on Hank Williams, and this has always been my favorite. How many haunted, lonely men have drunk themselves into a stupor listening to this?

"Loss Prevention" / "Revolution Blues" by Neil Young
This is another one from George. It was unavailable on CD for many years, but George gave it to me on a mix tape. It's supposedly about Charles Manson, L.A.'s original bogeyman. The ominous tone suits "Loss Prevention."

"The Hero Shot" / "Please Tell My Brother" by Golden Smog
This is by Jeff Tweedy of Wilco. It's about family, and it wrecks me every time I hear it.

"Blind-Made Products" / "Carmelita" by Warren Zevon
A chilling song about being strung out, desperate, and too tired to do anything about it. It also mentions Echo Park, where I live. The Pioneer Chicken stand is still there.

"Everything Beautiful Is Far Away" / "Everything Beautiful Is Far Away" by Grandaddy
This is off their first, and best, album. It's about a man stranded on the moon, pining for his old life on Earth. Perfect for this story, but I actually discovered the song after the story was written and stole the title.

"Dead Boys" / "I See a Darkness" by Bonnie Prince Billy
A great song from a great songwriter, Will Oldham. It's kind of about a yearning to explain yourself, and so is the story, kind of. By the way, I lied about the first record to ever really move me. It was Neil Diamond's soundtrack for *Jonathan Livingston Seagull*. Be a bro, though, and don't tell anybody else.

This essay first appeared on the Largehearted Boy music and literature blog, www.blog.largeheartedboy.com. Reprinted with permission.

Suggestions for further reading

Here are six of Richard Lange's favorite
short-story collections:

The Complete Short Stories of Guy de Maupassant (Hanover
House edition, 1955)

Dubliners by James Joyce

In Our Time by Ernest Hemingway

The Stories of John Cheever

What We Talk About When We Talk About Love by Raymond
Carver

Jesus' Son by Denis Johnson